*Please turn the page
for more reviews. . . .*

"FAST AND FUNNY."
—*Kirkus Reviews*

"You may not know Don Winslow, but you will. He is a former private investigator who has produced a wild, throw-everything-at-the-reader, very surprising first novel. . . . He certainly knows how to make a plot move and twist. . . . It reads like *It's a Mad, Mad, Mad, Mad World* played—just one crazy thing after another. . . . This novel is great fun . . . almost magical."
            —*Morning Star-Telegram* (Dallas, TX)

"A riveting tale of lost hopes, mistaken identities, and redemption . . . A big part of the book's lure is its elegant, fast-paced prose. It sparkles with images, great use of language, and nonstop black humor that has led critics to compare Winslow to masters like Elmore Leonard and Carl Hiaasen."
            —*Bergen Sunday Record*

THE DEATH AND LIFE OF BOBBY Z

Don Winslow

IVY BOOKS • NEW YORK

An Ivy Book
Published by The Ballantine Publishing Group
Copyright © 1997 by Don Winslow

This is a work of fiction. Names, characters, and incidents are the product of the author's imagination or are used fictitiously. Any resemblance to actual events or people, living or dead, is entirely coincidental.

http://www.randomhouse.com

Library of Congress Catalog Card Number: 97-97105

ISBN 0-8041-1610-5

This edition published by arrangement with Alfred A. Knopf, Inc.

Manufactured in the United States of America

First Ballantine Books Edition: May 1998

10   9   8   7   6   5   4   3   2   1

To Jimmy Vines,
the agent who does everything he says he will

Thank you to Dave Schniepp for sharing his knowledge of the Southern California surfing scene.

1.

Here's how Tim Kearney gets to be the legendary Bobby Z.

How Tim Kearney gets to be Bobby Z is that he sharpens a license plate to a razor's edge and draws it across the throat of a humongous Hell's Angel named Stinkdog, making Stinkdog instantly dead and a DEA agent named Tad Gruzsa instantly happy.

"That'll make him a lot easier to persuade," Gruzsa says when he hears about it, meaning Kearney, of course, because Stinkdog is beyond persuasion by that point.

Gruzsa is right. Not only does the murder rap make Tim Kearney a three-time loser, but killing a Hell's Angel also makes him a dead man on any prison yard in California, so "life without possibility of parole" really means "life without possibility of life" once Tim gets back into the general prison population.

Not that Tim wanted to kill Stinkdog. He didn't. It's just that Stinkdog came to him on the yard and told him to join the Aryan Brotherhood "or else," and Tim said "else," and that's when Tim knew that he'd better hone that license plate to a surgical edge.

The California Corrections Department isn't all that thrilled, although a few of its officials admit to mixed feelings over Stinkdog's demise. What pisses them off is

that Tim used the supposed tool of his rehabilitation—
honest work making license plates—to commit premeditated murder inside the correctional facility at San Quentin.

"It wasn't murder," Tim tells his court-appointed public defender. "It was self-defense."

"You walked up to him on the yard, took a sharpened license plate out of your sweatshirt and slashed his throat," the lawyer reminds him. "And you planned it."

"Carefully," Tim agrees. Stinkdog had about ten inches and a hundred and fifty pounds on him. *Used* to, anyway. Lying dead on a gurney he is considerably shorter than Tim. And much slower.

"That makes it murder," the lawyer says.

"Self-defense," Tim insists.

He doesn't expect the young lawyer or the justice system to appreciate the subtle difference between a preemptive strike and premeditated murder. But Stinkdog had given Tim a choice: Join the Aryan Brotherhood or die. Tim didn't want to do either, so his only option was to take preventive action.

"The Israelis do it all the time," Tim says to the lawyer.

"They're a country," the lawyer answers. "You're a career criminal."

It hasn't been much of a career: Three juvenile B&Es, a short stay with the California Youth Authority, a court-suggested stint in the Marines that ends in a dishonorable discharge, a burglary that ends up in Chino and then the beef that Tim's prior PD referred to as "the Beaut."

"This is a beaut," Tim's prior attorney said. "Let me make sure I have this straight, because I want to get it right when I dine out on it for the next three years. Your buddy picks you up at Chino, and *on the way home* you rob a Gas n' Grub."

My buddy, Tim thought. Asshole Wayne LaPerriere.

"*He* robbed the Gas n' Grub," Tim said. "Told me to wait in the car while he just went in for cigarettes."

"He said you had the gun."

"*He* had the gun."

"Yeah, but he cut a deal first," the lawyer said, "so for all practical purposes *you* had the gun."

The trial was a joke. A regular laugh riot. Especially when the Pakistani night clerk testified.

"And what did the defendant say to you when he pulled the gun?" the DA had asked.

"Exactly?"

"Exactly."

"His precise words?"

"Please."

"He said, 'Don't stickin' move, this is a fuck-up.' "

The jury laughed, the judge laughed, even Tim had to admit it was pretty funny. It was so fucking comical that it landed Tim an eight-to-twelve in San Quentin in the proximity of Stinkdog. And a murder beef.

"Can you plead it down?" Tim asks *this* public defender. "Maybe third-degree?"

"Tim, I could plead it down to pissing in a phone booth, and you're still looking at life without parole," the lawyer says. "You're a three-time loser. A monumental career fuck-up."

A lifetime ambition realized, Tim thinks. And I'm only twenty-seven.

That's where Tad Gruzsa comes in.

Tim's reading a Wolverine comic book in solitary one day when the guards take him out, put him in a black van with blacked-out windows, drive him to an underground garage someplace, then take him in an elevator to a room with no windows and handcuff him to a cheap plastic chair.

A blue chair.

Tim is sitting there for about thirty minutes when a squat muscular man with a bullet-shaped head comes in, followed by a tall, thin Hispanic man with bad skin.

At first Tim thinks that the squat man is bald, but his hair is just shaved close to his head. He has cold blue eyes, a bad blue suit and a smirk, and he looks Tim over like a piece of garbage and then says to the other guy, "I think this is the one."

"There's a definite resemblance," the beaner agrees.

That said, the squat guy sits down next to Tim. Smiles, then takes a big cupped right hand and whacks Tim on the ear—hard. Pain is like fucking *unreal*, but Tim, keeling over, manages to keep his ass on the chair. Which is a minor victory, but he knows that a minor victory is about the best he's going to get.

"You're a career fuck-up," Tad Gruzsa says when Tim straightens back up.

"Thank you."

"You're also a dead fucker when you get back to the yard," Gruzsa says. "Isn't he a dead fucker, Jorge?"

"He's a dead fucker," Jorge Escobar echoes with a grin.

"I'm a dead fucker." Tim smiles.

Gruzsa says, "So we're all agreed you're a dead fucker. The question now is, What, if anything, are we going to do about it?"

"I'm not rolling over on anyone," Tim says. Unless it's LaPerriere, then just show me where to sign.

"You killed a guy, Kearney," Gruzsa says.

Tim shrugs. He killed a lot of guys in the Gulf and no one seemed to get too uptight about it.

"We don't want you to roll over on anyone," Gruzsa says. "We want you to be somebody."

"So does my mother," Tim says.

This time Gruzsa hits Tim with his left hand.

To show he's versatile, Tim thinks.

"Just for a little while," Escobar says. "Then you walk away."

"And you keep walking," Gruzsa says.

Tim doesn't know what the fuck they're talking about, but the "keep walking" part sounds interesting.

"What are you guys talking about?" he asks.

Gruzsa tosses a thin manila file folder onto the table.

Tim opens it and sees a picture of a thin-faced, tanned, handsome man with his long black hair pulled sleekly back into a ponytail.

"He kind of looks like me," Tim observes.

"Duh," says Gruzsa.

Gruzsa's fucking with him, but Tim doesn't care. When you're a three-time loser people get to fuck with you and that's just the way it is.

"Try to pay attention, dummy," Gruzsa says. "What you're going to do is you're going to pretend you're a certain person, then you can split. The world thinks the Angels whacked you on the yard. You get a new identity, the whole works."

"What 'certain person'?" Tim asks.

Tim thinks Gruzsa's eyes sparkle like those of an old con who sees a fresh piece of chicken on the yard.

"Bobby Z," Gruzsa answers.

"Who's Bobby Z?" Tim asks.

2.

"You never heard of Bobby Z?" Escobar asks. His jaw's hanging open like he just can't believe what he's hearing.

"See, you're such a moke you never even heard of Bobby Z," Gruzsa says.

Escobar says proudly, "Bobby Z is a *legend*."

They tell him the legend of Bobby Z.

Robert James Zacharias grew up in Laguna Beach, and like most other kids in Laguna Beach he was *very* cool. He had a skateboard, then a boogie board, then a belly board, then a long board, and by the time he was a sophomore at the aptly named Laguna High he was an accomplished surfer and a more accomplished drug merchant.

Bobby Z could *read* the water, read it like it was "See Spot run." He knew if the waves were coming in sets of three or four, knew when they were going to peak, break right or left, A-frame, backwash or tube, and it was that sense of anticipation that made him such a promising young surfer on the circuit as well as a successful entrepreneur.

Bobby Z couldn't even get a driver's license and was already a legend. Part of the legend was that Z had hitchhiked to his first big marijuana buy and *hitchhiked back*, just stood out there on the Pacific Coast Highway with his thumb out and two Nike gym bags stuffed with Maui Wowie at his feet.

"Bobby Z is ice," intones One Way, resident lunatic of Laguna's public beach and self-appointed Homer to Bobby's Ulysses. "One Way" is short for "One-Way Trip," the story being that One Way took a trip on six dots of blotter acid and never really came back. He wanders the streets of Laguna annoying tourists with his endless stream-of-consciousness soliloquies about the legend of Bobby Z.

"Those skinny Russian babes could skate on Bobby Z," One Way might typically pronounce. "He's that cold. Bobby Z is the Antarctica, except no penguins shit on him. He's pristine. Placid. Nothing worries Bobby Z."

The legend continued that Bobby Z converted the profits of those two Nike bags into four more Nike bags, then sixteen, then thirty-two, and by that time he'd given some money to a flunky adult to buy a classic '66 Mustang and drive him around.

Other kids are worried about what college they're going to get into and Z is thinking *fuck college*, because he's already making more than your third-year MBA, and he's just getting started when Washington declares this war on drugs, which is a major boon to Z, because not only does it keep the prices high, it also puts in jail that layer of semipro incompetents who would otherwise be competition.

And Z figures out early, even before he skips his graduation ceremony, *fuck retail*, retail is where you get to lean against your car and spread 'em. Wholesale is where it's at: Supply the supplier who supplies the supplier. Get to that level and become a non-person just managing the orderly flow of the product and the money and never ever put your own ass on the line. Like buy sell, buy sell, and Z is an organizational genius and he has it figured out.

Bobby Z has it figured out.

"Unlike you, dipstick," Gruzsa says to Tim. "You know how Bobby Z spends his high school graduation night? He rents a suite—a *suite*—at the Ritz-Carlton in Laguna Niguel and has his friends over for the whole weekend."

Tim remembers how *he'd* spent graduation night. Not graduating, for one. While most of his classmates were at the prom, Tim and a buddy and two loser girls parked in a Charger up by the recycling center in Thousand Palms with a few six-packs and a low-grade joint. He hadn't even gotten laid—the girl just puked on his lap and passed out.

"Like you're a moke from fucking birth," Gruzsa adds.

What can I say? Tim thinks. It's true.

Tim grew up—or failed to—in the shithole town of Desert Hot Springs, California, just across Interstate 10 from the resort town of Palm Springs, where the rich people got to live. The people who lived in Desert Hot Springs got to clean toilets in Palm Springs and wash dishes and carry golf bags, and they were mostly Mexicans, except for a few white-trash drunks like Tim Kearney Sr., who on his rare visits home used to beat the shit out of Tim with a belt while pointing to the lights of Palm Springs and hollering, "See that? That's where the money is!"

Tim figured he had that just about right, so by the time he was fourteen he was breaking into those Palm Springs houses where the money was, nailing TV sets, VCRs, cameras, cash and jewelry and tripping off silent alarms.

On his first juvenile B&E, the family judge asked Tim if he had a drinking problem, and Tim, who was not stupid despite being a monumental fuck-up, knew an out when he heard one and worked up a few crocodile tears and said he was afraid that he was an alcoholic. So he got probation and some AA meetings and a pounding from his old man, instead of the CYA and a pounding from his old man.

Tim went to the meetings, and of course the judge was there, smiling on Tim like he was his own fucking son or something, which made the judge a little irritated when Tim appeared before him on his second juvie B&E, which included among the usual TV sets, VCRs, cameras, cash and jewelry, most of the contents of the victim's extensive liquor cabinet.

But the judge rose above his sense of personal betrayal and sent young Tim to a nearby rehab. Tim spent a month in group therapy learning to fall backward into someone's arms and therefore to trust that person, and all about his good and bad character points, and various "life skills."

The social worker at the rehab asked Tim if he thought he had "low self-esteem," and Tim was willing to accept the suggestion.

"Why do you think you have low self-esteem?" she asked kindly.

Tim answered, "Because I keep breaking into houses . . ."

"I agree."

". . . and getting caught."

So the social worker did more work with Tim.

Tim had almost completed the program when he had a little slip and burgled the rehab's petty cash box and went out and bought some good boo and the social worker asked Tim rhetorically, "Do you know what your real problem is?"

Tim said that he didn't.

"You have a problem with impulse control," she said. "You don't have any."

But this time the judge was *pissed* and mumbled through clenched jaws something about "tough love" and sent Tim to Chino.

Where Tim did his stretch and picked up a lot of useful life skills, and he was out about a month when the glittering lights of Palm Springs winked at him again. He was looking for jewelry this time and was almost out of the house and away with the goods when he tripped on a lawn sprinkler and sprained his ankle and WestTech Security grabbed him.

"Only you," his father said, "could get fucked up by *water* on *grass* in the middle of a fucking *desert*."

At that point the old man got the belt out, but Tim had learned a lot of useful life skills in Chino, and in a couple of seconds the old man was falling backward and there wasn't anyone there to keep him from hitting the floor.

So Tim got ready to go back to Chino, but he drew a different judge this time.

"What's your story, anyway?" the judge asked Tim.

"The problem is," Tim said, "I have a lack of impulse control."

The judge disagreed: "Your problem is breaking and entering."

"There's no problem breaking and entering," said Tim. "The problem is breaking and *exiting*."

The judge thought that Tim was such a smartass that maybe instead of learning new material at Chino he should become one of the few and the proud instead.

"You won't make it through basic," his old man told him. "You're too much of a pussy."

Tim thought the same thing. He had a problem finishing things (high school, rehab, burglaries) and figured the Marines would be the same thing.

It wasn't.

Tim liked the Corps. He even liked basic training.

"It's simple," he told his unbelieving barracks mates. "You do your job and they don't mess with you too much. Unlike real life."

Plus it got him out of Desert Hot Springs. Out of that shithole town and out of the fucking desert. At Camp Pendleton Tim woke up and got to see the ocean every morning, which was very cool, because it made him feel like one of those *cool* Californians who live by the ocean.

So Tim stuck it out. Stuck out his whole enlistment and even re-upped for a second tour. Got his GED, corporal's stripes and an assignment to Desert Warfare School at Twentynine Palms, about fifty miles from his dear old hometown of Desert Hot Springs.

Of course, Tim thought. Right back in the fucking desert, and he thought about going AWOL but then figured what the fuck, it's only one assignment. He figured maybe next tour he gets Hawaii.

Then Saddam Hussein invaded Kuwait in order to fuck Tim personally, and Tim got shipped to Saudi Arabia, which was like *major* desert.

"I can't believe you were a Marine," Gruzsa says.

"Semper fido," Tim answers.

Of course Gruzsa already knows—Tim knows he knows, shit, his file is sitting right there—all about Tim's career in the Marine Corps.

It's the one thing about Tim that Gruzsa can't figure out because it doesn't fit. Here you got your prototypical skell, a born-to-lose moke who can't pull off a simple B&E, and the guy wins a Navy Cross in the Gulf.

At the battle of Khafji, before the big U.S. buildup. Iraqi armored division comes pouring across the Saudi border at night and Kearney's recon unit is the only thing in the way. Unit is hanging out there all by its lonesome and it gets rolled over.

Corporal Tim Kearney pulls four wounded Marines out from under Iraqi tanks. Citation says he's running around out there in the desert night like he's John Wayne— shooting, throwing grenades and getting his buddies to safety.

Then he *counterattacks*.

Against tanks.

A one-man wrecking crew, a witness says.

He doesn't win, of course, but takes out a couple of tanks and his unit is still intact when the cavalry arrives in the morning.

Kearney wins the Navy Cross, followed by—in classic Kearney fashion—a dishonorable discharge.

For beating up on a Saudi colonel.

Shit, Gruzsa thinks, they should have given him another medal.

"They threw you out, huh? Go figure," Gruzsa says. "I was a Marine."

"What happened?"

"What happened?!" Gruzsa asks. "Fucking Vietnam happened, that's what happened. Fucked up my leg. That was a *real* war, not like that pussy CNN videogame war you were in."

Tim shrugs. "I'm a pussy."

Jorge grins. "A pussy."

Gruzsa leans over and sticks his face into Tim's. His breath smells like Italian sausage.

"But you're *my* pussy, Pussy," Gruzsa whispers. "Aren't you?"

"Depends."

"On what?"

"On what you want me to do."

"I told you," Gruzsa says. "I want you to be Bobby Z."

"Why?" Tim asks.

"You probably don't know who Don Huertero is, either," Gruzsa says.

Tim shrugs.

Escobar sneers.

"Don Huertero is the biggest drug lord in northern Mexico," Gruzsa explains.

"Oh," Tim says.

"And he's holding a buddy of mine down there," Gruzsa adds. "A damned good agent named Arthur Moreno."

"Carnal," Jorge says. Spanish—"blood of my blood."

"I want Art back," Gruzsa says.

"Oh."

"And Huertero wants to swap him for . . ."

"Bobby Z," Tim answers.

"They do big business together, and Huertero wants him out and making money," Gruzsa explains.

"You have him?"

"We got him."

Got him in Thailand in exchange for returning a heroin shipment to its original owner. The Thais fucking *hated* Z.

"The deal's done," Gruzsa says.

"So why do you need me?" Tim asks.

"He croaked," Gruzsa says.

"Who croaked?"

"Bobby Z."

Escobar looks almost sad about it.

"Heart attack," Gruzsa says. "Ka-fucking-boom. Face-first on the bathroom floor."

"A young man," Escobar says.

Gruzsa says, "Don Huertero has no sense of humor about this stuff. He'd give us dead for dead."

"This is where you come in," Escobar says.

Dead for dead? Tim thinks. And that's where I come *in*? Like what's wrong with this picture?

He asks, "Won't Huertero figure out kind of quick that I'm not the real thing?"

"No," Gruzsa says.

"No?"

"No, because he's never seen Bobby Z."

"You said they did business."

"Phones, faxes, computers, cut-outs," Gruzsa says like he's talking to a moron, which he kind of thinks he is. "He's never seen Z."

"No one has," Jorge says. "Not since high school."

"Until we picked the sleazy cocksucker up in the jungle," Gruzsa adds, "no one could really say that they'd actually *seen* the real Bobby Z."

"A legend," Jorge repeats.

3.

Escobar keeps it up as Tim's lying on a gurney with a sterile field over his face and some doctor is working off his cocaine beef by giving Tim a little scar like the one Z got when he bounced his head off a rock surfing the reef break in Three Arch Bay.

"Z didn't have any tattoos, did he?" Tim asks, because even with the local anesthetic this shit hurts, and anyway he's tired of lying there with this white cloth on his face.

"No," Gruzsa answers; then, as an alarmed afterthought, "*You* don't, do you?"

"No."

Which is a real good thing, Tim thinks, because Gruzsa would probably want to burn them off. But he figures the other option is the Angels on the yard, so what's another scar?

So he's lying there and Gruzsa's supervising the job and Escobar is yapping about Bobby Z.

About how Z gets out of high school and he's already a rich little mother and he's got a bunch of his little friends running dope all over your basic Southern California marketing area, which gets him some unwanted attention not from the cops but from rival businessmen. These are the days when the Mexican gangs are still a joke, the Vietnamese don't have it together, there's like maybe *one* Chinaman in Orange County and the Italians can still find their own dicks in their own pants. And it's probably one of the last, although Z never does find out, but two of his runners get taken out near Riverside and Z thinks this is a *très* bad sign.

Two young pretty cool kids lying facedown in a drainage ditch and it's like "Do not send to ask for whom the bell tolls," right?

But what to do, what to do? Z's sitting there in his condo he got a grownup to front for him, with his '66 'Stang likewise acquired and he figures, You know what? I don't exist anywhere on paper.

So he splits. Disappears.

"Like the morning mist," One Way describes in awed tones as his synapses pop like Rice Krispies. He's dogging four nervous German tourists down Forest Avenue in Laguna, telling them, "It's like Z *recedes* back over the ocean. Who knows where? Some say China, some say Japan, a few even claim they saw him on the beach in *Indonesia*, he's like Lord *Jim*, right. Or maybe he's on a boat sailing the ocean or maybe it's a *submarine*, like Z is Captain *Nemo*—James fucking *Mason*—but it's like one day he's on the beach and the next day he *isn't*, he's just *gone*, man. Gone. Like paddling out on his board he goes over the top of the wave and . . . *sayonara*."

But the dope keeps coming. Z has set up a marketing system using cut-outs and agents and bonuses and profit sharing. Z brings in the sweetest boo on the West Coast. Only primo stuff. By the bale. Bringing it in on boats like he's a smuggler of old, and every once in a while he loses one, a mule gets popped, but the DEA can't get near Z.

"We thought we had him about five fucking times," Gruzsa says. "And it turns out to be someone else."

"Grabbing Z is like grabbing fog," Escobar echoes. His hand makes a fist as he illustrates.

Z becomes huge. Enormous. Z is turning on the whole coast, the whole west. You got five yuppies smoking a bowl after their poached salmon, you gotta figure it's Z's dope.

"He's smart," Gruzsa explains. "No coke, no smack, no speed, no acid. Just high-quality grass. Opium. Thai sticks. Only sells to people who sell to money. So you aren't getting some pimpled kid or Deadhead or wanna-be biker who's gonna roll over for you. You bust someone with Z's dope, they're on probation and at Betty Ford before you can get back to the office. Z has a preferred-customer base."

"The Nordstrom of dope," Escobar says.

Z is landing dope from Alaska to Costa Rica.

"Who knows when a boat's going to hit the beach?" One Way asks the tourists as he strides beside them in Laguna. "Like, Z can look at a map, Z can figure out there's no way the Coast Guard can spot a little boat here, a little boat there on a coastline that big. Thousands of fucking miles for Z's dope, man. Do you see what I'm saying? Look out there, that's the *Pacific*, friends, that is Z's territory. Z knows the rhythm of the water, man. He knows it and rides it. Z is like Poseidon. Fucking Neptune, friends. Pacific means like *peaceful*, man. Z is peaceful with it."

"So what happens?" Tim asks. Because wonder boy dies in custody, right? Like the rest of the losers.

"Dunno," Gruzsa says. "Turns himself in in Thailand. Sick as a dog, got some sort of intestinal bug and walks into the embassy and asks to see someone from DEA. Says his name is Robert Zacharias. I was on a plane in about fifteen minutes."

"Then he dies in the shower," Tim says.

"Right?" Gruzsa says. Like, life sucks.

The doctor finishes up and tells Tim not to scratch it. Holds up a mirror and shows Tim the little scar on the left side of his forehead. Looks like a little "z."

Of fucking course, Tim thinks.

"What am I supposed to do," Tim asks, "if Huertero takes me across the border because he thinks I'm his partner Bobby?"

Gruzsa looks annoyed.

"The fuck do I care?" he asks.

"What do I do when he figures out I'm not?" Tim persists.

"That's your problem," Gruzsa says.

So there it is, Tim thinks. I can go back to the joint and definitely get killed or impersonate the great Bobby Z and probably get killed.

I'll take Door Number Two, Tim decides.

4.

But first some training.

"What kind of training?" Tim asks. Nobody mentioned anything about any training. The nice thing about the joint is that you don't have to do much of anything.

Unless you count making license plates.

"You got to know some stuff about Bobby Z," Escobar says. "And some basic vocabulary."

So Escobar becomes Tim's baby-sitter and trainer for the next two weeks, trying to implant Bobby Z into Tim's brain. They hold him at some camp somewhere around San Clemente to let the scar heal, and Escobar—Tim figures Escobar is like in *love* with the late Bobby Z, because Escobar just can't shut up about the guy.

Tells Tim everything the DEA ever learned about Z. What kind of food he likes, what he drinks, what he wears. Old friends, old haunts, old girlfriends.

Quizzes Tim on it until Tim feels like he's flunking high school again. Escobar's like Jiminy fucking Cricket, he's always over Tim's shoulder asking him questions, and all Tim is trying to do is check out the pussy on MTV.

"What kind of beer?" Escobar asks.

"Budweiser."

"Corona," Escobar moans, and he's like pissed.

Tim's in the fucking *shower* and Escobar slides the door open and asks, "Football team?"

"Doesn't have one," Tim answers. "Hates football."

"What sports then?" Escobar asks.

"Surfing," Tim says. It's a given. "And beach volleyball."

Or Tim's taking a nap, just stretching out on the couch catching the afternoon sun, and Escobar grabs him by the shirt, yanks him to the floor and shouts, "School colors!"

"Blue and gold," Tim mumbles.

Escobar screams, *"Maroon and white!"* and kicks Tim straight in the gut—hard—with one of those beaner pointed-toe shoes. Tim's curled up on the carpet in a fetal position and Escobar squats beside him and says, "You better get your shit together, *pendejo.* What you think Don Huertero's going to do with you, he finds out you're a fake? Kick you in the gut? Maybe he chains you to the wall and starts in with a blowtorch. Maybe he starts chopping off fingers. Maybe worse. Don Huertero is serious shit, *ese.*"

So Tim tightens it down, starts studying this stuff. Learns all this shit that Don Huertero may or may not know about Bobby Z. Starts looking more like Z, too. The scar blends in and Tim grows his hair out. They won't let him out in the sun, though. They want him to look prison pale. So Tim watches a lot of TV and does his homework.

Bobby Z homework. What clothes, what movies, what books? High school yearbook, there's this picture of Z with this little smirk on his face, like he knows this is bullshit and he's pimping it, right? High school friends, surfer friends, girlfriends. Lots of girlfriends, Tim finds out and it pisses him off. Not loser girls, either, but your classic Southern California cool girls. Sleek, good-looking, sloop-around-the-beach girls. Girls with that confident look in their eyes, the look that says they know the world is theirs, just for showing up.

"Z liked his *chucha*, *ese*." Escobar leers as they look at the pictures together, each of them speculating on which of the chicks Z actually banged. Escobar points out the ones they know were Z's girls: an Ashley, two Jennifers, a Brittany, an Elizabeth, one named Sky. "And the *chuch*, they liked Bobby."

Like this is some big revelation to Tim. It was like a well-known scientific fact that girls will put out for dope. Good looks, cool, money and dope, Tim thinks. But whoever said life was going to be fair?

Escobar briefs Tim on Z's male buddies, too. Surfer buddies, doper buddies, some of them—even the girls—became employees, sales representatives for Bobby's boo. A Jason, a Chad, two Shanes and a Free, who was—go figure—the brother of Sky. Hip-looking guys, cool guys, Tim sees. Guys who rightly figure they own the world because they own the beach. Bobby's friends.

Good friends, too, Escobar tells him. Bobby's *carnal*.

So *carnal*, Tim thinks, that two of them—one of the Shanes and the Brittany—end up facedown in an irrigation ditch.

Tim studies their pictures, their names. He studies books on surfing, he gets lectures from Escobar on how Bobby Z's empire runs. As much as they learned, Escobar says sadly, before Z's heart banged out.

"Bobby's head guy in the States is someone called the Monk," Escobar tells him.

The Monk? Tim thinks. The fuck is this? Only monk Tim knows is the fat guy in Robin Hood.

So he asks, "Who's he?"

Escobar shakes his head.

"If we knew that, we'd grab him, wouldn't we?" Escobar asks.

"I dunno," Tim says. Cops have cop brains, and who knows what's going on in there.

It's all too much for Tim. He shuts the yearbook and closes his eyes.

"You better learn this shit," Escobar warns. "Huertero's men will ask questions, make sure you're the real deal, before they make the trade. They better make the trade, *ese,* or Gruzsa'll burn you bad. Things can happen on the border at night, you know?"

Tim knows that. Tim was on the fucking Kuwait-Saudi border when the Iraqi tanks poured in. Yeah, Jorge, bad things can happen on the border at night, *pendejo, ese*?

So Tim studies and learns the shit. Couple of weeks he knows everything there is to know about the legendary Bobby Z. And not because he's so entranced with the boy wonder, but because Tim wants to have at least a shot of living through this little scam on the border.

Boring couple of weeks, though. They won't let him go out, of course, and won't let him bring anyone in. Won't even bring a working girl up from Oceanside to let him get his rocks off, even though they know he's been in the joint for months and didn't go the fag route. Tim asks, though, and Escobar just sneers, "You can get laid *after* the trade."

If I'm alive after the trade, Tim thinks.

It wouldn't be half so bad if they'd feed him some real food, but Bobby became a vegetarian and Escobar doesn't want Huertero to smell any rotten meat on Tim's breath.

"That's stupid," Tim argues.

"Isn't," Escobar says. "Huertero had Indians working for him. Cahuila. They can smell that kind of shit, man. They're like coyotes."

So no cheeseburgers, no hot dogs, no *tacos al carne* that Tim's been dreaming about. Escobar tells him he can have a fish taco if he wants and Tim tells him to fuck himself with his fucking fish taco. Hurts Escobar's feelings and for three days all Tim gets is pita bread and rice and vegetables and Tim says *I know all the shit now, let's do this thing*.

So Gruzsa shows up and gives Tim a little test. Escobar's standing there like a nervous father, smoking a cigarette and rooting for his boy as Gruzsa asks Tim a shitload of questions about the late great Z.

Escobar's grinning like an idiot when Tim 4.0's the test.

Gruzsa doesn't get all warm and gushy.

"I guess you're ready, dumb fuck," is what Gruzsa says.

So one night they stick him back in the van and haul him out.

5.

Late night in some canyon on the border.

Tim figures they're somewhere east of San Diego.

The moon is out and the sky is not black but silver as Escobar walks Tim down the slope to the canyon floor. Gruzsa's sitting in his jeep back up on top, watching through a nightscope, a small battalion of DEA guys with M-16s, shotguns and maybe mortars, for all Tim knows, there to back them up.

The INS guys must have taken a prearranged hike because there's no green-and-whites around, and Huertero must have cleared the Mexican side because there are no illegals crouched behind the wire to make the dash for the dollars. The usual game is off tonight, it's just this session of swap and trade with your friends, Tim thinks, and now he can see some figures coming toward them across the canyon from the Mexican side.

Tim feels the butterflies he used to get in his stomach just before a B&E, the same feeling he had that night when the fucking Iraqis came pouring into Khafji before the troop buildup and it was just a few Marines and the Saudis and all hell broke loose, and he can *feel* Gruzsa's nightscope on his back.

Now he can make out a couple of Mexicans holding up

what must be Art Moreno, like semi-dragging him between them, and Tim figures Moreno has had a rough ride. It sure doesn't look like his legs work real well anymore, and as they get closer he can see the agent's face and it looks some fucking tired.

So Tim's happy for Moreno cuz the guy is coming home and happy for himself, too, although he doesn't want to get too happy until it's over. But he has to admit to himself that he's excited about the prospect of freedom.

He's spent the two weeks waiting for the scar to heal reading *Consumer's Digest* and other useful magazines, trying to decide where to move after this is over. One of the magazines rated cities by quality of life, and it's mostly midsized cities in the Midwest that rank high. A lot of that, though, is the school systems and similar shit Tim doesn't care about.

He's now tending toward Eugene, Oregon, because it rains a lot, so he's concentrating on that and on how he's going to say to Don Huertero's boys basically *"Vaya con Dios,"* I like it here in America, and what kind of job can he get in Eugene. And they're close enough now he can see Art Moreno's eyes and they look bad, like *out of it*, like they've seen some shit they don't ever want to see again.

Escobar sees them, too, because Tim hears him hiss *pendejos*, then the whoosh of a bullet and Escobar's brains splatter onto Tim's face and Tim drops to the deck.

It's Khafji all over again, Tim thinks as he flattens himself against the desert floor and starts looking for cover. Tracers streak through the night sky, the noise fucking *paralyzes*, guys are yelling, feet are stomping and the two Mexicans turn back for the border, still dragging Moreno, except one of them catches a burst in the back and sort of *melts* like that witch in *The Wizard of Oz* that used to scare the bejesus out of Tim every Easter. The other guy like *freaks*, pushes Moreno to the ground and drops behind him like Moreno's a horse in a western, and starts shooting.

At Tim.

Tim's basic training takes over and he starts crawling to cover and makes it into some mesquite. He thinks for a second about going back to try to help Escobar, but he can see that the body doesn't have a face anymore so Escobar doesn't need any help that Tim can give. And anyway, Tim sees fucking Gruzsa roaring down the slope in a jeep, steering with one hand and blasting with the other, and Tim thinks it's about time to leave.

He rolls backward out of the mesquite and down into a narrow *barranca* that runs parallel to the border and must be an illegals *highway* because it's got tennis shoe tracks all over it. Which is just what Tim has in mind, to tennis-shoe it out of there because when the whole mess is cleaned up he knows Gruzsa's gonna blame someone and that someone is going to be named Tim Kearney.

So Tim starts to trot.

All of a sudden it's a zoo out on the border. Now everybody and his dog are out running around in the moonlight. Illegals appear from nowhere to use the chaos as a diversion, the DEA and Huertero's desperados are punching out a sharp little small-arms engagement, and Tim even startles a coyote that doesn't know which way to run because the noise is coming from all sides.

Tim is running with a stream of illegals—men, women, kids—which is okay with him, but then the INS Broncos start rolling in, agents jump out and try to scoop them up some wetbacks, and Tim figures this ain't gonna get it so he dives into a smoke-tree bush to wait it out.

As soon as the INS finishes up, Tim thinks, I can just trot out of here and head east and it's sayonara. Like they wanted me to be Bobby Z for a few minutes and I did and whatever went sick and wrong here is their problem and not mine.

I'm done.

Then he hears the hammer click behind his ear and a Mexican voice ask, "Mr. Z?"

Of course.

"That's me," Tim sighs.

6.

Tim wakes up in starched purple sheets in a guest room bigger than the house he grew up in. He pulls the thick white drapes—the whole room is bone white—and looks out the window at the pale early-morning desert, where sunlight has just started to paint the surrounding mountains lavender.

The compound—that's what it is, Tim decides now that he sees it for the first time in daylight—is surrounded by an eight-foot-high adobe wall with guard towers at the corners and parapets. It reminds him of some movie he saw on TV one Saturday afternoon, about three brothers who run away and join the Foreign Legion, but he can't remember the name of the movie.

He does remember getting here.

The Mexican who pulled the gun on him put it away when he confirmed that Tim was Bobby Z, and with great deference ushered Tim to a fucking *humvee* and drove for hours over some tortuous mountain trails until they reached what seemed like an oasis in the middle of the desert. They'd passed through an electric barbed-wire gate past some armed guards and then down a road into the compound. The man showed Tim to his room and said that Brian, whoever the fuck Brian was, would see Tim in the morning.

Tim, looking at luxury for the first time in his whole fucking life, sank into the circular bathtub for about an hour, dried himself with a towel the size of a flag and then plopped into bed and channel-surfed until he fell asleep. Tomorrow would take care of tomorrow.

So here I am, he thinks now as he puts on the white terry-cloth robe and slides open the glass door and steps out onto the little patio outside his room. He sits on the cane deck chair and puts his feet up on the little wrought-iron table and tries to remember some of the orienteering shit he learned in the Marines. He doesn't try real hard, though, because the sun is hotting up and that feels fine, and it just feels so damn good to be alone and outside.

Sort of alone, anyway. Off to his left, inside the compound, he hears the sound of someone whacking a tennis ball and from the same general direction the sound of someone swimming smooth, steady laps. A Mexican woman walks by holding fresh linen, spots him, and with a worried look comes over.

"Lo siento," she says. "I did not know that you are awake."

"That's okay," Tim answers. "I'm not so sure myself."

"¿Café?" she asks.

"Sounds great."

"¿Solo o con leche?"

"Con leche, por favor," Tim answers.

With milk, he thinks, lots of milk.

"¿Y azúcar?" he adds. He wants it thick and sweet.

She smiles at his Spanish.

"¿Desayuno?" she asks him. Her teeth are snowy white against her full lips and brown skin and that's what

makes Tim realize that he's finally *out*. Not out of the
jam, maybe, but out of the joint. Into the world of milk,
sugar and women.

"*¿Desayuno?*" he asks, not understanding.

"Breakfast?" she translates.

Not knowing now whether he looks like more of a dick
if he answers in Spanish or English he just nods his head
and smiles.

"What you like?" she asks.

Which confuses the hell out of him. No one's asked
him that question about anything for a long time.

"Whatever."

"*Huevos,* toast . . ." She struggles for the next word.
"Bacon?"

"No, thanks," he says, pissed at Z for being a
vegetarian.

"I will tell the cook," she says, then adds apologeti-
cally, "It will take a few minutes, but I will bring your
coffee right away."

"Hey?" he asks after her.

"*¿Sí?*"

"Where am I?"

She thinks for a second before she answers, "In a nice
place."

No shit, Tim thinks. And thinks also that he'd have
started being Bobby Z years ago if he'd known it was
going to be like this.

He glances at her legs and breasts as she comes back
with the tray but looks away when she bends down to put
it on the table.

"*Gracias,*" he murmurs, feeling stupid.

"*De nada,*" she answers, and off she goes, leaving him
with just himself and the sounds of money, the hollow

thunk of racquet meeting ball and the whoosh of a body gliding through water. A child's laugh.

Not bad, he thinks, for a dead fucker.

After coffee and breakfast and no word from Brian, he meanders back into his room and starts looking in closets and drawers. They're filled with clothes that fit him.

Nikes, Gucci loafers, fucking Calvin Klein polo shirts in pastel colors. Two Armani suits the color of sand. A white Adolfo blazer. Stacks of folded T-shirts, most of them black, one plum, one yellow, a few white. No advertising slogans on them, either, just pure color.

He showers and shaves—no aerosol can but a sleek gray tube of shaving cream from something just called M—then gets dressed. He puts on some Ocean Pacific trunks, a cotton Mexican peasant pullover, the Armani shades and a khaki ball hat, and heads toward the sound of the water.

A fucking waterfall in the desert. Cascading down rocks into a pool that's shaped like a Saudi window—a long oval with circles on the top, bottom and two sides. Tiled at the bottom. In the center in Arabic-style script the letters BC. The pool's big enough to hold a Mormon family reunion and there's a Jacuzzi you could do laps in. Big tall fucking date palm trees in case you get tired of lying in the sun.

Good view of the house here, too. It looks just like a goddamn Arab fort. One central building with two wings. Arched doorways, windows, the whole nine yards. He half expects to hear the imam calling the faithful to prayer. Tennis courts—not court, courts—swimming pool, an emerald-green rectangle of clipped lawn with croquet shit on it. A couple of adobe outbuildings. All surrounded by the adobe wall, in which Tim can make out motion and sound detectors.

So Brian C must have himself some enemies, Tim thinks.

And some nice friends, too, because now Tim sees her, lying on her stomach on a chaise, her top unstrapped, her back evenly tanned, her dark auburn hair pulled up off her neck. Long legs and a small ass.

She senses him there and cranes her neck a couple of inches off the chaise to check him out. She smiles at him under her wraparound shades.

A secret smile, Tim thinks.

He smiles back.

She drops her head back down.

He peels off the peasant shirt. He's in good shape. Good prison shape anyway, lots of push-ups and sit-ups. Pale, though.

She sees it. She says, "Jesus, you're *white*."

Low voice. Very sexy.

Without looking up she reaches under her chaise and hands him a tube of 30 blocker.

He mumbles, "Thanks," stretches out on a chaise behind her and starts lathering his body.

He's getting down to his feet when a Mexican boy comes out and says, "Mr. Z? Brian would like to see you if it's convenient."

Of fucking course.

He slips his shirt back on and follows the kid into the house.

7.

Brian turns out to be Brian Cervier, "with a hard C like 'curvier' not a soft C like 'servier,'" but Tim figures that C is the only thing hard about Brian.

Brian is obese, like *round*, like the Pillsbury doughboy on a Twinkie binge. Tim makes Brian to be maybe in his late twenties, already balding—there's some red Brillo clinging to the sides of his head—and if Tim is pale, Brian is a freaking albino. Not really, Tim thinks—Brian doesn't have pink eyes or anything—but the guy is like Casper the Friendly Ghost he's so white.

For one thing, he's wearing a full-length white caftan you could hold a revival meeting in and he still looks fat. He's got these fat toes shoved into sandals and his cheeks are sinking down into his fat neck, and Tim figures that if Brian-with-a-hard-C Cervier has like one more dough-nut, it's going to be a Richard Simmons suicide situation.

Right now Brian's sitting in a big wooden chair and he's drinking some fruity shit with vodka in it and he's just about wetting his pants he's so happy to meet the legendary Bobby Z.

"An honor," Brian trills. "Would you like a drink?"

Tim would. He asks for a beer and a Mexican boy appears the next second like the room is miked. The boy could be seventeen or twenty-three, and he and Brian share a glance that Tim recognizes from the joint. The boy hands Tim an icy Corona.

Tim sits down in another wooden chair. He and Brian look at each other for a few seconds, a real love fest, and finally Brian says, "Don Huertero sends his apologies he couldn't come in person. But he's asked me to extend you every hospitality. He's going to make it up over the weekend. So, *mi casa, su casa.*"

"It's some *casa*," Tim says.

"Thank you."

"Reminds me of a movie . . ."

Brian is pleased. He smiles and says, "*Beau Geste.* My favorite film. I watch it all the time. I had the place designed like the fort, *sans* the dead bodies, of course."

"That's wild," Tim says. What he's thinking is that Brian Cervier has too much money and not enough to do.

"Well," Brian says, "I wanted to go with a desert theme and you get so tired of the Mexican shit, you know. And the Santa Fe thing has been done to death—"

"To death."

The fuck we talking about? Tim thinks.

"—likewise the Taliesen West bit," Brian continues, "soooo . . ."

"Here we are," Tim says. He's afraid to really ask where exactly "here" is, because maybe Z is supposed to know.

"What *happened* last night?!" Brian suddenly screeches. When he grins, his piggy eyes roll up into fat and disappear.

Tim shrugs.

"A lot of shooting is all I know."

Brian shrugs. "It can get edgy on the border."

"Were you there?"

"No. I sent representatives," Brian says. "Call it an overabundance of caution."

Tim raises his beer in a salute.

Brian goes on, "Don Huertero is *furious* at his people for botching the exchange."

"A couple of his people are dead."

"They're better off," Brian says. Then he adds, "Of course, Don Huertero is *thrilled* with me. Which is good for business."

Tim raises his beer and toasts, "Business."

"You know the one product Mexico produces really well?" Brian asks.

"What?"

"Mexicans."

"Mexicans."

Brian says, "Mexico fucks up its oil, its gold mines are shot, it can't market a *frijol*, but it poops out Mexicans like Japan shits cars. Mexicans are Mexico's one export."

"And you import," Tim says.

"Well, we're importers, aren't we?" Brian purrs. "Anything the government makes illegal makes us money. Drugs, people, sex. I'm hoping they outlaw oxygen next."

Tim smiles what he figures is a Z-like, knowing smile. Which is like the thing to do when you *don't* know. There's at least a shot that people will figure you know so well that you don't need to say.

Tim stays cool and silent and drains the rest of his beer.

A smile plays on the edges of Brian's lips. Smile flutters there for a second and then Brian just can't contain himself.

"I shouldn't be telling you this," he says, "but . . . Don Huertero has a big business proposition for you. *Big*."

"What's that?"

"Meth," Brian says. "The new big high."

"Meth?"

Brian nods. "Don Huertero's setting up meth labs all over the Southland. He provides the chemicals, I supply the labor, and we're hoping that you . . ."

Brian is just breathless.

". . . that *you* will supply the market."

"I don't do meth," Tim says. "I do dope."

"I know, I know," Brian says. "But use your imagination, Bobby. Don Huertero's organization? With my labor supply? Tapped into your high-end market? We could print our own currency."

So that's the deal, Tim thinks. That's what's worth giving back poor fucked-up Art Moreno. Turn Bobby's mellow grass network on to crystal meth.

Get you a West Coast full of hopped-up yuppies whacking each other's heads off, going bad fucking crazy. But getting a shitload of work done.

And let the money roll in.

"I'll have to give it some thought," Tim says.

"Of course," Brian coos. "Kick back, chill out, put your feet up. *Mi casa, su casa.* Anything you desire, Bobby, just nod or lift a finger, let your desire be known and it shall be done."

"Okay."

"This is an oasis. A perfumed garden. A house of pleasure."

Tim says, "The DEA might be looking for me."

"They won't find you," Brian answers. "Not here."

Tim takes the chance. "Where *is* here?"

"Anza-Borrego State Park," Brian answers.

"A state park?"

Like with rangers and shit?! State-owned land?! Hey, Brian, I've spent just about all the time I want to on state-owned property.

"This is freehold land," Brian answers. "Two thousand acres of desert my grandparents left me. Surrounded by the great nothing. Desert flats and desert mountains. A jackrabbit couldn't get in here without my knowing about it."

"Or out?"

Brian's smile gives Tim the creeps. "Or out."

"And convenient to the Mexican border," Tim says.

"A border," Brian answers, "is a state of mind."

He lets Z ponder this for a moment, then says, "So welcome to the Hotel California."

8.

They step outside, where the sun has bleached the world white.

Sunlight so harsh it burns the eye. Tim puts on his shades and sees through blue filters a party in progress at the pool. Against the noon-faded pastels of the desert the guests are bright primary colors, rectangles of blues, reds and yellows standing around the bright turquoise of the pool.

Beautiful people in angles of repose.

Even the ones standing up look like they're resting, Tim thinks. Their arms bent in the leisurely angle of drink to lips, hips swiveled and knees flexed, ready to move on to the next conversation, eyes lazily scanning the crowd for sights more interesting or pleasurable.

Tim hates them instantly.

They look—and *are*, he supposes—rich. The men are mostly tall and thin and look strong from pushing on machines in air-conditioned gyms. They're cocoa-butter tan, too—not farmer tan or working-guy tan, tans that stop at the shirt line—these guys are tanned from lying around pools and boats. They sport trendy haircuts, either long with a ponytail, or sides shaved with a ponytail, or sides shaved with no ponytail. A few goatees. A couple have carefully manicured two-day stubble.

The women are a convict's wet dream. Mostly blondes with big straw hats over two-hundred-buck hairstyles from José Ebert. Big jewelry—chains, earrings, bracelets over expensive bathing suits, mostly black two-piece. Or topless over wraparounds, beads of sweat dripping between brown breasts.

Men or women, they turn to look at Tim as he comes into the pool area with Brian. It startles him at first. Shit, *scares* him, but then he realizes he isn't loser Tim Kearney from Desert Hot Springs, he's ultimate-cool Bobby Z from Laguna and he doesn't have to carry their garbage anymore. In fact, he doesn't have to do *anything*.

That's California cool, Tim thinks—*do* nothing but *look* good.

Let the legend do the work.

So he stops and lets them get a good look at the legend. Shielded by the shades he meets their gaze, one lazy pair of rich lazy eyes at a time.

And for the first time in his life sees . . . what?

Not fear, exactly. Not exactly respect. What is it? Tim asks himself as he looks at their pampered faces look at him. *Inferiority,* he realizes. They think he's better than they are.

Except for *her*. Standing at the far end of the pool, hand on cocked hip. She meets his eyes and gives him that knowing, mocking smile again. He takes the time to stare back. Check her out. A gauze skirt is wrapped around her long legs now, an unbuttoned linen blouse hangs over her black bikini top. He likes it that she's covered up, her breasts not like everybody's in some *Playboy* pictorial.

Her hair is still up, her neck long and lovely. But it's that smile, man, that gets Tim going.

He feels his own lips twist into a smile of their own.

She laughs and turns away.

It breaks the tableau. Most of the guests change partners or approach the Mexican bartender for a fresh drink. Through the breaking crowd Tim's gaze stays on *her* as she squats down to speak to a small boy who is putting a toy boat into the water.

The boy looks so out of place here, Tim thinks. *Is* out of place. The fuck are his parents thinking? Tim wonders. The scent of marijuana pierces the hot air. Dope and semi-naked women and they're letting a little kid run around. He hopes *she's* not his mother.

The kid doesn't look like her. He's blond, for one thing. His hair long and chopped at the bottom like some Deadhead's kid, surf bum's kid. Blue eyes—it's hard to tell behind the blue shades—and hers are what, green?

It ain't her kid, Tim thinks. If it's her kid she takes him out of here, takes him home because she has class. Tim looks around for the parents, but there doesn't seem to be a pair of adults with special eyes for the boy. There is another young woman, looks South American, watching the boy. Looking at a magazine and watching the boy, and Tim wants to go ask her what the fuck she's thinking about.

Fucking pools are dangerous for kids, Tim thinks. Dangerous for him, too, because even in the Marines he never learned to swim. Switched with a guy on the test. But you got to watch a kid around a pool, not be looking at some magazine reading about having a better sex life in ten minutes.

But it ain't my kid, he thinks, and none of my business.

The boy pushes the boat into the pool, then steps back and points a black box with an antenna at it.

Kid's got a radio-controlled boat, Tim thinks, so the kid's got him some money. A nanny and a radio-controlled boat, he thinks, and a buddy: her, because the kid is clearly showing off for her.

Don't blame you, kid, Tim thinks. You can pick 'em.

Brian is ushering the guests to a big open tent where Mexicans sweat under white jackets behind big platters of *carne asada* and pots of *chile verde*. Tim smells the moist scent of fresh flour tortillas and it makes him hungry again.

And horny, he thinks. The smell, the sun, all the naked flesh, and her.

"Just a small brunch," Brian says to him. "We'll have a *real* party for you when Don Huertero can be here. A barbecue."

"Who are all these people?" Tim asks.

"My friends," Brian answers. "Mostly Eurotrash. Most of them from the import-export community. A few Germans who live in Borrego Springs. A few weekend guests. A few more permanent houseguests."

"Who's the kid?"

"Kid?" Brian asks. He turns to look at the boy.

"That's Olivia's boy," he answers.

"Which one is Olivia?"

"Olivia's not here." Brian chuckles. "Olivia's back in Betty Ford. For the *eightieth* time. She asked Elizabeth to look after Kit, and Elizabeth asked me if she could bring the boy and the nanny here, so here we all are, one great big happy extended dysfunctional family, *chez* Cervier."

Elizabeth, Tim thinks.

"Cute kid," he says.

"Isn't he?"

Brian's practically licking his lips, Tim thinks.

"Kid got a father?"

Brian shrugs. "In theory."

Tim realizes that they're all waiting for him to start, so he gets a big bowl of vegetarian chili and some tortillas and sits down. A waiter brings him a margarita.

He eats and drinks and watches the slave traders and drug dealers line up for their food.

Something else: A tall man strides into the pool area. Tim watches him. The man wears an old cowboy hat, a thick green work shirt, khaki jeans and cowboy boots. The sleeves are rolled up and show a cowboy's tan. The man takes off his reflective sunglasses and smirks at the party guests. He squints until he finds Brian, then walks under the canopy, takes off his hat and talks to Brian. Hat in hand, Tim thinks, employee to employer.

Brian nods, nods, and nods again. He gestures for the man to eat, but the man smirks, shakes his head and points the hat out there, toward the desert.

He has *work* to do, Tim thinks.

Then the man looks over Brian's shoulder and stares at Tim. And smirks. He doesn't think he's inferior.

He's middle-aged, Tim sees. Big sun-wrinkled face and he's been working his whole life. Out there. He looks at Tim like Tim's one of his cattle that he's sizing up.

The man doesn't put his hat back on until he's out from under the canopy.

Tim thinks the same thing he'd think if he saw the guy on the yard.

The man is trouble, Tim thinks.

Then he goes back to eating. A rule that holds up in the joint or in the Corps: When there's food, eat. When there's a party, party.

9.

Tim watches the sunset from a parapet on the wall.

Behind and beneath him the pool party sputters toward
an end. Beyond the wall the mountains turn from sienna
to chocolate brown as the light fades.

He's interested now in watching the sun set because he
wants to mark true west for himself. Something he
remembers from all that orienteering shit in the Corps.
So he watches the sun go down over the nearest mountains and he figures he's somewhere in the southern
dogleg of Borrego, near the Mexican border. There's a
long stretch of desert between Cervier's ranch and those
mountains.

He can also see that the *Beau Geste* fort is a make-
believe fort set inside a real one, a small compound
encircled by a much larger one. The larger circle is bor-
dered by thick rows of tamarisk trees. He can make out
the high barbed-wire fence inside the trees. Soda cans,
probably filled with pebbles, he thinks, are strung from
the lower strands of wire. The top of the fence is
stretched with double wire and a single strand of electri-
fied fence. In a thicker grove of tamarisk there's a
barbed-wire gate that leads to a dirt road.

Outside the trees, out in the scrub brush of the desert,

coils of barbed wire lie like snakes on the ground. And probably motion and sound detectors, Tim thinks.

Brian likes his privacy.

Not that there aren't a lot of people around. In the large outer compound Tim can make out several armed guards, at least five outbuildings that look like workers' quarters, garages and workshops. He sees several three-wheel all-terrain vehicles and a small fleet of dirt bikes. The humvee, and maybe there is more than one, is visible in a garage where a worker is checking the oil. There's even an ultralight aircraft that one of the Germans flew over from Borrego.

There's a stable with horses and the accompanying shit.

And way off in the southern end of the large compound, and Tim's had to look hard to see it, there are five rectangles of off-colored brush that look like overgrown tennis courts. But he doesn't think they are. He doesn't know what the fuck they are.

He climbs down and rejoins the party, which is gathered now around the Jacuzzi.

Brian is cuddled up with a pretty boy from Milan. Two lanky Germans are up to their shoulders in the hot swirling water. Another Luftwaffe type, a big strapping Aryan, is busy seducing a small dark-haired woman whose pert breasts peek through a gauzy poncho. The women who remain are at least dressed, Tim sees, as the desert night turns cold. And *she*'s sipping a glass of dark red wine and sitting back on the chaise, watching.

The kid—what's his name? Tim asks himself—is at it with the boat again, zooming it around the pool in some sort of imaginary race. Against nobody. A lonely kid, with no other kids around to play with and no one seems to care.

The nanny's toking on a joint.

Tim pulls a chair up and sits down.

Brian takes a thick spliff from his lips and says, "Your dope, Z."

Tim makes a sign of the cross and says, " 'Wherever two or more are gathered in my name . . .' "

They laugh and Brian offers Tim the joint. Tim waves it off and Brian slips it into the mouth of his pretty boy, who sucks hard and deep. And the kid's *seeing* this shit, Tim thinks.

The big German—Tim thinks of him as Hans even though he doesn't know his name—says to the minx lady, "You know what I'd like to do to you?"

He says it loud deliberately, Tim sees, so that everyone will stop and listen. Everyone does. She's tickled fucking pink. Her eyes light up and she asks, "What would you like to do with me?"

Tim sees the kid turn to watch.

Hans says, "I'd like to spank your little ass—"

"Why don't you keep it between you?" Tim asks Hans.

Hans's had enough to drink that he forgets who's talking to him, and he gives Tim an upper-class sneer, turns back to the lady and says, in this B-movie accent, "—eat you until you scream—"

"Shut up, Willy," Elizabeth says.

"—fuck you, then come all over your tits."

They all laugh, except the kid, Elizabeth and Tim.

Tim's not laughing.

What Tim does is he springs up and slaps Willy hard across the face. The slap knocks Willy off his chair. He's on his knees giving Tim this shocked look when Tim grabs him by the shirt collar, hauls him to the pool and pushes his head under the water.

And holds it there.

Even while Tim's thinking that it's the same bad temper that got him tossed out of the Corps. And even though he knows it's the same character flaw, all he feels is this red anger as he holds Willy's head under the pretty blue water.

Nobody moves, either. Not Brian or his boy, or the woman who had just now thought Willy was so hot. They just sit there watching him drown their friend.

Some fucking buddies, he thinks.

Then Elizabeth uncoils herself from her chaise, walks over and taps Tim on the shoulder.

"Bobby," she says quietly, and she's smiling again, "he's turning funny colors."

Tim hauls Willy up. Willy lays on his back gasping like a trout and Tim tells him, "You shouldn't talk that way in front of a kid."

Then, to sound more like Bobby Z, adds, "It's not cool."

He's about to tell the stoned nanny to do a better job when the cowboy is suddenly standing there. Now he has a revolver strapped to his hip.

Talks like a cowboy, too, Tim thinks, when the man says, "We're ready to go out, Mr. C."

And Tim hears himself say, "I want to go."

Brian sputters, "I don't think—"

"I want to go," Tim says. Cold, like Z, like *nobody fuck with me*.

The cowboy hears, too, because he asks, "You got any *real* clothes?"

"In my room," Tim answers.

"I can wait a bit."

Tim feels the kid watching him as he leaves. Her, too, but she's trying to hide it.

When he comes out again a few minutes later the party's broken up. But the kid is still playing with the boat and Elizabeth's keeping an eye on him. She gets up when she sees Tim and walks over to him.

She says, "I liked what you did."

"I was an asshole," he answered. "I lost my temper."

"He was thrilled someone stood up for him," she says. "Finally."

"He looks like a nice kid," Tim says. He can't think of anything else to say.

"You think so?" she asks, looking at him funny.

"Yeah, why not?" he answers, then says, "I mean, if you're into kids."

"Are you?"

"Not me, no."

"That's too bad," she says.

"Why's that too bad?" he asks, figuring he's being flirted with. Liking it.

She looks at him with those smart, knowing eyes.

"Because he's yours," she says.

And turns around and walks away.

10.

The cowboy's name is Bill Johnson. He's the ranch foreman. Brian actually has some cattle out there but cattle isn't the ranch business. Tim learns this riding with Johnson in the front of a Bedford truck, rumbling along a mountain trail toward the border.

The trip starts in the garages in the outer compound. Four big canvas-topped Bedfords gassed and ready to go. A humvee in front. Lights on only in the humvee as they pick their way along what has to be a sheep trail. It's around ten o'clock when they reach the back side of a ridge overlooking the border.

Johnson stops the trucks and signals the humvee ahead. The fourwheelers scutter up the ridge. The truck driver slips headsets on and scans the radio. He looks at Johnson, shakes his head and gives a thumbs-up. Johnson grabs a handheld radio and a pair of infrared glasses, which he loops around his neck.

"You wanna go for a walk?" he asks Tim.

"Sure."

Johnson walks to the back of the truck, opens the flaps and says something in rapid Spanish. Tim watches five Cahuilla Indians jump out, all of them armed with rifles and machetes. They trot down the ridge toward the canyon below.

"C'mon," Johnson says to Tim.

They climb the ridge where the humvee sits like one of those idiot guard dogs that used to annoy Tim so much in his B&E days. Lights off now and motor shut down. Tim lies down beside Johnson behind some rocks as the foreman scans the terrain with the night glasses. He hands Tim the binoculars and says, "Have a look."

To his right Tim sees Interstate 8 and the lights of the border town of Jacumba. Directly in front of him in the desert plain he sees four packs of people trotting away from the border. He watches as the Cahuillas run to meet them and start to steer them into the canyon.

Illegals. Coming to El Norte to find work.

Johnson gets up and crouches his way to the humvee. A window opens and Tim sees another headsetted driver.

"Anything?" Johnson asks.

The driver shakes his head.

Tim figures that they're monitoring the INS radios and that there'll be no problem tonight.

"Get down there," Johnson says to the driver. "Hurry them up."

Tim watches the humvee tear down into the valley and help herd the illegal immigrants into the mouth of a narrow canyon. Johnson grunts an order into his radio and Tim hears the truck motors start up behind him.

"Let's go," Johnson says.

They hike back to the road. The Cahuillas and the humvee driver are trying to jam the Mexicans into the backs of the trucks. Dozens of illegals stand in clumps, shivering and looking confused as hell. Whole families, it looks like to Tim—men, women, kids and grandparents. The families are trying to get into the same trucks and it's slowing things down.

Johnson gets into it, pushing, swearing under his breath, and kicking. The Cahuillas pick up on his anger and start swinging rifle stocks, not into heads, but into backs and buttocks. It takes about ten minutes to get the illegals packed in and the canvas flaps tied down.

"And make 'em *callar*," Johnson says to the truck drivers. *Make 'em shut up.* He climbs back into the truck.

"I used to herd cattle," Johnson says. "Now I herd people."

The convoy starts back. Johnson sends the humvee ahead, the Cahuillas riding on its running board. It's a slow process—the trucks cling to the side of the mountains for switchback after switchback. Tim can lean out the window on the curves and look several hundred feet straight down, and he wants to puke. Especially on the downhill grades, when he can hear the gravel slipping under the wheels.

Johnson smokes a cigarette and doesn't seem to mind the drive. He offers Tim a smoke and Tim's tempted, but he quit in solitary and is trying to stay off.

The only thing that seems to make Johnson nervous is his watch. He keeps glancing at it and frowning and after an hour says to Tim, "We're racing the sunrise."

It's such a fucking cowboy thing to say, such a cowboy *movie* thing to say, that Tim chuckles a little.

Johnson says, "There was a truck carrying a load of wetbacks through this desert a while back. Converted moving van that couldn't handle the roads. Sunrise found 'em halfway to nowhere and the INS has choppers. You know what the coyotes did?"

"No."

"Locked up the trucks and left," Johnson says. "The

wetbacks couldn't get out, sun beat down on that metal roof all day, and they cooked inside there."

One thing Mexico's always making is more Mexicans, Tim remembers Brian saying.

"So I'd kind of like to get back well before sunrise," Johnson says.

Johnson radios the driver ahead to put the foot down a little and radios the other trucks to keep up. They're hurtling around these fucking curves, wheels slipping on the gravel, and Johnson suddenly gets talkative.

"One of the most godforsaken places on earth," he says, "Anza-Borrego. And it leads right down to the border. A rustler's dream. Since the government boys clamped down on San Diego the action's moved east, out here, that's all. Perfect for us. The coyotes bring the wetbacks across, turn 'em loose in the desert, the wetbacks're scareder than shit and we pick 'em up and take 'em back to the barn.

"Easier 'n cattle, really, because cattle don't always *want* to come, you know?"

The convoy makes it down the grade and leaves the road altogether, driving across the packed desert ground to a riverbed where there's still a trickle of water in the late spring. They rattle up the creek for an hour, and leave it where a shelf of rock leads them back to the desert floor. A few more minutes, they hit another old mining road and make it back through the gate while the sky is safely black.

Brian waddles up in his white caftan.

To inspect his property, Tim thinks.

The drivers open the trucks and start herding the illegals into the camouflaged rectangles at the far end of the compound. Johnson hops out and motions for Tim to follow him.

They aren't tennis courts, Tim sees, but the roofs of underground barracks. He steps into one to see the tightly packed rows of bunk beds on the concrete floor. A room in the back has some drop toilets and a couple of shower heads. Some water that smells like sulfur drips from a leaky faucet head in the side of the concrete wall.

The place stinks of old sweat and Lysol, and the disinfectant just isn't getting it done. There's been too many fucking people jammed into an underground bunker with the ventilation of a submarine, Tim thinks.

And now they're jamming in a new bunch.

Pack them in and hide them under the ground and if there's a smell of misery, Tim's smelling it. He glances at the eyes of some of these poor bastards and thinks if you can see fear, he's seeing it.

Welcome to the Hotel California.

"It's not getting them *in*," Brian tells Tim as they walk back to the *Beau Geste* inner compound. "It's *hiding* them until you can place them. We have room for five hundred illegals here, and I can move them from here without worrying about checkpoints. North a few miles they pick dates in Indio, a few more miles they clean toilets in Palm Springs. I can truck them to factories in San Diego, L.A., Downey, Riverside . . ."

"You're a sweet guy, Brian."

"So," Brian asks. "You think you can get us some Thais?"

"You running out of Mexicans?"

"It's this fucking NAFTA thing," Brian says. "Next they'll legalize drugs."

"You high, Brian?"

"Just skin popping."

11.

When he gets back to his room she's waiting there for him.

Sitting on the bed, holding a glass of red wine, she's wearing a black silk nightgown with a jacket. Her auburn hair is down now, shoulder-length, and she looks like one of those Victoria's Secret women—three packs of cigs in the joint for a catalog—only better and a lot more real.

It's not all he has on his mind, though.

"The boy's mine?" he asks. Like Bobby Z has a fucking kid? Like why didn't Escobar have that in the book along with favorite sports and beer of preference?

"His name is Kit," she says. "Olivia thought you'd like that."

He decides to take a chance.

"She never told me," he says.

"Well, you'd have had to be around for that," she scolds. "Look, I don't blame you. If I were into women, I'd want to do her too. She's beautiful."

"And fucked up," he says.

"And fucked up."

"Does everyone know?" he asks.

"Olivia and me," she answers. "Now you."

Which is like, *good* news, right? Tim thinks.

"How come you told me?"

"I thought you should know."

He's thinking about this—hell, his head is fucking spinning—when she says, "I've been waiting a long time."

"Brian had a lot to show me."

The smile, the smirk, and "That's not what I meant."

"What did you mean?"

He has a hard-on that's threatening to tear his jeans open and he's hoping she doesn't notice.

But she looks right at his crotch and answers, "You know what I mean."

She gets up from the bed, uncoiling slowly, the way she did from the chaise, and pulls down his jeans. She cups his balls in her right hand and with her left hand grabs his dick and puts it in her mouth. She strokes him, and sucks, and rubs his balls as he looks down at her auburn hair and her beautiful face and reaches his hand down the top of her nightgown. She takes her hand from his balls and slaps his hand away, then she looks up at him as she runs her tongue up his dick and licks the tip.

"It's been a long time," Tim says hoarsely.

"Do you want to come in my mouth, baby?"

"No."

But she goes back to sucking until his balls throb and he doesn't think he can stop himself. She seems to sense it, stands up and strips off the nightgown.

He almost pops off looking at her. Her breasts are bigger than he thought, her stomach flat and her long legs shiny. She pushes him down on the bed and says, "I want to do it our old way."

Old way?! Tim thinks. Our *old* way?! She knows me? Or Bobby, anyway. They tell me no one here has even

seen this dude since like 1983 or something and this
babe's been *sleeping* with him?! So now I have to walk
like him, talk like him and *fuck* like him?!

And figures if he has any brains he'd throw her out, or
make some sort of excuse like he's got an STD or something, but right at this moment Tim isn't exactly thinking
with his brain.

So he lies down. She turns her back on him, squats
over him, then looks over her shoulder and smiles as she
eases herself onto him. She laughs and points to the
mirror and he realizes now that he can see everything.
Her neck and hair and back and beautiful small ass as it
rises and falls on him, and in the mirror her face and
breasts and pussy as it slides up and down his dick.

She sees him watching, laughs again and spreads herself for him. Then she takes her long fingers and starts to
stroke herself as she slides up and down. He grabs her
shoulders to set the pace and force her down hard on him
and they fuck this way until he says, "I can't last much
longer."

She groans for his pleasure then gasps, "Tell me when
you're about to come."

He figures this is so she can pull him out, but when he
tells her he's coming she presses down harder and asks,
"Is it good? Is it good?"

He answers, "It's *so* good," and that seems to set her
off and she arches her muscular back and asks again and
he answers and she goes, "Oh, oh, oh, oh!" and holds
herself on the tip of him and they can both see his dick
throb as he comes.

Later they're just lying there talking about old times,
about the suite at the Ritz, and lazy days on the beach and
hot nights at his mobile home at El Morro beach, just

north of Laguna, which is where she says she fell in love with him, and that she walked down there a few months ago and it doesn't look like it's changed, and does he still own it? And he bullshits for a while with stuff Escobar made him learn, and then they're talking about their lives and she's telling him how things have been since he split and left her hanging out in Laguna.

How she had a semester at UCLA but was too lazy to cut it and it seemed easier to find rich boyfriends and the rich boyfriends she found were rich because they were dealing dope so she gets back into that circle. Which is a hard orbit to leave, especially when you're lazy and what you do *really* well is fuck. And she prefers *courtesan* to *whore*. Anyway, that's how she ends up at Rancho Cervier with the drug-dealing, people-trading nouveau-riche Eurotrash.

"And the Monk helps out from time to time," she says.

Which gets Tim's attention.

If the Monk is Bobby's main man, maybe the Monk can help him get the hell out of the country before Gruzsa can nail him. So Tim's kind of pretty interested in hearing about the Monk.

"You been in touch with the Monk?" he asks.

"Every once in a while," she says. "I need a little hand, I call him. Sometimes he needs an errand run, he calls me."

"Which number do you use?" Tim asks.

"The backdoor number," she says like it's obvious.

He laughs. "Which back door number?"

She tells him 555-6665 like real casual and goes on with filling him in about her life, like she just left a guy and the guy is like stalking her so she's staying with

Brian for a while, which works out okay because she can help keep an eye on Kit.

"My life's been pretty fucked since you dumped me," she says casually. "But it's my own fault. I don't see it changing."

He does. He figures he's pulled this off pretty good so far, why not stretch it out. Take her with him. Get his hands on some of Z's money, announce his retirement and move up to Eugene.

So he says, real gallant like, "Why don't you come with me?"

She laughs, "You're not going anywhere."

"I'm not?"

She's smirking and he thinks she's running some game with him.

"No," she says.

"No?"

He reaches for her pussy and starts to stroke her. Feels her moisten. Loves looking at her green eyes as she gets wet.

"Because when Don Huertero gets here?" she says, with that California-girl upward inflection. She closes her eyes because she's digging what he's doing with his fingers.

"Yeah?"

"He's going to kill you," she says.

Of course.

"Which would be a shame," Elizabeth murmurs.

"I think so, too."

She grabs his dick and repeats, "A shame."

Before he knows what's happening, she's *moving* under him—like it's no work at all—like his dick is on remote control or something, she's doing ripply things

up and down the length of it and he doesn't care Don
Huertero wants him dead.

He just wants to fuck.

Which he guesses is what the prison social worker
meant by "lack of impulse control" and "inability to delay
gratification."

"They say I can't delay gratification," he tells her.

"Did they say you don't finish what you start?"

"They didn't say that."

"Good."

As to the delayed gratification, he does okay.

That done, he asks, "Huertero wants to *kill* me?" Good
job, Agent Gruzsa. Nice going. How come you know
everything there is to know about Bobby except that little
detail? Call *me* a dumb moke.

Elizabeth says, "Brian's just holding you for him until
he can get here."

"I thought they were planning a barbecue," Tim says.

"They are."

Of fucking course.

"How do you know all this?"

"You know Brian," she says casually. "He can't keep
his mouth shut. I hear things."

The situation is not, like, *good*. They have him trapped
in this movie fort and they got something in mind worse
than what the Angels do. All of a sudden Pelican Bay is
looking pretty good to him.

"Why?" he asks.

"Why what?"

Why fucking what?!

"Why does Don Huertero want to kill me?" he asks.

She shrugs her beautiful shoulders. "You're kidding,
right?"

Yeah, I'm just fucking around, he thinks. But he's afraid to push it because probably Bobby is supposed to know what the beef is with Don Huertero. Also Tim thinks that if he ups and tells them he isn't Bobby Z, only bad things can happen. They either don't believe him, in which case they kill him. Or they believe him, in which case they kill him.

So it's probably better to be Bobby Z and have some stroke—and maybe some bargaining power somewhere—than to be three-time loser and career fuck-up Tim Kearney.

With no stroke and less than zero bargaining power.

He's thinking about all this when she says, "So don't you think you'd better get going?"

"Yeah."

He does think that, now that he's basically fucked out and worried about staying alive again. And he's pissed off and scared, and it's a situation not all that different from the joint except this time the choice is die or die.

So he figures like, fuck you all, because he's getting pissed off.

So pissed off he feels the old impulse control slipping.

Like that night in the Gulf when the Rack tanks started shooting the shit out of them and Tim just got pissed off, that's all, and the old impulse control just went right out the old window.

He's feeling like that now.

It feels great.

12.

Tad Gruzsa isn't exactly the happiest camper in the greater Southern California coastal region.

Gruzsa's sitting in a shitty bar in Downey, knocking down his second bourbon with branch water, trying to drink enough nerve to hit the barrio for Escobar's calling hours.

The beaners love those open caskets, too, Gruzsa's thinking, and there was so little left of Jorge's face that Gruzsa had to lay three dimes on the undertaker so that Escobar would at least vaguely resemble a human being as he lay smiling up from the casket.

Gruzsa didn't mind paying for the Madame Tussaud job, he just didn't want to actually *see* it. Especially after the undertaker had called him to proudly announce that he had even cosmetically recreated Escobar's acne, for chrissakes.

Gruzsa hates beaner funerals, too. Too fucking emotional, with the mother and the sisters and the aunts wailing and the men—half of Escobar's male relatives are Mexican Mafia anyway—standing around pledging revenge. And they'd do a full mass, too, then the drive out to the cemetery and . . . Gruzsa's been to any number of Mexican funerals: it comes with the job in this part of the country.

So Gruzsa is trying to drink away the thought of the wake and the funeral and he's also very pissed at one Tim Kearney, career criminal and monumental fuck-up who has tennis-shoed it, leaving Art Moreno hanging and Tad Gruzsa in the deep shit.

Won't be easy to explain this mess to the suits back in Washington who don't understand just how complicated the business can get on the Left Coast. Sooner or later, Gruzsa broods, they're going to start asking just why it is that I keep losing beaners. First Art Moreno kidnapped and now Jorge Escobar splattered all over the old arroyo.

What can I say? Gruzsa mused. Life is a dangerous proposition for a beaner on the border.

Tim Kearney is another story. It's one thing to spring a three-time loser from the joint if you get results, another thing entirely to loose a career criminal on society and have nothing left in your hand but your dick.

Tim Kearney running around could fuck up all sorts of things, Gruzsa thinks. I'm just going to have to locate the skell and make him live up to his part of the bargain and that's all there is to it.

It just wouldn't do to have Tim Kearney running around shooting his mouth off. Tim Kearney's only useful role in life was to get himself dead.

Gruzsa polishes off his drink and knocks on the bar to order another. It arrives as an enormous mass of man in leathers plops onto the stool beside him.

"Hello, fuckwad," Gruzsa says. "How's the meth business?"

"I don't even want to be *seen* with you," the biker says. "Never mind exchange pleasantries."

"What? You think I'm thrilled?"

"What do you want?"

Gruzsa orders the biker a beer and says, "The guy who did your brother?"

Gruzsa sees he's got Boom-Boom's interest. Boom-Boom is like six-seven, about three-twenty and has mouse-brown hair down to his ass. The book on Boom-Boom is that he doesn't like to fight. Fists, knives or guns, Boom-Boom would rather take a pass.

What Boom-Boom likes is blowing people up.

Hence the name.

Now Boom-Boom's got a gleam in his eye.

"Kearney?" he asks.

"That the guy who killed your brother?"

"Tim Kearney murdered Stinkdog."

"Then that's who I'm talking about," Gruzsa says.

"What about him?"

"You been looking for him."

Boom-Boom doesn't answer. No point in wasting air on the obvious.

Gruzsa says, "You been searching the system for him, but you ain't found him. It's like he disappeared, right?"

"Figured he was stowed away out-of-state," Boom-Boom answers. "We'll find him."

Gruzsa shakes his head. "I cut him loose."

Gruzsa enjoys the surprise on Boom-Boom's fat stupid face as the biker asks, "Why'd you do that?"

And Gruzsa can't resist answering, "Because we were so thrilled with him greasing your trailer-trash brother."

Sees Boom-Boom's hand tighten around the neck of the beer bottle and adds, "You don't have the balls, Boom-Boom. Maybe you'd leave a package under my car and sneak away in the dark, but you don't have the balls to do me to my face."

Boom-Boom's hand loosens and he lifts the bottle to his lips. When he finishes the beer, he asks, "Why you telling me this?"

"Like the TV commercial," Gruzsa says. "Why ask why?"

"Cuz you could be setting me up."

Gruzsa laughs. "I want to set you up, I could do it without sitting down with you. By the way, did you ever hear of a shower? You smell."

"Fuck you, Gruzsa."

"You can dream," Gruzsa says. "Anyway, what I heard was that at Chino you were a catcher."

Boom-Boom looks at Gruzsa with a look that's pure hatred, which is fine with Gruzsa because he likes his hatred straight up. Boom-Boom's so mad Gruzsa figures what he heard about him is true, and Gruzsa laughs at the image.

"I can do a car bomb so that it takes off just your legs," Boom-Boom tells him, looking down at Gruzsa's crotch.

Gruzsa nods then hits him in the face with a chopping right hand. Can hear the cartilage in Boom-Boom's nose crack under his fist.

"We're doing business doesn't give you rights," Gruzsa explains.

Boom-Boom sits on the stool, his eyes watering and blood pouring out of his nose. But he doesn't go out and he doesn't go down. Gruzsa has to give it to him for that. Boom-Boom's a *tough* stupid son of a bitch.

The bartender's suddenly very busy counting the till and developing selective amnesia. Bar sells more meth than booze, anyway, so you ain't gonna see no videotape of this cop smacking a skell. This is all between grownups.

"Let's just say somebody drops off Kearney in a body bag," Gruzsa says, "I'm just going to figure it was Santa Claus and leave it at that."

Boom-Boom nods and wipes the blood onto his sleeve.

Gruzsa adds, "Soon."

"We want him worse than you do."

"I were you, I'd start looking down around the border," Gruzsa says. He slides off the stool and leaves a twenty on the bar. "Don't bother to thank me. My work is its own reward."

"Fuck you."

But it has a nasal twang this time.

Gruzsa leaves the bar feeling better than he has all day.

13.

Tim finds his way to Brian's room, sneaks open the door and sees Brian fixing himself up a speedball. Brian's Italian boy is naked, stretched out on the floor, propped up on one elbow, watching.

The room smells of incense and hashish.

Tim walks in.

"Z!" Brian squeals. "An unexpected pleasure!"

Tim looks at the Italian boy and says, "Is it cool if Brian and I have a private moment?"

The boy looks hesitant, but Brian says, "Run along."

When they're alone, Brian says, "Did Elizabeth find you? You smell like fucking."

Tim nods at the syringe and says, "Can I help you?"

"An honor."

Tim fiddles with the syringe as Brian ties off. When he sees a vein pop up nice and thick, Tim squeezes all the fluid out of the syringe and jams the needle into Brian's arm.

Brian's eyes bulge in fear.

"What the fuck—" he says, his teeth still clamped on the rubber hose.

"That's right, Bri," Tim says. "A fat syringe of pure air. I push the plunger here and an air bubble goes zinging right up to your heart and ... *bang*. Instant massive coronary."

"*Why—*"

"Look into my eyes, fuckwad," Tim says with a confidence he doesn't feel. "I'm Bobby Z and I'll know if you're lying. You know that, don't you?"

Brian nods. His face is red and Tim's afraid he might have a heart attack anyway.

"So what's up, Brian?" Tim asks.

"What's up?" Brian squeaks.

"Yeah, what's up with you and Don Huertero?" Tim asks. "What's the big hidalgo have in mind for me? And don't give me any more bullshit about the big meth deal, Brian, because I know that was just candy to keep me fat and happy while you set me up, right?"

Sweat's popping out of every fat pore in Brian's face.

"Right?" Tim asks. He pushes the needle in a little deeper.

Brian says, "We can make a deal, Z."

"The deal is you're going to tell me right now or your heart's going to explode like an M-80 in a trash can," Tim says.

A common way for guys to go in the joint, Tim recalls. No muss, no fuss, and the guards can say that another junkie con OD'd.

"Death is just another trip," Brian says, trying to bluff.

"Well, *adiós*, my friend," Tim says.

He starts to press the plunger.

Brian's arm jumps, his eyes about pop out of their fat, and he says, "Don Huertero wants to kill you himself."

"Is that why he traded Moreno for me?"

"I guess."

"Keep talking."

"He's coming this weekend," Brian gushes. "Talked about putting you on a spit and roasting you over a fire."

Swell, Tim thinks.

"Why?"

"Why?" Brian asks. He giggles. "Don Huertero doesn't tell 'why.' He tells 'what.' "

"You don't know what his beef is?!" Tim asks.

"Just that you took something from him."

"What?!"

"I don't know, Z." Brian starts crying now. "I don't. He just said you took his treasure."

"His treasure?" Tim asks. "The fuck is he? Long John Silver?"

"Come on, Bobby," Brian whines. "We're friends."

"But you were going to just hand me over, right?"

"I didn't have a choice."

Yeah, Tim thinks. He wants to press the plunger but doesn't. He asks, "You have a gun in here, Brian?"

"No."

"Don't lie to me. I don't like it."

"Desk," Brian says. "Top drawer."

Tim pulls out the needle. Brian slumps to the floor and sits there crying while Tim gets the gun from the drawer. It's a 9mm automatic. Tim would have preferred a service .45, but it'll have to do. Tim also finds a money clip with cash, and he puts both in his pocket.

Because cash is always in good taste and you never know when you'll need a piece.

"Tell Don Huertero *gracias* but *no gracias*, Brian," Tim says. "I'm checking out now."

And Tim knows he's being like *stupid*—he ought to whack Brian or at least take him along as a hostage—but he's just like sick of this shit, sick of these people, and all he really wants to do is walk away from here *alone*.

I mean *fuck*, he thinks. A kid, an old girlfriend, some fucking Mexican thinks he's god wants to cook me over a fire. I mean, *fuck this shit. Fuck Bobby Z.*

So he even knows he's fucking up massively—what's new—but he just takes the gun and walks back to his room and starts to throw a few clothes together. Khaki L.L. Bean shirt, jeans, denim jacket, Doc Martens. He grabs a couple of bottles of Evian from his little fridge and shoves them in his pockets along with a few other necessities.

Then he pulls the gun and walks out into the compound. Nobody's called the dogs out yet—Brian's probably still changing his underwear—so it's cool so far.

The night is desert warm. Soft and inky black. The stars look so close you could kiss them.

Tim wants to. He's wild now. Really free for the first time maybe ever.

There's a guard at the *Beau Geste* gate.

"Coming through," Tim says.

The guard starts to go for his own gun, but Tim's smiling like a *loco* and the guard figures it ain't worth dying for. He drops his gun and pushes a button and the gate swings open.

Tim steps through into the outer compound, and now he can hear a commotion behind him. Fucking alarm going off and he reminds himself not to trip over any lawn sprinklers and now they're all coming.

He hears Brian running along the parapet screeching, "Stop him! Stop him!" but Brian's a moron because he's also yelling, "Don't kill him! Don't kill him!" so the guards don't know what the hell they're supposed to do.

"Don't stickin' move!" Tim yells. "This is a fuck-up!"

He laughs like a crazy bastard and looks back up at the parapet and there's Brian running back and forth screeching and Elizabeth just standing there watching.

And that's truly cool but Tim doesn't know how the fuck he's going to get through the main gate, and now he realizes that they don't have to shoot him, they only have to keep him in the compound.

Which is when he spots the truck and that gives him a bunch of ideas.

He walks over and lets three rounds loose, which gets everyone's head down, and it takes him maybe five seconds to hot-wire the truck. He steers for the gate and there's Johnson standing there in his boxers looking sleepy and irritable with a Winchester in his hands.

"Where do you think you're going, son?" he drawls.

"Out there," Tim answers.

"Ain't nothing out there," Johnson says.

"That's what I like about it."

Johnson just shakes his head and says, "Well, I can't let you go."

"You're not going to shoot me."

"I don't have to."

Johnson's raising the rifle to shoot out the tires when Tim points the 9mm at him.

Johnson smiles. "You ain't the type."

So Tim squeezes one right past his ear. Johnson hits the deck and that gives Tim time to put the truck in reverse and get himself some room. Then he fucking *stands* on the gas and heads toward the gate.

Johnson's trying to get a shot from the old prone position but now he's too busy rolling out of the way, and the guards are jumping clear of the gate and Brian's screaming and Tim can feel Elizabeth smiling as he rams through the gate, and he's free and clear.

Except he sees the kid.

Sees the kid in the rearview mirror. Just standing there in the outer compound looking at the back of the truck. Looking real sad.

And Tim's thinking *fuck it, man,* it ain't my kid.

But his foot hits the brake anyway, and he's telling himself, You're free and clear, man. Take your shot. You'll never make it with a kid in tow. No way.

"Fuck it," he says to himself, and steps on the gas.

And he's still thinking *fuck it* as he puts the truck in reverse and the kid starts trotting toward him. Trotting and then *running* as he sees the truck coming back. Little legs pumping it out, man, and Tim can see Brian's boys scrambling for their wheels and Johnson's standing there, but even he's not going to try to shoot over the kid.

Tim stops the truck and opens the door.

The kid stops running and just stands there looking at him.

Of course, Tim thinks. Of fucking course.

"You wanna come?" he asks the kid.

"Yes."

"Shit, come on."

He reaches down and scoops the boy up and sets him in the passenger seat. He shifts into first as the kid grabs the shoulder strap and clicks the buckle in.

Tim is shoving the truck into third as the kid says, "You don't have your seat belt on."

"Shut up," Tim says.

But he buckles up, then races into the desert night.

14.

He's in a race he can't win and he knows it.

First, he doesn't know where he is. Two, he doesn't know where he's going. Three, he's driving a slow truck on a bad road. Four, he's saddled with a kid. Five, the other side has a fleet of off-road vehicles. Six, he's just a loser, that's all. He figures there's probably a seven and an eight but he's too stupid to think of what they are.

Okay, first things first, he tells himself. One: You don't know where you are. Big deal. Two: You don't know where you're going. Well, that's not exactly true. You know you're heading off fucking Rancho Cervier. The road's leading roughly north and it must connect with an east–west road that leads out of the park. Three: You're driving a slow truck on a bad road . . . Okay, let's skip to four. Four: You're saddled with a kid . . . Okay, let's skip to five: The other side has a fleet of off-road vehicles . . .

He brakes the truck and turns off the engine.

"What—" the kid starts to say.

"Quiet, I want to listen."

"What for?"

"Engine sounds."

"What for?"

"Shut up," Tim snaps, then adds, "I need your help. Be

real quiet and see if you can tell how many different sounds there are. Can you count?"

"I'm six years old," the kid says with some annoyance.

But he shuts up and starts to listen.

So does Tim. What he hears is pretty interesting. He can hear a shitload of activity way the hell off to his left, roughly east, running parallel to him. In fact getting out ahead. The high-pitched whines of dune buggies. Maybe a couple of dirt bikes. Maybe six or seven vehicles total. Enough, anyway.

Headed for the road junction, Tim thinks. Cut him off there.

Okay, what's behind me?

Two, maybe three, dirt bikes, close. But not trying to catch up necessarily. Just herding me to the junction. Behind the dirt bikes, what? Maybe the fucking humvee.

"Well?" he asks the kid.

"Sounds like eighty-seven engines," the kid says seriously.

"I counted eighty-six," Tim says, "but I think you're probably right."

Tim starts the truck up again and stamps on the gas.

"Your belt on tight?" he asks the kid.

"Yes."

"Hold on."

Tim jerks the wheel to the right and the truck slides off the road. He keeps gunning the engine until the wheels spin in the sand.

They're waiting at the road junction? Tim thinks. Fuck 'em. Let 'em wait.

Who do they think they're dealing with, a fucking moron?

He gets out of the truck, walks to the other side and

pulls the kid out. Whispers, "We got a little surprise for these guys."

The kid's grinning from ear to ear. Say "surprise" to a kid, it's like saying "beer" to a sailor. Anyway, the kid's into it.

Kid nods and whispers, "Try to act nonchalant."

They climb into the back of the truck.

Tim starts getting shit together, like *quickly*, because they don't have a lot of time before the boys catch up. Someone who knows what he's doing has thought things out, because the essential stuff is there. Tim takes a blanket, two bottles of sterilized water and a flashlight and shoves them into the compartment behind the dirt bike's seat. Then he finds a fold-up shovel and sticks it under the bungee cord. Finds some wire, duct tape and other repair crap, and crams it in with the other stuff.

"You ever ride on one of these babies before?" Tim asks.

The kid's so blown away he just shakes his head.

"Well, you're about to."

"Cool."

"Way cool."

If we get lucky, Tim thinks. If the bikers behind us fuck up and try to be heroes. Don't do what they should do.

What they should do when they see the truck is lay back, radio ahead and let the rest of the boys close in. What I'm hoping they do is try to get up the promotion list by checking it out themselves.

"You have to be real quiet," Tim whispers as he plops the kid onto the seat.

"Okaaay," the kid says, struggling to say it through his giggles.

"No, *real* quiet."

"Okay."

Because Tim's heard the bikes sputter to a stop. Figures the boys have seen the truck crashed off the road and are deciding what the fuck they're supposed to do now.

C'mon, boys, Tim thinks. Come be heroes.

He hears their boots crunching on the gravel. Slowly.

Come on, Tim's thinking. Closer.

So close now he can hear them lock and load.

"Hold on," Tim mutters.

He feels the kid's arms tighten around his waist.

He guns the throttle and they come *flying* out the back of the truck. Land and bounce and the kid almost loses it but holds on. Tim steers the bike off the road into the arroyo and off they go, full fucking throttle. The boys are scrambling back for their own bikes, and it's like *chase city* out there on the desert.

These boys are *good*, Tim thinks, because it isn't long before they're on his tail in the arroyo, catching up to him. They're whooping it up like *vaqueros*, having just a wonderful time out there, probably figuring that they'll get beside him and have a little rodeo, and in fact one of them pulls alongside then jumps up out of the arroyo so he's riding along about head-high with Tim while the other guy pushes from behind, and the humvee is coming up fast on the other side.

Tim wrenches the handlebars and skids to a stop, then throttles it and heads back the other way, straight at the boy behind him, who chickens out and crashes his bike into the side of the arroyo.

But a few seconds later it's the same game only in the opposite direction, and now the first guy is riding beside Tim on his left side and the other guy has about caught up from behind.

Fuck it, Tim thinks, and he jumps the bike out the right side of the arroyo back up to the desert floor. The guy behind follows him up so Tim spins the bike again and zooms straight at the arroyo this time, hollers "Hold on!" and jumps the bike over the fucking thing just as the other biker's jumping it the other way.

Tim figures the kid's about had it, going to freak, but he can hear the kid giggling like crazy, *giggling,* so Tim keeps on gunning the bike and he's jazzing it straight ahead now, dodging rocks and cactus and mesquite bushes, and the boys are zooming in behind him.

Tim spots one huge mother of a sand dune off to his left and figures *What the hell, we're going to lose anyway,* and heads straight for it. He stops for a second at the base of the thing and asks, "Are you okay?" like it makes any difference anyway.

"I'm fine!" the kid says.

"We're going up this thing," Tim says, pointing to the sand dune.

"Cool!"

Yeah, cool, Tim thinks, until we lose momentum and flip over backward, or tip sideways and roll back down it, or just plain can't make it up and get caught by our playmates, but he guns the throttle and up they go.

Climbing steeper and steeper, the back wheel trying to slide out but Tim just won't fucking let it. The motor screaming, the boys coming up behind, sounds like they're having problems of their own, and Tim about flips the bike five times but he makes it to the top, stops and watches the boys coming up behind him.

Real cute, too, because they've spread out to cut him off on the top of the dune. So Tim figures *fuck you* and just heads right back down again, not on the wussy *side* but just straight down the dune, like it's almost skydiving on a motorcycle and if the boys don't want to lose him they have to do the same.

The kid's giggling like a crazy little motherfucker and the bike is falling out of the night sky like falling off the earth on a big pile of sand and the boys aren't whooping anymore, they're just pissing their pants, because it is *steep*, and sure enough the first bike coming down *loses* it. Poor bastard just flips that thing end over end and it must be a wicked spill because he doesn't get up.

Tim reaches the bottom and starts racing for nowhere with the other bike behind him and that fucking humvee out there somewhere and Tim realizes he just can't beat this other biker, the guy's too good. And has a rifle, a beautiful M-16 strapped over his back. Looks like some German in an old movie but the guy is one good rider and this isn't going to work out.

So I gotta do something else, Tim thinks, and the sand dune bit's maybe bought me a little space to do it. So he heads for a stretch of thick bush, mesquite and smoke tree and all that shit, and finds a little corridor through it and guns like hell. Hears the other guy pick up on his throttle and knows the guy's scared of losing him in the brush.

Tim lays the bike down in the brush. Grabs the kid and sets him down under a mesquite and says, "Stay here and be quiet."

Doesn't wait for any argument but grabs the shovel, unscrews it, flaps the blade open and waits beside the bush. Times it, steps out, swings that little shovel and smacks it right into the guy's face. Guy's like *out* even before he tumbles backward off the bike.

Tim takes the M-16, straps it over his own back, picks

up the kid and gets back on the bike. Steers her back onto the open desert to make some time. Making time like crazy, things looking pretty good, and then he looks back and sees that fucking humvee coming up behind.

Knows he isn't going to take it out with any shovel. Maybe, *maybe* could lay the bike down and shoot the humvee's tires out, but they might freak and start shooting back and there's the kid to think about.

So he just tries to outrun it, knows it's a loser game because the humvee doesn't have to catch him, just maintain contact until daylight, until the reinforcements come, but he can at least make that a race.

So he's cruising, racing through the night, the humvee racing behind him, closing in, *real* close now, but Tim's making a run for it and then the world just disappears.

Tim screams, *"Shiiiiiiiiiitttt!"* because he's just run out of desert. The whole world like just ends at the knife edge of this huge fucking canyon, like a three-hundred-foot straight drop, and Tim about tears the damn handlebars off he turns so hard, and hits the brakes and lays the bike into a wicked skid. He figures they're both dead, the front wheel's dangling off the edge of the world and he's afraid to move and the humvee just keeps going, just flies off the edge and there's like *silence* for a few seconds, then *boom* and the sky's glowing orange.

The kid isn't giggling.

He's crying.

"Are you okay?"

"My leg hurts."

Tim disentangles himself from the bike, carefully lifts the boy up and sets him down again. He gets the flashlight from the back, rolls the boy's pants leg up and sees blood. It's mostly scrapes, nothing seems broken, and the boy is just sniffling now.

"I'm okay," the boy says.

"You're a brave boy."

Kid smiles.

Tim takes the stuff from the back of the bike. He rolls up the blanket and ties it around his waist, takes out the bottles of Evian. Hands one to the kid.

"I'll bet I can drink this before you can," Tim says.

The kid takes the bet and starts to guzzle. Times it so the kid just beats him. Then Tim refills the water bottles.

"You want to play a game?" Tim asks.

"Sure. What?"

"You know what a Marine is?"

"Some kind of soldier, right?"

"Don't ever say that again, kid," Tim warns. "A Marine is not a soldier. Those are Army pukes. A Marine is the toughest, roughest, finest fighting man the world has ever seen. You wanna play Marine?"

"Yes."

"Okay. We're gonna play Marine for the next couple of days and we're going to be on a secret hike. We can't let the other guys find us. Got it?"

"Got it."

"You up to it?"

"I'm up to it."

"There's going to be a lot of walking."

"Okay."

Tim pushes the bike off the edge of the cliff, down to where the orange glow is fading into a blood red.

"Let's go," he says.

He can make out the silhouette of the mountains to the

west. He figures if they can make it over those mountains they'll be home free. So they start walking.

After a few minutes the kid looks exhausted and Tim decides they can make better time if he carries him. He picks him up and sets him on his shoulders. The kid's no heavier than a fully loaded field pack.

"*What's* your name?" Tim asks, because he's forgotten again.

"Kit," the kid answers. "What's yours?"

"Call me Bobby," Tim says.

He sets a strong pace. He wants to be as close as he can to those mountains before the sun comes up.

15.

Brian Cervier is pissed.

And worried—sphincter-gripping scared—because he *had* Bobby Z and let him get loose.

"Find him," he tells Johnson.

Johnson's standing there in the parlor, hat in his hand from old-fashioned manners, not from respect. The hat band leaves a red welt on his forehead where his receding hair is going to gray. He stares at Brian. Johnson doesn't say it but his look says it for him. The look says *Listen you fat queer, it's a big goddamn desert out there.*

Brian reads the look—even the faggot part—and answers the unspoken words.

"Bobby's a surfer-boy dope peddler," Brian says. "He's soft. He doesn't know the desert. Won't be no day at the beach."

"He did himself pretty good last night," Johnson says. Johnson's seen the bodies already. Seen the wreckage.

"The sun's not out at night," Brian snaps.

Johnson just smiles. He figures he knew that already.

"Ain't all that hot this time of year," he says.

"It's still the desert!" Brian screeches.

Fat Boy wouldn't know the desert from his dessert, Johnson thinks. Fat Boy lives in the desert and hates the sun. Wears them big hats and old-lady dresses all the time and hides from the sun. Stays inside most of the day watching those movies. Black-and-white desert movies. That's what Fat Boy knows about the desert.

"I'll catch him," Johnson says. Not because it's the desert and not because the man is soft, but because the man is dragging along a kid. And that ain't gonna get it.

"Woman must have told him," Johnson says.

"No shit?" Brian asks.

Johnson figures he's had enough of Fat Boy's sarcastic crap so he says, "Don Huertero's gonna be one unhappy hidalgo."

And watches Brian's skin crawl. A visible shimmer across the white fatty flesh. Like a shadow racing across the sand flats.

Brian's just terrified of Don Huertero.

"Find him," Brian whines.

"I got two of the boys tracking now," Johnson says. "And I'm goin' into town to pick up Rojas."

"Rojas is probably drunk."

"Probably," Johnson says.

Drunk or sober, Johnson thinks, Rojas could track a fly across eighty acres of shit.

"What about the woman?" Johnson asks.

"I'll take care of the woman," Brian says.

Johnson's smile says *Well, that'll be a first.* But otherwise he keeps his mouth shut and just puts his hat back on his head.

"I need him alive," Brian says.

Johnson already knows this but thinks it's too bad. Hard to catch a man like that, especially if the man knows you ain't going to risk shooting him from a range. And you could bring a man down from a long ways away in the desert. Long flat country with no wind blowing. But catching him, putting your arm on him and haulin' him back like some wild spring calf, that's a different story altogether.

"What about the little boy?" Johnson asks.

"What *about* the little boy?"

"You want him alive, too?"

"I don't want him at all," Brian says.

Johnson knows better but doesn't say anything.

"I won't kill a kid," says Johnson.

Brian shrugs. "Rojas will."

Rojas will, Johnson muses. Rojas'd kill anything.

Brian watches Johnson's lanky frame duck under the Arab doorway and Brian hates the big cowboy. Just fucking detests the Gary Cooper act and if he didn't need Johnson to run the place he'd fire his ass pronto. But he does need him and there's trouble ahead just sure-as-shit so it's no time for any major personnel changes.

Another time, though, and Brian is looking forward to kicking Johnson's ass clear off the ranch. Fantasizes about Johnson ending his days as some broken-down drunk in the Gaslamp Quarter in San Diego. Pictures the cowboy eating his beans off some hot plate in an SRO hotel with the smell of recent urine and imminent death unwashable from the walls.

Fucking cowboy.

For another time, though.

As the young Milanese boy is now edging his way into the room, spying with almond eyes to see if the temper tantrum is done.

"Not now," Brian snaps, and the boy disappears from the doorway. Brian can hear his footsteps padding quickly down the hallway.

Later, but not now, Brian thinks.

Now he has to deal with his dear old friend Elizabeth, who got him into this trouble.

The cunt.

16.

Brian comes into Elizabeth's room and sits down in the big wicker chair and looks at her.

She's sitting up in the bed, her right wrist and left ankle cuffed to the bedposts. She delicately crosses her right leg, as if her nudity would mean anything to him, but doesn't bother to cover her breasts.

Brian can appreciate her body on a purely intellectual level. It is firm and well toned, and Brian can appreciate the hard work, the gym time he won't do himself but insists upon in his young men. For a moment he idly wonders whether, if turned on her stomach . . .

"You've *ruined* the weekend," he says.

"May I have some clothes, please, Bri?"

He shakes his head. "I've always found that naked people are easier to talk to. Something about vulnerability, I suppose."

"I feel pretty vulnerable."

"Well, girl, you *should*."

They look at each for a few seconds, then Brian sighs. "Love is a fucked-up thing, isn't it?"

"You got that right, Bri."

"You told him."

"Told him what?"

"Come on."

"I don't know what you're talking about, Bri."

"Something to do with Bobby, maybe?"

"Well, I figured that."

"I've always liked you, Elizabeth," Brian said. "Admired you, even."

"It's mutual, Brian."

"Haven't I treated you well?" he asks.

"Very well."

"Given you a place to stay?" he asks.

She nods.

"And then you do this to me?" he whispers. "Betray me? Put my business in jeopardy? My life in danger?"

She starts to lie again but sees he's not going to believe her, so she goes the other way. "Love's a fucked-up thing, isn't it, Bri?"

"Don't I know it, girl?" he sighs. "Don't I know it?"

This hangs in the air until he asks, "Where's he headed?"

"I don't know," Elizabeth answers. "Honestly."

"I believe you," Brian says. "Trouble is, Don Huertero won't."

"No?"

"No. Although it would be more convincing if I at least made an effort to get it out of you."

"I understand."

"Oh, good," he says, oozing up from the chair. He slips his belt from the loops and wraps the tongue end around his hand. The buckle hangs loose and ready.

"Not my face, okay, Bri?" she asks, her voice breaking. "Just not my face?"

He shrugs and starts in, asking *Where's he headed* only lethargically. He doesn't think to ask why Bobby Z took the boy.

17.

The boy is asleep on Tim's back. Tim's hefting him piggyback style and can feel the weight of the boy's sleeping head on his shoulder. The boy is easier to carry this way, dead weight like a pack. And Tim carried heavier in the war, in that other desert.

But in that other desert they were delivering cheeseburgers and corn on the cob, pink lemonade and chocolate ice cream. Ice cream in the damn desert, Tim thinks, which is when he was sure they were going to win, when old Uncle started to bring them chocolate ice cream in the desert.

Not here. Here he knows he can expect no help from Uncle Sam—just the reverse, come to think of it—so he keeps the pace up and heads toward the mountains he can just start to see to the west.

Head toward the mountains, Tim thinks. Isn't that some sort of beer commercial? Head toward the mountains of some kind of beer. But he can't let himself think about beer just now, as good as it sounds, because there ain't gonna be no beer and there ain't gonna be no ice cream, either. At least not until they get out of this desert.

If they get out of this desert.

Anyway, Tim thinks, if he didn't have the kid he'd be

jogging, pounding it out like at Pendleton or Twentynine Palms, and making good time. Beat his pursuers to the high ground and give 'em the AMF, *adiós*, mother-fuckers. *Vaya con Dios*.

But jogging just doesn't make sense carrying this kind of load. Sweat too much, Tim figures. Lose too much body water, and the sun will be up soon. Just like in all those desert movies where they show you the sun, then the guy staggering across the sand, then the sun again and the guy drinking his last water, then the sun again, and the guy dropping. Then the sun with the vultures circling.

Well shove that, Tim thinks, and fuck your *Beau Geste*. Make it to this next ridge line before dawn and find a place to lay up. Get off the ground a little into some shade.

He knows what he's looking for: a little hole under some rock with some shade and a view.

See what's coming after him.

But he needs the high ground to do that and he's in a race with the sunrise so he decides to jog for a little bit. The boy wakes briefly but gets used to the new rhythm and falls back to sleep.

Tim jogs toward the hills just turning chocolate brown in the dim light.

18.

Johnson drives his truck about ten miles in the direction of Ocotillo Wells, turns onto an old dirt road and follows it another mile and a half into the brush. Pulls off at a dilapidated adobe shack with a corrugated tin roof about half pulled off.

Parks the truck and goes in.

The place is dark. There ain't no windows and the only light is from one kerosene lamp stinking and sputtering on an old cable spool they've been using for a table. The whole bar is furnished with your basic forage material. Chairs pulled out of someone's garbage heap, the cable spools from when they put the phone lines into Borrego, some old soda-pop cartons from the days they put soda pop in bottles.

The bar itself is just a bunch of plywood hammered onto some sawhorses, but it doesn't make a shitload of difference, because the local Indians just go in there to load up on mescal anyway.

There's three or four of them asleep in there right now, sleeping off last night's drunk.

Place stinks, Johnson thinks. Smells like shit, and he wonders when the last time was anyone dropped some gasoline and a match down the hole in the outhouse just outside the bar.

Johnson puts a boot into one of the Indians asleep on the floor.

"Where's Rojas?" Johnson asks.

Runty Indian looks up at him and blinks.

Johnson figures on the scale of things around here these boys are on the lowest order. If the whites are on top, which they sure as hell are, and the Mexicans a distant second, and the Cahuillas third, then it is just hard to say where these little brown brothers are.

They aren't even Cahuillas. Come from a tribe so small they've either forgotten their name or just plain aren't saying. Just so goddamn miserable a group of people that they all just got lost somewhere. Slipped into a haze of mescal, glue sniffing and snorting on them spray-paint cans, and became worthless for just about anything except tracking.

They can track better than a coyote, which is why Johnson has made the trip here to find Rojas.

Rojas' real name is Lobo Rojas—"Red Wolf"— after that little Mexican wolf they've just about succeeded in shooting out in these parts. Fucking little shits were murder on the calves in the spring, so it was a good thing the local ranchers had just about exterminated them before the EPA could come in, rescue the murderous fuckers.

Anyway, Johnson figures that Rojas has picked himself an apt nickname, because he is as murderous a little fucker as ever walked barely upright.

"Rojas, where is he?" Johnson demands.

"In back," the man croaks. His eyes are crossed and

there's a little ring of gold paint around his mouth. Gold is their favorite color for snorting, for some reason.

In back.

Johnson slips his pistol from its holster and kicks the door to the small back room open.

Rojas rolls off the woman he's lying on and lands on his feet, his big goddamn knife held back near his ribs where no one can kick it out of his hand.

His eyes are bloodshot and puffy but still coal-black and burning hot.

It's true, Johnson thinks as he looks at the naked runty Indian pointing a knife at him, Rojas *wakes up* angry.

Johnson thumbs the hammer back and points the pistol at Rojas' square forehead.

"You spit at me, you little cocksucker," Johnson warns, "I'll blow your head off."

Rojas, he likes to spit when you first wake him up.

"I'll cut your balls off and feed them to this whore."

"She don't look like she's missed a lot of meals to me," Johnson says. "Are you sure she's hungry?"

The woman is still asleep.

"I have work for you," Johnson says.

Rojas shakes his head. "I'm drinking and fucking."

"Need you to track someone."

Rojas shrugs.

It's what they always need him for. Some wetback bolts in the desert and they can't find him, they get Rojas. Or some coyote gets smartassed, camps himself out in their part of the desert and starts rustling their wetbacks, they send Rojas out.

Rojas finds the coyote and leaves his head stuck on a mesquite pole.

Discourages that kind of thing.

"You want to fuck her, Johnson?" Rojas asks. "You can."

"No, I don't think I could," Johnson answers. "Come on and get some clothes on before the track gets cold."

"Track gets cold for you, Johnson. Not for me."

"Yeah, yeah, yeah. Come on."

"I rather fuck instead."

"Me, too," Johnson says. "But I got an old boy out there's already killed about three of my Cahuillas."

Knowing that would goad Rojas. Not that he'd want to get revenge for the Cahuillas, but because he'd want to show that he could do what they couldn't.

Rojas has an ego.

"I don't care," Rojas says. "I'm drunk."

"You was born drunk."

"My mother, she was drunk."

"Elsewise she'd've aborted you."

And true enough, Rojas is an ugly man. Short, squat, with a flat nose and eyes set too wide apart. Hands and feet like paws.

But shit, that nose could smell.

"Am I going to have to shoot you?" Johnson asks.

"You're too slow to shoot me," Rojas says, and Johnson sees him draw that knife back a little like he's getting ready to come ahead with it.

And he might be right, Johnson thinks. He might just be able to stick me with that thing before I can put him down.

"Okay," Johnson says. He lowers the gun. "I'll get me somebody else. You go back to that fat woman."

Johnson watches as Rojas grabs his mescal bottle off the floor and takes a long defiant pull. Climbs back onto the filthy matress, lays the knife by his hand and slaps the woman awake. Tells her something in Spanish, which Johnson don't quite know the words to but the meaning of which is clear.

Johnson lets Rojas get into it a little bit, until Rojas' ugly face is all screwed up and his eyes are closed, then Johnson whacks him behind the ear with the pistol butt. Once, *whack,* twice, *whack,* and watches Rojas' little body go limp.

Johnson holsters his gun, hefts Rojas over his shoulder and grabs his clothes with his other hand. Tips his hat to the woman and carries Rojas outside and dumps him onto the bed of the truck.

There's already three of Rojas' buddies sitting like dogs in the truck, waiting. Already figure there was maybe some work, they could make some money and buy some mescal or a case or two of Testor.

Johnson gets behind the wheel and heads back to the ranch and sighs.

19.

Escobar's funeral is everything Gruzsa expected and more.

The women are wailing like someone took their welfare checks from them, and the men are standing in their cheap suits looking grim-faced even under the wraparound shades. To make Gruzsa's afternoon even happier, Escobar's younger male relatives are decked out in their very best Monday-Go-to-Funeral gang attire—clean white T-shirts, pressed jeans two sizes too large and Raiders jackets. Raiders jackets, Gruzsa thinks, like any of these glue-sniffing mokes would know Kenny Stabler from a pimple on their asses. And they got the shaved heads, the badass *cholo* attitude, and they're giving Gruzsa—the sole Anglo in the congregation—their very best teenage murderous looks.

And if it wasn't Jorge's funeral Gruzsa would like to take one or two of them outside in the alley and wash their mouths out with the barrel of his 9mm Glock, leave their teeth like Chiclets on the pavement and walk away whistling, but it *is* a funeral and there's a truce of sorts on.

Which is also a good thing, Gruzsa muses as the priest babbles on in Spanish, because not only are Escobar's younger male relatives gang bangers, they bang for at least two different gangs that Gruzsa can recognize. There's a bunch from Quatro Flats there, and TMC and maybe even East Coast Crips. And all it would take is for one of these mental defectives to start throwing down for them to start blowing each other away.

Which ordinarily Gruzsa would consider not only entertainment but a real benefit to society, except today would be a real pain in the ass because he has business to do.

So he sits ignoring the dirty stares and concentrates on the big photo of Escobar staring back at him from an easel by the coffin. Wonders what the beaners did in the days before Kodak, whether they stuck a painting of the deceased up there or what, and after an endless goddamn sermon by the Mexican priest, Gruzsa joins the line to file past the casket and pay his respects.

Gives his sympathies to Jorge's weeping mother, a couple of sniffling aunts, two or three cousins, and then Jorge's brother asks to speak to him outside, which is what Gruzsa's been counting on.

Jorge's brother is serious people. Old-time *cholo* ETA from the days when the Mexican gangs defended themselves instead of killing each other. Luis Escobar hasn't been crying, either. Eyes dry as a stone, man, but black with anger. Luis has done long, stand-up stretches in the joint: a murder two and an aggravated assault, and he was an ETA leader in the joint, Gruzsa knows. Those black eyes have stared down the Panthers and the Aryan Brotherhood and the mob and now he's out and running the old network. And the man is wearing a suit, Gruzsa notes. A real suit, not some baby-gang clown outfit. He's wearing a good suit and showing his brother some real respect.

You have to respect Luis Escobar, and Gruzsa isn't going to give him any shit.

"How'd this happen?" Luis asks.

Gruzsa shrugs. "Jorge got fucked, Luis."

"By who?"

"Informer he was working with."

"Name of?"

Gruzsa looks up and shakes his head sadly. "Bobby Z, Luis."

"Bobby Z killed my brother?" Luis asks. "Bobby Z is not a killer."

"I don't know he pulled the trigger," Gruzsa warned. "He might have had one of Huertero's men do that."

"Why?"

"They had some kind of beef, I guess," Gruzsa says. "You knew Jorge; he could be rough sometimes. Could make people angry. Anyway, don't worry—we're going to find him. The agency is leaving no rock unturned until we find Bobby Z and bring him to—"

"You won't find him," Luis says calmly. It's not a complaint, just a matter of fact. "We'll find him."

Which is what Gruzsa figures. Gruzsa knows most people think that California is more or less part of the United States, but if you see what Tad Gruzsa sees you know it's really part of Mexico. The beaners go around all but invisible, but they see everything, hear everything, say nothing except to each other.

Luis Escobar would have an army out there, a few soldiers actively looking but a whole fucking county reporting anything they saw.

You don't really see the Mexicans in California, Gruzsa muses as he looks at the stone-cold figure of Luis Escobar, but they see you.

Good luck, Tim Kearney.

"Now, Luis," Gruzsa says, "I have to warn you against taking the law into—"

"You would come after me?"

Gruzsa pretends to think about that for a few seconds before he answers. "No, Luis. You do what you do. Jorge was my friend."

"Carnal."

"Blood of my blood, Luis."

Blood of my blood, my ass.

The blood in my dick.

20.

One Way stirs under the park bench and pokes his eyes out from under his poncho hood. The clouds over the ocean are a rosy pink and the beach is deserted.

He sniffs the air, looks around and sniffs the air again. Then he crawls out from under the bench, straightens his stiff, cold knees and contemplates the ocean.

Something's different.

He smells the air again, scratches his scraggly beard and runs his fingers through his long, dirty hair. He turns his back to the ocean and looks east at where the sun is just beginning to top the Laguna hills. Smells the air to the east.

Looks back at the ocean again.

Then jumps in the air and shouts, "He's back! He's back!"

Runs down to the ocean, jumps ankle-deep into the low surf and starts splashing himself with the freezing water. Yelling, "He's back! He's back! Bobby Z has returned!"

This goes on long enough to attract the attention of the Laguna police, who are just so pleased that One Way is washing himself that they let it go on for a while before hauling him to the clinic.

One Way doesn't mind. Soaked with seawater, draped in a blanket, he sits handcuffed in the back of the cruiser smiling, laughing and exclaiming the good news to all who will hear.

Bobby Z has returned.

"He's coming from the east," One Way confides to the nurse.

21.

Tim finds what he's looking for about an hour after dawn. He risked moving in daylight because he figured he had a decent lead, and anyway he'd trade that risk for the right location to lay up.

The right location is about fifty yards up a canyon in the lower reaches of the hills. It's a small depression underneath a rock shelf and it's got a nice big rock in front of it. Peeking out from beside that rock, Tim can see the flats below, and he figures what he can see he can shoot.

He sets Kit down on the slope and checks the tiny cave for snakes before bringing the boy in. He sets him down, tells him not to be afraid, he'll be back in a minute, then breaks off a smoke-tree branch and spends a good half-hour cleaning up his tracks and making a new trail deeper in the canyon that comes back into the cave from above.

Give the bad guys at least a chance of walking past the cave, and anyway it's always preferable to shoot an enemy in the back if you have that opportunity.

When he climbs back into the cave Kit says he's tired of playing Marine.

"How about Batman and Robin?" Tim asks.

Kit dismisses this with a polite frown. "How about X-Men?" Kit asks.

Tim's not entirely displeased, because he whiled away a shitload of time in Saudi reading X-Men comics while waiting for the A-10s to pound the Iraqis into wet sand. "You like X-Men?"

Kit nods. "Who do you want to be?" he asks.

"Wolverine," Tim says. "Unless you wanna be."

"You can be Wolverine," Kit says. "How about if I'm Cyclops?"

"Okay."

"Okay."

A minute later Tim asks, "Cyclops, are you hungry?"

"I sure am, Wolverine."

Tim unwraps two of the energy bars and hands one to the boy, with a bottle of water. Then he starts to field strip and clean the rifle, an act as automatic and comforting to an ex-Marine as saying the rosary is to a priest.

The kid devours the energy bar, swallows some water and asks, "How about we're trapped in the desert? And bad guys are chasing us? And we hide in this cave?"

"Okay," says Tim.

It sounds about right.

22.

Monk's on his way to get a latte and *The Economist* and to sit outside savoring both when he hears the news of Bobby Z's return.

The prophecy comes from One Way, of course, freshly released from the mental health clinic and now striding the sidewalks of the PCH proclaiming the good news to modern man.

As a longtime Laguna resident, Monk knows One Way only too well and is used to his lunatic rendition of the legend of Bobby Z. This morning he even gives One Way a dollar and is a little unsettled when the wack job crumples the bill and tosses it into the gutter, exclaiming, "Who needs money? Bobby Z has returned! To claim his kingdom!"

This last bit unsettles Monk some more, mostly for the reason that *he* has pretty much claimed Bobby's kingdom since the latter went off the screen about four months ago.

Off the screen literally, because Monk is the computer wiz who controls Bobby's interests stateside. On Monk's hard drives, floppy disks and CD-ROMs are the codes that tell the whereabouts of the wages of sin, the immense fortune built on smoke, lots of it, wafting skyward from the best living rooms, patios and hot tubs of the West Coast.

Monk know where the treasure be, aye Jim. Knows further who the retailers are, knows further that the Z empire—always on the cutting edge—is on the verge of going completely electric.

Except, of course, for the hard cash that has been stored away against a rainy day. Which Monk has decided has arrived since Bobby went off the screen somewhere in Southeast Asia. Monk tried for months to raise a signal, tapping away at the keyboard like *Come in, Rangoon,* but Bobby didn't come in. So after a while Monk figured that his best friend Bobby had met his fate in the treacherous mountains of Southeast Asia—as had so many other American boys—and now the empire was Monk's own. As was the stash of cash—Carl Sagan numbers—hidden for posterity.

So Monk has—to his acknowledged shame—mixed feelings about One Way prophesying Bobby's return.

It's human nature, Monk muses. Original sin, perhaps, but man is just prone to the idea that if you hold someone else's money long enough, you start to think it's yours.

Monk knows about original sin because he used to be a real monk. Left Laguna High for Notre Dame and took it all pretty seriously, as evidenced by the fact that he then entered the seminary and emerged a Jesuit priest. But even that level of commitment wasn't serious enough for James P. McGoyne, so down the line he entered a monastery deep in the desert of New Mexico, where the monks basically dug irrigation ditches, cultivated agave plants and marketed agave jam to the health food market. One day the senior monk took James aside, noted that he'd taken computer courses at Notre Dame, and asked him to develop a mailing list of customers.

Although Monk wouldn't realize it for months, this was the beginning of the end for him as an actual monk, because Monk found a new religion: the computer. Within two years, the good brothers were marketing their foul jam in locations as diverse as New York, Amsterdam and Santa Fe, and Monk even had the good brothers producing a catalog, a newsletter and a recipe book, and the brothers were making money hand over fist, and Monk was in charge of counting it.

Monk wakes up one morning, and in the midst of his silent contemplation—what other kind is there in a monastery?—loses his faith.

Just like that.

Elusive as morning mist. Here and then gone, his faith deserts him. On this early-morning walk in the desert, Monk pulls a reverse Moses. There's no burning bush or anything—Monk's just walking along looking at the brown mountains and suddenly decides that there is no God.

Doesn't realize why it didn't occur to him before.

He's been in this dump for years, digging ditches, eating shitty food, keeping monklike silence for all but essential communications and the usual chanting, and for what? For *nihil*, that's what. For nothing. *Nada*. For the great emptiness.

Ever the fanatic, Monk becomes not just an atheist but a nihilist. Leaves the brothers that afternoon, in a bus headed west. Bumps into his old classmate Bobby Z and they get talking computers. And mailing lists.

A monster is born. Monk attacks the dope trade with all the single-minded fervor he once gave to God. Monk creates a worldwide communications and accounting system impenetrable to the mere mortals of the DEA, the FBI or Interpol. The one entity he fears is the Society of Jesus—he knows from personal experience how thorough they are—but they're too busy with their own rackets to take an interest in the Z empire.

Out of which flows everything Monk now possesses: an interesting career, an enormous house on Emerald Bay on a cliff hanging over the blue Pacific, and a seemingly endless supply of money.

His own and now Bobby's.

"You've seen him?" Monk asks One Way.

"In here," One Way answers, pointing at his own head.

Monk figures that encompasses an entire universe of possibilities and starts to breathe a little easier.

"But you haven't actually *seen* him," Monk presses, "in the flesh."

"Who has?" One Way answers, nothing deterred.

Actually, Monk has—several times—but not for years.

"Do you know Bobby?" Monk asks.

"Does anybody?"

With this, One Way paces exuberantly away to accost the tourists who are just now emerging from the hotels for their morning coffee. He's so exuberant that he gets picked up again by the Laguna cops. Familiar with this problem—although not always to this degree—the Laguna cops know how to deal with it. They drive One Way south on the PCH and drop him off.

Then it's Dana Point's problem.

For Monk the issue isn't that simple.

He gets his latte and his *Economist* and sits outside at the bookstore-cum-café but can't quite concentrate on the future of the Eurodollar.

If Bobby's back, he contemplates, if the random elements of the universe have lined up in that precise order that would make One Way for once cogent, then some interesting and unsettling questions must be answered.

Why, for instance, hasn't Bobby contacted him? By fax, by computer, by messenger, even by the antiquated dead-drop along the walk at Dana Point?

Could Bobby the Boy Wonder have smelled a rat? Sussed out Monk's Prince John to his King Richard? If Z is back, Monk wonders, where is he?

And what, pray tell, to do about him?

23.

Johnson figures Bobby Z has gone to ground.

Either that or he's wandering around lost in the sage-brush and they're going to find him dead in a day or two. Which might fry Brian but ain't no sweat off his own dick, because riding around in the desert watching Rojas and his three compadres sniff around like dogs gets positively tedious after a while.

They'd picked up his tracks by the cliffside. Didn't seem like much point climbing down to see what was left of the morons who'd flown the humvee off the edge. And Rojas, even drunker than a skunk, could tell Johnson that the white man they were looking for hadn't gone over the edge with the motorcycle. He'd walked west with the boy, then the boy's tracks stopped.

And it didn't take no damn Indian to look at those tracks and figure that the man had hefted the boy and was carrying him. The footprints in the sand were that much deeper.

So Bobby Z was on the move, but a lot slower than he oughta be, so Johnson had sent Rojas and friends out on the trot while he followed at a walk and on horseback.

Let Rojas run him down, pin him, and then figure out just how the hell to bag him.

That old Mex wants him alive.

So they're tracking him west, across the flats and into the foothills and then up into a canyon, and the Indians are getting excited because they can sense the quarry slowing by his tracks. Johnson watching them work way out in front of him like dogs.

Rojas starts up the canyon wall, then stops and starts backtracking, and Johnson takes that moment to wipe his sunglasses on the front of his shirt while the Indians are conferring. He puts the glasses back on in time to see one of the Indians drop like he's been shot.

Shit, Johnson thinks, I forgot about that missing rifle.

He wonders just where the hell a beach-bum dope dealer learned to shoot like that, and even though he's probably out of range, slides off his horse and finds a rock to get behind.

Shit, Johnson thinks as he watches Rojas and the other Indians run to shelter, it has all the makings of a long day.

24.

"That's a real gun, isn't it?" Kit asks.

"Pretend," Tim answers, a little preoccupied with what's going on below him on the canyon floor. One of the trackers is down and the other two are behind rocks.

"Real," Kit insists. "That man fell down when you shot."

"That's the rules," Tim answers. "Anyway, I told you not to peek."

"Is that blood on his leg?"

"Red paint," Tim says. "Now get back and lay down. I don't want the bad mutants to know there are two of us."

This is Bobby Z's kid, all right, Tim thinks, because the boy has like *no fear* as he slides to the back of the cave. Which is a good thing, because Tim needs to concentrate.

On the wounded man. Who should by now be screaming for help, because that's the idea. Get one man down and pick off the others when they come to help him.

That's the game.

This is one tough little fucker out there, though, because he's lying there tearing off a piece of his pants leg with his teeth and making it into a tourniquet.

Smart, tough little fucker and no one's coming for him, either.

I guess, Tim thinks, they know the game.

And Tim just doesn't have the heart to put one in the guy's head. It seems pointless, and anyway, a wounded man's better than a dead man. They're going to have to deal with him one way or another.

"You stay back," he says to the boy.

"I'm staying, I'm staying."

But they aren't shooting, Tim thinks. That would be the thing to do, just start blasting away at the cave while one guy runs out and brings back his buddy.

Unless they haven't figured out where the shot came from yet, which is a possibility.

Or they're already in the brush, working their way around.

Which is another possibility.

Bad mutants.

Why do they want to kill me, anyway? Tim wonders with some annoyance. Why are people always putting me in this position?

Why ask why, he tells himself.

He puts the crosshairs on the downed man's head and takes a deep breath.

25.

Boy's got a soft side to him, Johnson decides.

He's gotta know by now that none of us is gonna risk his ass to go out and help that old Indian, so the next best thing is to put him down for good so you don't have to worry about him.

But there ain't been no shot.

Boy's got a soft side to him.

So Johnson slips the Winchester from its saddle holster, takes his handkerchief and ties it around the barrel. Then he steps out from behind the rock and starts walking toward the canyon floor.

Counting on the boy's soft side.

Johnson reaches the wounded man and sees he's probably going to live. Your basic Cahuilla is a tough little fucker.

Johnson looks up at the cave and is annoyed that Rojas was so goddamn stupid as to walk into this trap. On the bright side, they did have old Bobby gone to ground.

"Looks like we got us a situation here!" Johnson yells.

Tim knows what the situation is, too. The situation is that he's fucked up again and got himself trapped in a cave in the middle of the desert. Shit, there might as well be lawn sprinklers out there.

But he doesn't think he needs an answer so he just sights in on the cowboy's chest and waits.

"Shit, Mr. Z, we got you trapped!" Johnson hollers.

Tim lowers the sight and puts a round into the dirt by Johnson's boots just to remind him that things aren't maybe all that one-sided.

"Now why did you do that?!" Johnson hollers.

"I have a problem with impulse control!" Tim yells back.

Johnson's all of a sudden thinking that maybe the boy's soft side might have a hard edge, and isn't all that enthused about feeling that hard edge slice smack into his head in the form of a 7.62 bullet. Also, the boy's got himself a pretty good position up there—tough nut to crack—so Johnson decides to take another tack.

"How about we make a deal, Mr. Z?!" he yells.

Tim hollers back, "What kind of a deal?!"

26.

Just walk away.

Like most deals it sounds too good to be true, but Tim doesn't see where he has a better choice so he takes it.

So the cowboy pulls his Indians off, they pick up their wounded, and Tim keeps his finger on the trigger until they're a long way off down on the flats and headed away. They'll stow the wounded guy away somewhere and the cowboy'll just tell fat Brian that, sorry, but he just couldn't find old Bobby Z.

That's the deal, anyway, and Tim doesn't believe it for a second. But he's got the kid to think about, and whatever sleazy trick Johnson has in mind it gives him a better chance than sitting in that cave till he runs out of food and water.

"You shot that guy," Kit says. Like matter-of-fact, Tim thinks, not like he's upset about it.

"Nah," Tim answers. "I pretended to shoot him and he pretended to be wounded. That's the game."

"Oh," Kit says.

Tim knows the kid's pretending to believe it, so he pretends to believe the kid believes it, because that seems to make it easier on both of them.

"We gonna stay in this cave?" Kit asks.

"I don't know yet," Tim says. "What do you think?"

"I think we should get out of here."

Tim thinks this over for a few seconds. It would be better to wait until night and then go, but it leaves them with a long afternoon to wait it out and maybe Johnson decides that he comes back with reinforcements.

"Let's wait a little bit," Tim says, then adds, "if that's okay with you, Cyclops."

Wait for the sun to go down a little.

"Okay with me, Wolverine," Kit says.

Neither of them thinks this is a comic book anymore, but it's easier to deal with this way.

So they sit it out and wait. Wait until Johnson and his posse become small dots on the desert flats, wait until the noontime sun sinks a little. Sit and wait and talk X-Men, Batman, Silver Surfer, radio-controlled boats—which Tim knows, like, shit about—and dirt bikes. Talk about everything but their situation, which just ain't no comic book.

Finally Tim hands Kit one of the two water bottles and says, "Drink it."

"All of it?"

"All of it," Tim affirms. "In the desert you store water in your belly, not your canteen."

Not like the movies, where they ration it and take a sip every other day. No wonder the dumb fucks die in the movies, Tim thinks. They got the water in their canteen and not in their bellies.

Die of thirst with water in their canteens.

Beau fucking *Geste*. Some joke.

"Guzzle it," Tim says.

"That's bad manners," Kit says, delighted.

Tim's not real impressed, having seen what passes for

good behavior around Kit's set of adults. Like don't double-snort off the same twenty, and foreplay *only* in front of the kids, please.

"How your legs feel?" he asks Kit.

"Fine!"

"Truth?"

The kid puts his hand up like he's about to take the stand. Something he saw in a movie, must be. Something Tim saw other people—cops mostly—do in court, because he never had the chance to take the stand in his own defense. Lawyers thought it inadvisable.

Only one of the problems of being guilty.

The kid interrupts this reverie. "Why are you asking about my legs?"

"Because we have some climbing to do."

A lot of climbing, Tim thinks.

Because the easiest thing to do would be to go back down the canyon, onto the flats and follow the wash out of the desert. Any idiot knows that a riverbed, even a dry one, will take you out of the desert.

They'll be waiting for me in the wash.

So we're just going to have to climb out.

It'd be nice to have a map, Tim thinks. Course, it would have been nice never to have gotten into this mess in the first place, but that was another deal and a done one so it's best not to think about it and just concentrate on getting out of this deal.

Life, he thinks: One shitty deal after another.

He looks at the boy and thinks, You don't know what you've got to look forward to, kid.

"You're sure you wanna come with me?" Tim asks.

"I'm sure," the kid says quickly.

Looks scared for the first time. Scared that one more grownup's thinking of dumping him.

"Because I can bring you back if you want."

"They'd kill you," Kit says.

No game, no pretend, no comic book.

"No way," Tim says. "I'm tough to kill."

Ask Stinkdog.

Kid looks up at him with those big blue eyes.

"I want to come with you," he says.

"Let's climb," Tim answers.

They've only gone a few feet when he asks, "What are we? Marines or X-Men?"

Kit thinks it over, then asks, "Can't we be both?"

"Why not?"

"Cool!"

A mutant Marine, Tim thinks.

Cool.

27.

One Way's not all that busted up about being dumped in Dana Point.

For one thing, the garbage is better, he thinks as he searches through a Dumpster behind the Chart House restaurant. He finds the remnants of a nice Caesar salad, some overly buttered Texas toast that he decides to eat anyway, and some leftover poached salmon. There are any number of steak bones, half-eaten prime ribs and hunks of cheeseburgers, but One Way doesn't eat red meat because there are health issues to consider.

He picks the Chart House not only for the cuisine but for the view: It sits on the bluffs and offers a serene and splendid view of Dana Point harbor with its hundreds of yachts, pleasure boats and sports-fishing craft.

One Way knows boats.

Or thinks he does, anyway, because somewhere back in time, before what he considers the Enlightenment, he had his own charter license and sailed the *turistas* around the Caribbean. He dimly recalls it as a fallow time of sweet rum and tangy Jamaican boo, sailing the bourgeoisie from one port to another and occasionally nailing their wives, daughters and sweethearts.

A sweet time, but unenlightened.

Still, he enjoys the view. Likes to watch, as he dines, the boats come in and out of the harbor, sailing along the long stone jetty that separates the harbor from the raw Pacific. Likes to look at the boats and critique their structure and lines.

Also, he decides that somewhere among those hundreds of boats is hidden the boat of Bobby Z.

Must be, otherwise the fates—the cops, the ignorant tools thereof—would not have driven him to Dana Point just on this auspicious day.

Finishing his entree, he descends the bluffs and walks down to the harbor itself, to the broad pier that supports several restaurants. Finds in a trash can that treat of treats: a still-cold ice-cream cone—chocolate—snatched from a child by an irritated father with stained white slacks.

His mustache and beard smeared with chocolate, he starts his bit with the tourists. Can't help himself, the words boil inside him and bubble over out of his mouth just as the Japanese tourists start spilling out of their bus.

One Way is there to greet them.

"Welcome to Dana Point!" he shouts at a startled rubber-products salesman from Kyoto. He takes the worried man's arm by the elbow and guides him down to the pier. "Sometime home of the legendary Bobby Z, who even as we speak is wending his way home to us. Bobby Z disappeared into the ocean mists and shall sail away again, but first he has come to tell us the good news, my friend!

"How do I know?" One Way asks rhetorically, because the rubber-products salesman from Kyoto is too shocked to ask anything. "Well might you ask and well might I answer!"

One Way leans in and whispers with foul breath into the man's ear, "Many years ago when just a young sailor, I was second mate aboard a sloop that plied the wilder reaches of the southern sea. Cargo we had on board this otherwise sheer pleasure craft, I do confess it, cargo that would have gained the unfavorable attention of government officials if ever stopped and searched in port or open water—not to mention pirates, my friend, *pirates*—"

A desperate tour guide tries to head One Way off because he's leading the group the wrong way.

But he's pleased to have an additional audience and just says to the guide, "Hello, I was just telling my friend here about how I came to actually speak to Bobby Z. I *knew* him, you know."

"No, no, no, no . . ."

" 'Twas on the good ship Something-or-Other and I was sitting on the deck one soft silky night splicing a line, my hands busy and my lips around a roach of the sweetest Hawaiian boo, when I am joined by a man whom you would otherwise think was just a youth except that he had even then the bearing of a king.

"You're ahead of me, I see. Yes, Bobby Z it was, and he sat down beside me, a humble sailor I, and we said words to each other as we watched the stars sparkle on the phosphorescent water. We spoke as men. I was deeply moved.

"The next day we sailed to an uncharted island . . ."

One Way stops not only because the tour guide is yelling for help and the Japanese tourists are stacking up like cordwood at the edge of the pier, but because he sees a tall, skinny man with thin hair unlock the gate to Slip ZZ and hurriedly walk down.

He watches as the man hurries to the very last boat, a

small but elegant sloop, get on board and go down into the cabin.

One Way juts his bearded chin to the sky and sniffs the air.

"As I was saying," he starts, but the hand on his elbow is not the tour guide but the security guard, whose gloved hand soon turns him over to the custody of the Dana Point police.

On the drive back to Laguna, One Way tells the cops, "Bobby Z has returned, you know."

"Sure he has." The driver laughs.

"He has!" One Way yelps indignantly.

"How do you know?" the cop asks. He's losing his good humor and is just a tad annoyed that the Laguna cops keep dropping One Way off on the PCH just south of the town border. Why can't they drive him north for a change, where he could be a pain in Newport Beach's ass?

"How do you know?" the cop repeats.

"I smelled it in the air."

"Oh."

"And I saw his high priest," One Way says. "I saw the Monk."

"Yippee."

"The first time I saw him I didn't recognize him," One Way confesses. "But when I saw him get on the boat . . ."

"That cinched it, huh?"

"Definitely."

The cop pulls over just across the Laguna line and opens the door.

"Out," he says.

That cinches it, One Way thinks as he starts walking toward downtown Laguna. Cinches it—he likes the cop's words and adopts them.

That cinches it, One Way tells himself. The Monk getting on the boat cinches it.

And the name of the boat!

The *Nowhere*.

Pure Z.

A legend.

28.

"You had Bobby and you let him go?!" Brian screeches.

He's red in the face and Johnson thinks he might have a heart attack and die right there.

Johnson wouldn't half mind.

Would be a lot of people show up at the funeral, too. Mexicans just love a good party, and there'd be a lot of singing and dancing at this one. Might even put a toe in myself, he thinks.

"He had the high ground," Johnson explains.

"The fuck does that mean?" Brian whines.

"Means it would have been a bitch to dig him out of there."

"It means you were too chicken to do it!"

"Maybe." Johnson shrugs. He thinks of taking Brian out right there. Just pulling his pistol and putting one right between those piggy eyes.

"We did have a man shot," Johnson says instead.

"Big yip."

"Don't worry. We got him patched up."

Brian's worried, though. Not about some lame Tonto but about the hidalgo across the border. Brian's eyes are bugged out and he's huffing and puffing and Johnson hopes again that his heart'll tap out and save them all a lot of trouble.

"And we didn't let him get away," Johnson drawls. "Rojas looped back. He's trailing him."

"What's he going to do?" Brian asks. "Send up smoke signals?"

"Gave him a radio."

"And?"

"He headed up Hapaha Canyon—"

"Didn't he shoot your man in Hapaha Canyon?"

"Yup," Johnson says patiently. "Then he kept heading up Hapaha Canyon."

"What did he do that for?"

Johnson takes a deep breath. He's running out of patience. "Because he probably figured that's the opposite of what we'd expect him to do."

"Yeah, but Hapaha Canyon's just going to take him up to Hapaha Flats."

"He don't know that, though."

"I guess not." Brian's thinking real hard. "Can you take him on the flats?"

"I expect so," Johnson says. "Course, the flats ain't so much flat as they are like a bowl."

"Should be easy then," Brian says. He likes the idea of Bobby Z trapped in a bowl.

Hell of a lot easier if I could just shoot him, Johnson thinks. Or send Rojas in to cut his throat. But that makes Johnson think about the boy and he doesn't like thinking about that.

"Think we can surprise Mr. Z on Hapaha Flats?" Brian asks no one in particular. His morale's rapidly improving.

Smile spreading across his fat face.

"Maybe Willy would like to help . . ." Brian purrs.

"After all, he owes Bobby a dose of pain and humiliation, *n'est-ce pas*? I think we should make an afternoon of it. I'll do the Foreign Legion sartorial thing—kepi, neck scarf, jodhpured slacks—and Willy . . . I'm sure Willy would love to put the ultralight to some practical use for a change."

Johnson worries when Brian's in this voice. It usually means that something dumb is coming up.

"What are you thinking about?" Johnson asks.

Brian's smile is all over his face as he hums that tune from that old Vietnam movie.

" 'Death from the sky,' " Brian answers.

Death from the sky? Johnson wonders.

The hell is that supposed to mean?

29.

Tim and Kit stand on the rim of a big bowl and look down.

"Holy shit," Tim says.

"It's beautiful!" Kit gasps.

Five miles of flowers bloom beneath them.

A bowl of flowers.

Tim's seen springtime in the desert before but he's never seen anything like this. Fucking Mardi Gras down there in that bowl. Bright reds, purples, yellows, golds and colors he doesn't know the words for. Doesn't know if there *are* words.

In contrast to the usual desert brown, these colors glow from a carpet of green. Tim knows it's heavy brush—sage, smoke tree, desert tobacco, creosote, brittlebush and mesquite—but from here it looks like a green carpet.

Under thousands and thousands of wildflowers.

Like whatever rain the desert gets has poured down into this bowl and *voilà*, *springtime*. Like give some acid-crazed painter a five-square-mile canvas and let him paint his craziness out.

"If you make your eyes cross," Kit is saying, "it looks like a what-do-you-call-it?"

"Kaleidoscope?"

"Yeah. Kaleidoscope."

Tim sees the kid form the word with his lips a couple of times to memorize it.

Tim looks out across the crazy painting. Smack dab in the center sits a huge goddamn rock, looks to be about the size of a big house. Like it's been plopped out there like some goofy lawn ornament.

It's like a big movie shot, Tim thinks, but he's not wild about seeing the close-up. Not at all crazy about walking down into a bowl because what happens is that people sit on the rim of the bowl and pick you off. Or they come down into the bowl with more guys than you have—and shit, he has one little kid—and outflank you and you don't have the high ground and it's *adiós*, motherfucker.

But there isn't any other choice but to double back and that isn't a other choice. The canyon walls are too steep to climb with a kid in tow. Besides which, the kid is tired—game but about played out—and Tim knows he'll probably end up carrying the boy most of the way across. Also knows that if he had any fucking brains at all he'd dump the kid, but the fact that he doesn't have any brains at all has already been well established so there isn't any choice but to cross this bowl into the hills on the far side.

There are a lot of advantages to living alone, Tim thinks, one of them being that you usually get to live longer.

"Let's go into the kaleidoscope," Tim says.

"Cool. I like kaleidoscopes."

"Gonna be hot."

The kid shrugs. "It's the desert."

Tim feels a little better about things once they're down in the bowl, because the brush is so high it'd be hard to see them unless you had an airplane or a helicopter or something. And they're on some sort of game trail or something, Tim figures, maybe where the coyote hunt jackrabbits or the deer move through, so it's easy walking and the kid is doing okay so far.

And there's color everywhere they look, near and far: the fiery red blooms of the ocotillo cactus, the bright yellow flowers on the creosote, the greenish-yellow flowers of silver cholla, and the bright rose-colored blooms of the beaver tail. There's desert lavender and indigo bush and the green spiky yucca and a tall plant with yellow flowers—the century plant that legend says blooms only once in a hundred years.

And maybe that's a good-luck sign, Tim thinks. Plant only blooms once every hundred years and here we are to see it. That has to be *some* kind of luck, and I'm due for a little of the good variety.

He hears the airplane before he sees it.

30.

Johnson's standing on the rim of the bowl watching the little ultralight putt-putt over the desert floor. Brian standing right beside him in his French Foreign Legion gear, peering through binoculars, looking like that sergeant from that movie he likes so much. Brian says the sergeant in *Beau Geste* is the first great homosexual villain in cinematic history, but Johnson wouldn't know about that.

Johnson's watching Willy putting around in that ultra-light aircraft of his, which looks to Johnson like an aerial go-cart. Sure ain't nothing *he* would want to fly in.

"He looks like a hawk circling his prey," Brian says without taking his eyes from the glasses.

He looks like a moron, Johnson thinks. He himself has more confidence in old Rojas trotting behind old Bobby Z and keeping his distance. Rojas don't need no idiot Kraut zooming around in the sky relaying radio messages as to Bobby's position. Rojas already knows Bobby's goddamn position.

But you give a boy a toy and the boy just has to play with it, Johnson thinks. Brian's too chickenshit to go up in the little airplane himself and Heinz or Hans or Shit-head or whatever his name is is just dying to give the thing a try and says he knows all about them from the Bavarian Aerialist Club or some such thing, so here they are watching the circus.

He hears the Kraut's voice over the radio whisper *Zuh supject iss proceeting at tventy-sefen dekrees south-southvest* and Johnson wonders *What the hell is he whispering for?* Who's gonna hear him, the goddamn hummingbirds?

"He's proceeding at twenty-seven degrees south-southwest," Brian says breathlessly.

"I heard," Johnson says.

"Relay it to Rojas," Brian orders.

Johnson knows Rojas wouldn't know twenty-seven degrees from his own asshole but does what he's told. The only harm is it will annoy Rojas, but who gives a shit whether Rojas is annoyed?

He hears Brian ask the Kraut, "Do we have him trapped?"

Ja, vee half him trapped.

Brian's so gleeful it about makes Johnson sick.

"Let's fuck with his head," Brian says.

Johnson's not sure what that means but he sees the ultralight swoop down. Sees the fucking idiot lean out and wave.

Then the fucking idiot starts shooting.

31.

"Don't look up," Tim tells Kit.

"But—"

"I know," Tim says. "But don't look up."

Fucking ultralight has them pinned. Goofy pilot flying right over them, leaning out the cockpit winging pistol shots.

Dumb fuck, Tim thinks. He knows there's a kid down here.

And the kid's scared now, Tim can see it in his eyes.

"Shit," Tim says.

Kit nods.

"Magneto," Tim says ominously, naming the head bad guy from X-Men.

Kit brightens right away.

"What're we gonna *do*?!" he asks, his voice urgent with mock desperation.

"We're gonna run to that big rock!" Tim says. "It has a force field over it and Magneto can't get through it!"

"Let's go!"

They start running. The game takes the boy past his tired legs and they run with the crazy pilot zooming overhead, whooping and shouting and shooting, and Tim knows it's hard enough to hit a moving target with a pistol when you're standing still, never mind when you're flying a toy plane, so he's not all that worried about the bullets but still . . . And the whooping has a funny sound to it, like whooping with a German accent like some old cable-movie villain, and Tim decides it must be the German from the pool so this is personal.

Okay with me, he thinks.

Now the German's singing that "da-da-da-*dah*-da," "Death from the sky" music the assault chopper guys used to blast from speakers in the Gulf—scared the Iraqis shitless—and blasting away and Tim's thinking *These guys are nuts*.

We better get to that rock.

Not that he knows what he's going to do when he gets there but it has to be better than running like jackrabbits from a hawk.

He decides they need to get there faster so he stops and shouts, "Cyclops, hop on my back!"

"I'm okay!"

"I know! But your super-magnetized spinal protection armor will shield both of us!"

"Good idea, Wolverine!"

Fuckin' A, Tim thinks.

Kit hops on his back and they start running again, Tim giving it his best Semper Fi sprint like on the obstacle course at Pendleton, like some motherfucking DI is screaming at him and firing live rounds as a motivational tool. Pretty soon he can see the rock close up and maybe there is something to this century plant business, because the rock looks like good luck.

With that big split running smack down the center.

32.

"Where's he going?" Brian asks urgently.

"Looks like he ran into Split Rock," Johnson says.

This is good news. Smartass damn Bobby Z just ran into a trap. Ran right into the middle of a fifty-foot-high boulder and there's only two ways out. One end of the narrow crack or the other, and it'd be real easy to seal off one end and go in the other. Boy might as well have run into a corral.

This game, Johnson thinks, is about over.

"Do we *know* that?" Brian asks. He's concerned because he sees the ultralight pull up, gain altitude and start to circle again. "Are you sure we didn't lose him?"

"No, he's in there."

And come night we'll take him out of there.

But Brian's jabbering into his radio, "Confirm the subject's position. Confirm the subject's position."

He gets his binoculars up again and watches the ultralight circle the rock.

33.

Tim's watching him, too.

Lying on his back in the split, which is about as wide across as two small men standing shoulder to shoulder, he's looking up at the sky. The rock is so fucking weird, he thinks as he tries to catch his breath. Like God took an ax and just slammed it down on the rock and cut it in half. And there are weird little pictures carved in the walls.

"Why are you lying down?" Kit asked.

"Catching my breath."

"Are you out of shape?"

"Yup."

The kid lies down beside him. They watch as the ultra-light appears in the crack of blue sky above and then disappears again.

"He's pretty high up there," Kit says. "Do you think he spotted us?"

"Not exactly," Tim answers. "But if he knows where we're not, pretty soon he's gonna know where we are."

"Huh?"

"I dunno," Tim says. "Listen, no offense, but I don't want to talk. I want to catch my breath."

"Me, too."

The ultralight appears again and Tim figures he about has the guy's timing down. *One or two more orbits and I'll have my breath nice and steady.*

He waits until there's no shudder at all in his chest and says, "Do me a favor, Cyclops? Close your eyes?"

"You mean my *eye*."

"Yeah, okay. Your eye."

"Why?"

"Just do it."

Tim thinks he can hear the guy laughing up there but maybe it's just his imagination. *Doesn't make any fucking difference,* as he slowly raises the rifle to his shoulder, sights straight up and waits.

He sees the ultralight—straight above—high up.

Tim hums "Da-da-da-*dah*-da" quietly to himself and squeezes the trigger.

34.

Johnson doesn't hear the gunshot, just the engine sputtering.

Sees black smoke belching out of the ultralight and can just make out the Kraut about halfway out the cockpit like he's looking for somewhere to jump.

"He have a parachute?" he asks Brian.

"Too low for a parachute," Brian murmurs.

Then the ultralight sputters, stops in midair for a second, then just drops from the sky.

Like a shot bird, Johnson thinks.

It falls on the far side of Split Rock so they can't see it crash.

"You think he could be still alive?" Brian asks.

"Shit, he must've fell a hundred feet," Johnson says.

A second later they hear the explosion, then see a tower of red-and-orange flame shoot up.

Johnson can't help himself. "Your friend," he says, "he wasn't one of them rocket scientists, was he?"

"Shut up."

"I mean, back in the old country?"

Brian's all red in the face. Looks like a tomato that's about to go *kablooey*. He's trying to sputter some words, but nothing's coming out of his mouth but flecks of spit.

Satisfying as it might be to see Brian expire from a massive coronary, Johnson figures the potential trouble outweighs the possible entertainment value so he decides he'd better say something.

"I dunno, Commander," Johnson drawls, "but I'd say it was about time to send in the infantry, wouldn't you?"

Unless, Johnson thinks, you got a speedboat or something you want to try out.

35.

Kit hears the crash, too.

"What happened to Magneto?" he asks.

"I guess he fell," Tim says.

Kit thinks about this for a few seconds, then says, "Like Icarus."

Tim's impressed. "You read the book?"

Kit shakes his head. "I saw the cartoon on TV."

"Oh."

Still, it's a pretty good story, Tim thinks. With a practical lesson. You get too close to the muzzle end of an M-16, it's very likely to melt your dumb-ass wings.

"How old did you say you are?" he asks Kit.

"Six," the boy insists. "Elizabeth says, 'Going on twenty-six.' "

"I'll bet."

"What's she mean?"

"She means you're old for your age," Tim says.

"Oh."

Tim takes the entrenching tool off his belt, unscrews the blade, locks it back down and hands it to Kit.

"In fact," Tim says, "you're so big you can start digging."

"Digging?"

"A hole."

"Why?"

"To sleep in," Tim lies.

What he's really thinking—except he doesn't want to scare the boy to death—is that unless Willy was out there playing von Richthofen all by himself, Johnson and the boys would be coming for them tonight.

And while the split in the rock seemed like a good idea at the time—like a lot of things, Tim thought ruefully—it also meant that they were trapped.

The smart thing for Brian and his boys to do would be to wait them out, but Brian didn't have the discipline to do that. The next best thing would be to climb up on top of that rock and lob explosives down the split. But if they still wanted him alive they wouldn't do that.

So they'll be coming in. And if the bad news is that there's only two ways out of this rock, the good news is that there's only two ways in.

But only one of me.

Because even if the kid could shoot—and Mister Magoo could hardly miss shooting down this crack—Tim isn't going to ask a child to kill anybody.

Kid probably has nightmares enough of his own already.

So he'd dig the kid in nice and deep. Safe as he could be if the rounds start bouncing off the walls. Going to be like fighting in a hallway.

Also, he has to figure out how to make himself be two troops.

Isn't going to be easy, he thinks, especially for a monumental fuck-up.

"Keep digging," Tim says. "I'm going to get some firewood."

"We're going to have a fire?" Kit asks, enthused.

"Yup," Tim says.

At *least* one fire.

36.

The kid gets tired of digging pretty quickly, so Tim takes over. Digs a foxhole Hulk Hogan could hide in. Then he weaves together some smoke-tree branches to make a lid and lays it on top of the hole.

"What's that for?" Kit asks.

"To keep you warm."

"What about you?"

"I'm warm-blooded."

Tim takes some of the mesquite he's gathered and prepares a campfire. Then he piles dry brush across the split at the far end of the rock.

Kit gets bored watching him do this and spends his time looking over the carvings in the walls.

"Who do you think made these?" he asks.

"Some old Indians!" Tim shouts.

"How do you know?!"

"They're all over these deserts!" Tim answers. "They're called pictographs!"

"Oh."

"Indians made 'em!"

"I'm going to get in my fort!"

"Good idea!"

He watches the kid lie down in the hole and pull the lid

over himself. Hopes the kid'll sleep, because there's lots of work to do and he doesn't really want the boy seeing it.

He finds himself a forked branch and digs it into the ground. Then he takes the pistol and duct-tapes it into the fork so it's as steady as it's going to get. He digs the spool of wire out of the canvas bag, ties one end around the trigger, cocks the hammer and then carefully counter-wraps and stretches the wire ankle-high across the split. He brings the wire back across and ties it tightly onto the branch.

So there's one shot, he thinks, I'll get off at the back door without having to be there. Make the motherfucker jump through fire to get shot in the chest.

He scoops the gunpowder out of three rounds and pours a line of cordite from the pile of brush back to the center of the split. Then he takes the entrenching tool and digs a shallow trench a little farther in. Not as deep as Kit's hole, just deep enough for him to lie in and not necessarily be seen in the dark. Finishes that and then digs himself a narrow, shallow firing position at the other end of the rock.

Tries to think of anything else he can do to give them a better chance and can't.

So he puts his mind to why old Don Huertero is so sweaty to have Bobby Z alive when it would be so much easier to have him dead. Decides that it must be because Bobby has something he wants, *knows* something he can't tell if he's dead.

What had Elizabeth said? *You took something from him?*

And Don Huertero wants it back.

And if I ever want to live through this, I'd better find

out what it is, locate it and give it back. World ain't big enough to hide from a guy like Huertero forever.

Then he hears Kit crying softly. Crying quietly, like a kid who's used to crying so no one will hear.

"You okay?" Tim asks.

"I miss my mom."

"She'll be out of the hospital soon," Tim says. "I'll see that you get to her."

Tim doesn't have a fucking clue just how he's going to do that but decides that he will.

"She's not my mom," Kit says.

"Sure she is."

"I heard Elizabeth say."

"That's not what Elizabeth meant."

"What's she mean?"

"She meant that maybe Olivia isn't always a great mom."

"Oh."

"Sorry."

"It's okay."

Tim sits with this for a minute, then says, "Why don't you get up and we'll cook some dinner? Yummy Q-rations."

"Like Marines eat?"

'Fraid so, kid.

"Yeah."

"Okay."

So Tim lights the fire and it has that great mesquite smell and they heat up some Q-rations that are turkey-something with rice and have the energy bars for dessert.

They tell each other stories to pass the time and Kit's better at it than Tim is. Kid has an imagination that just won't quit and actually entertains Tim with a story about an island somewhere full of treasure and the pirate who hid it there.

The pirate's name is Bobby and Tim doesn't know if he should be like flattered or freaked out.

37.

Johnson rolls a cigarette as he waits for the moon to come up. Sits up on the ridge looking down at Split Rock and thinks that Bobby Z has his dick *stuck* in the wringer this time.

Johnson's feeling pretty relaxed. For one thing, Brian got bored and went home, which is a damn good thing, because Johnson thinks Brian was gonna be more trouble than help in a fight. Also, Johnson thinks he's about had it with this "take him alive" shit.

Come to think of it, he's had it with all Brian's shit.

Johnson spent forty years of his life doing *real* ranching. Which in the desert took some genuine skill, shifting cattle around the sparse foliage until the stupid damn beasts were fat enough to sell for enough money to keep the bankers off the ranch. Pulled that trick off for forty damn years, and never got rich, but had enough for beans, coffee, tobacco and whiskey. He had his land and his cattle and his damn self-respect, and then the government booted the ranchers off the federal land. No more grazing cattle lest they "ruin the pristine vegetation of the natural desert," and that just kicked it for the small ranchers like Johnson.

The bankers were on him like stink on shit.

Took the ranch and everything on it, didn't leave him with as much as a horse to ride away on.

And, Johnson thinks, I end up renting myself out to this fat fag on his so-called ranch.

Ranch, my callused ass.

He finishes rolling his smoke, lights it up, and as he takes in that first relaxing draw he's thinking that they'll just take old Bobby about any way they can get him.

And the boy . . . well, now.

Rojas is sitting beside him like some mean old dog.

Johnson rolls a smoke for Rojas and hands it to him. Lights it for him and says, "We'll wait for the moon . . ."

Rojas don't say nothing.

Rojas ain't big on words, anyway. Tends to be a bit spare in the word department when he's sober. Plus, Johnson thinks, I ain't really said anything that needs responding to.

And Rojas is sulking. Johnson can tell just sittin' next to the man that the man is steaming. Doesn't really blame him. Rojas has spent a whole hot day tracking the man and the boy and then the boss brings in some asshole in a toy airplane and fucks everything up.

And Johnson's thinking what Rojas is thinking: They should've just let Rojas run 'em down and kill 'em.

It's what you got yourself a Rojas for.

Otherwise what's the use of havin' him; he's such a pain in the ass to bail out of jail all the time.

Just a goddamn danger to himself and others.

Johnson says, "You know, I been thinking. I'm not so sure we need to take this old boy alive. I'm thinking if you have the chance you just might as well kill him."

But Johnson hasn't reckoned on just how pissed off Rojas really is.

Figures it out when Rojas says, "I take him alive."

"No, really, you don't—"

Rojas holds up that big knife and twists it in the starlight.

"I stick this," he says, "into his neck and the man feels nothing ever again."

Jesus shit, Johnson thinks.

"The man is alive," Rojas continues, "but when he shits himself he doesn't know."

"That some old Indian thing?"

"I think we take Bobby Z to Don Huertero that way," Rojas says. "I think that will make Don Huertero happy."

"I expect."

"Me, too," Rojas says.

Johnson stares out to where the rising moon is turning Hapaha Flats into a silver bowl.

"Well, you do what you want," Johnson says. "Me, I'm telling the boys to go in shooting. To 'wound,' of course. If you get to Bobby before a bullet does, well, that's your good luck."

"Luck," Rojas spits. "I don't need no airplane to fly."

Johnson doesn't know what the hell he means by that but lets it go as some sort of mystical Indian shit. The Cahuillas're always like that—turning themselves into coyotes and badgers and jackrabbits and shit.

Least when they've been at the mescal.

"Well, if you can, take him alive," Johnson says. He takes a few moments to get to the next part. "The boy, on the other hand . . ."

Rojas, the mean son of a bitch, waits him out. Wants to make him say it.

Johnson's more stubborn. He sucks on his smoke and watches the moon rise.

Finally Rojas laughs.

"The boy," he says.

He takes the knife and draws it in front of his throat.

"You want the boy's head?" Rojas asks.

Johnson can tell Rojas is fucking with him.

"I don't think that'll be necessary," Johnson says.

He gets his nightscope out and looks down into the flat. Can see his boys getting in position around Split Rock.

Give it another half hour or so and it'll be time to finish this thing.

38.

Tim shoots the first guy the second he appears, like a green ghost in the nightscope. Knows he hits him because the guy drops in that awkward way guys do when they've taken a round.

Tim's shooting for the chest: It's the broadest part of the target. None of this shoot-to-wound crap tonight. Tonight it's the real deal.

Khafji all over again.

He hears the kid stir behind him.

"You stay *in* that hole," Tim orders. Voice like a sergeant, no bullshit, 'cause they're returning fire now. Tim hears the rounds smack like drumbeats against the rock. One or two rounds come zooming in above his head.

"You stay in that hole," Tim repeats.

Another figure dashes across his thin corridor of vision and Tim squeezes off a round. Hears the air go out of the guy when he hits the ground.

Tries to listen over the sound of his pounding heart. Adrenaline rush and all that happy crap, but it's important that he can hear them coming around the other side.

Through the old backdoor.

Sees another figure, shoots and misses.

Can hear them out there, though, and they've hit the

dirt. They have any brains they'll crawl around the side and take some snap shots around the edge of the split.

He listens for footsteps.

Doesn't hear any in front or in back.

Then he hears the pistol shot.

Shot, hell, it's more like a fucking roar, echoing behind him in the narrow corridor of the rock, and he hears the guy yell, "Oh, shit!" like he's heard guys yell before when they're surprised they're shot.

Here we go, Tim thinks. It's the fucking Alamo now, and he crawls backward out of his firing hole.

"Stay in that hole," he orders again as he belly-crawls past Kit toward the backdoor. Sees the guy sitting against the rock wall, can just make out the entry wound in the front of his chest. Doesn't *want* to see the exit wound, not from a 9mm at that range, and the guy's just sitting there with that glazed look in his eye and Tim yells, "Medic!" out of sheer habit and doesn't even realize that he shouts it.

Tim flicks a flame from the cigarette lighter and touches it to the line of gunpowder just as he hears feet running toward the opening in the rock. Watches the spark crackle and then the pile of brush ignites so bright it hurts his eyes.

"What's that?!" Kit yells.

"Keep down!" Tim yells back.

He doesn't hear any footsteps now, isn't sure whether he could hear them through the fire's roar, so he takes a gamble that the guys have stopped at the fire's edge. Flips the lever on the M-16 to bush rake and lets loose.

Even through the fire he can hear the pop-pop sound of rounds smacking into bodies.

Tim throws himself down.

Good fucking idea because rounds come winging back through the fire.

Bullets and curses in Spanish and Tim realizes that the "take him alive" order is probably forgotten now that the blood is up and people are dead.

He remembers that a lot of orders get forgotten when a buddy or two's been hit and the fear and adrenaline and rage are *screaming* like his is now. But he makes himself wait and he crawls into the shallow trench he dug earlier.

And reaches for the K-Bar at his belt and gathers his knees under him.

Guy comes leaping *through* the fire—through the fucking fire—shit, he's *on* fire, little flames licking out his sleeve and on his hat—he looks like some sort of comic book villain—the Human Torch or something—as Tim lunges up with the knife in both hands.

Pushes the blade into the guy's stomach, twists it sideways, straightens it, then kicks the guy's body off the blade.

Hits the dirt and listens.

Tim decides to believe the backdoor attack is history. No choice anyway because he can hear someone coming in at the front. They must have brought an army and Tim figures he's fucked anyway.

Same old Tim Kearney, he thinks: Good at getting into places, fucking hopeless at getting out.

He eases the rifle into the old supine firing position and looks through the scope. Sees another green ghost edging along the side of the rock wall. Not giving him much to shoot at but enough, and Tim has just about applied the requisite pressure on the trigger when he hears something above him and looks up just in time to see a body hurtling down the split from the top of the rock.

Motherfucker just dropping from the sky like some kind of berserk bat.

Crazy motherfucker, Tim thinks, as he tries to squeeze out of the way, but the crazy motherfucker lands square on him. Knocks the wind out of him. Tim can't fucking breathe and the rifle's pinned beneath him and so are his arms so he can't reach the K-Bar.

Feels a knife against the back of his neck.

Guy's lying flat on him, trying to catch his own breath, but is cool enough to get the knife where it can make Tim a quad in about a second and a half and this crazy motherfucker's so cool he has the stones to say, "Señor Z *pendejo* fuck."

Then straightens up to get some leverage, which is like an error because the guy pinned against the wall is so wigged out he raises his gun.

Rojas screams, "No!" but it's too late because that just startles the other guy, who squeezes off his whole clip.

Tim feels the weight fly off him, and the other green ghost is just standing there in shock with an empty gun and he's still fumbling for that spare clip as Tim gets up and butt-strokes him across the face.

Now the adrenaline is like *singing* in Tim.

Khafji all over again, like the night he won the Cross, like no impulse control whatsoever, and he pushes the guy against the rock wall, strips him of his ammo and shit, what's this, *grenades*? You should have used them, Tim thinks as he grabs the guy by the back of the neck and pushes him in front toward the opening. Pushes the guy out and another green ghost lets his buddy have it with a shotgun blast across the legs before he realizes it ain't Bobby Z, and he's standing there in the open when Tim puts a round in his face.

Then it gets real quiet.

Tim drops and crawls back to his firing hole in front of Kit.

"You okay?" he asks the boy, because he can hear the boy crying.

"I'm okay," Kit says.

Brave little fucker, Tim thinks.

"You're a good Marine," Tim says.

"I didn't do anything."

"Exactly."

If the kid had started jumping around screaming and shit they'd both be dead. Lying there covered up in that hole while the shit's flying and you don't know *what* the fuck's going on, that takes some serious stones.

It's all like quiet, except that fire at the other end is blazing. A wall of fire, which is just what Tim intended, except that they still have to get out of there and Tim isn't so sure they can just go waltzing out the front door.

Might be lawn sprinklers, he's thinking just as he hears the cowboy holler, "Looks like we got us another situation here, Mr. Z!"

Tim hauls the kid out of the hole and whispers, "We got to do something that's going to be really hard and we got to do it *now*. You up for it?"

Little bastard just nods.

"Okay," Tim says, "we gotta run as fast as we can through that fire."

"Can't do *that*."

"Got to."

The kid shakes his head.

Tim looks him in the eyes. "Yes, you can."

He strips the kid's shirt off and puts it over his head. Then he takes the last of the water and pours it all over the kid. Then he says, "We're gonna run as fast as we can straight through that fire and when we get through you just keep on running. You keep on running into that brush out there and hide—"

"I—"

"I'll find you, I promise. In just a few minutes," Tim says. "But just in case I get lost or something, you hide till morning, then you walk into those hills. Get yourself on top of one and sit until someone finds you. Understand?"

"Understand."

"Ready?"

"Ready."

"Let's make some noise first."

Tim lets off a clip through the fire to soften up the darkness a little, then they run. He holds Kit's hand as they run through the flames.

Tim breathes again as he sees the boy has made it through clean and he pushes him forward and yells, *"Run!"*

Tim watches the boy make it into the brush and then takes a quick look around. Two KIAs and one about to be.

Tim starts climbing the rock. Figures if that crazy motherfucker could do it he can, too. Slips a couple of times and scrapes himself up pretty good but holds on and makes it to the top. Looks down and sees the cowboy with three of his Indians picking their way through the debris at the bottom of the split. One of the Indians sees the body of one of his comrades and howls, howls like a red wolf when he sees that the man is dead.

Tim pulls the pin on the grenade and drops it down the split. Buries his head in his arms and hears the loud but dull thud.

Hears the screams.

He opens his eyes and sees a weird, eerie green glow from inside the rock. Like from a space-alien movie except this is from a phosphorus grenade.

He eases his way down the rock and heads for the brush.

Finds the boy huddled like a jackrabbit underneath some sage.

Tim thinks he should say something but doesn't know what to say that won't make it worse for the boy so he just says, "Can you walk for a while?"

Kit asks, "Can you?"

"Let's get out of here," Tim says. "I'm kind of sick of the desert."

"So am I."

The moon comes up and the desert's all silvery and quiet as they walk toward the hills.

39.

By the time Johnson makes it back to the hacienda it's mid-morning and the sun is high. He sends the woman for their bought-and-paid-for doctor in Ocotillo Wells and the man shows up an hour later more or less sober.

Man stinks of vodka but does a good enough job of picking fragments out of Johnson's arm and shoulder while the cowboy sits pulling on a bottle of tequila. The doctor's paid to keep his mouth shut, does his job, puts Johnson's broken right arm in a sling, gives him some pills and leaves, which is just fine with Johnson, who doesn't want any excess conversation anyway.

Johnson's in an ornery mood. Took a goddamn army of Cahuillas to bag Bobby Z and Bobby Z bags his army. Kills every damn one of them except him.

As for Johnson, he's feeling blown-up and bleeding and raw and to add to that he has the aggravation of having to deal with Brian.

There's no use putting it off, so Johnson takes a long draw on the bottle, ignores his *mejicana*'s entreaties to lay down, and hauls himself over to the main house to give fat Brian the cheerful news.

Don Huertero's already there. Johnson doesn't see him, but sees his men stationed all around the house.

Standing there all macho with their carbines and Mach-10 machine pistols and shit, reflective sunglasses and those beaner straw cowboy hats, and the head beaner won't let Johnson go into the house.

"I just wanted to tell him that we didn't get Bobby Z," Johnson says in English.

"I think he knows," the honcho answers, and they all stand out there in the sun until Don Huertero and a few more boys come out with Brian.

Naked as the day he was born. One big fat white blob of flesh, and he's crying like a baby as one of Huertero's bodyguards gives him a boot in the ass that sends him sprawling into the dust.

"We didn't catch Bobby Z," Johnson says to him.

Brian just looks up at him, all red-eyed and puffy, and Johnson can see he's been slapped around a little. Johnson's glad he's had the tequila, because judging by the look on Huertero's face it's probably the last tequila he's ever gonna get unless the next world's a whole lot different than those old Baptist preachers said it was.

Old Huertero's standing in the shade of the porch, all cool in his white suit, ocean-blue shirt and six-hundred-dollar loafers. Blue wraparound shades, salt-and-pepper hair combed straight back, but not greasy-looking like Johnson's used to seeing Mexicans'. He looks down at Johnson and says, "So you tried to catch Bobby Z?"

"Yessir."

"And what happened?"

"He killed us," Johnson says. "Most of us."

Huertero nods.

Then says, "He didn't kill you."

"No," Johnson says.

Huertero nods again, then says, "Yet."

Johnson shrugs.

"And yet you had him trapped," Huertero says.

Johnson figures this is the moment he's about to get the drop, but there's nothing to do about it so he just says, "Thought I did."

But Huertero smiles and says, "Ah, well, I know the feeling. Mr. Zacharias is like starshine. You reach for him and . . ."

He trails off into some kind of reverie, then his voice gets hidalgo big and he announces, "But Brian had him. A guest of the house. Brian had him and let him go and it makes me wonder if Mr. Z did not offer Brian something more than he thought he could get from me."

Brian's snuffling something that sounds like a denial, but Huertero's having none of it.

"How do I know the truth from Brian, who is an accomplished liar?" Huertero asks the assembled crowd. "Do I give him the same as I was going to give Bobby Z?"

Brian picks himself up and tries to run but one of the honchos stops that with a gun butt to the stomach and Brian's left on all fours, gasping for air.

"Let's let Brian be out in the sun for a while," Huertero says pleasantly. "Mr. Johnson, will you come in the house?"

Johnson doesn't know if he has much choice so he follows Huertero into the big old Arab living room, where one of Brian's servants is already pouring the drug lord some coffee.

Elizabeth's sitting in one of the big chairs. She's dressed in a green silk robe and hasn't brushed her hair or done her makeup, but she's still a handsome woman. Looks pale, though. Scared.

"Coffee?" Huertero asks.

"Wouldn't mind."

The maid trips all over herself pouring Johnson some coffee with cream and sugar. Her hand shakes and the cup rattles on the saucer. Somehow Johnson finds it more unsettling than all last night's gunfire: It's pretty clear that Brian's old servants are now Huertero's new servants, and Johnson guesses that applies to him, too.

Hopes so, anyway.

It's just as possible that Huertero's going to just kill him.

Old bastard sits there in silence like he's just savoring the old richness of Juan Valdez, but Johnson knows that he's just letting the silence spook them.

Well, fuck you, Don Huertero, Johnson thinks. You know what you get when you give a beaner a couple of hundred million dollars? A rich beaner.

Huertero finally opens his mouth.

"Brian is a deeply stupid and degenerate man," he says. "He believes that he can make an arrangement with Bobby Z and fool me. I must believe that such stupidity springs from the degenerate nature of his lifestyle."

Well, Johnson thinks, if corn-holing Italian boys makes you stupid, Brian'd be pretty near a moron by now, that's true.

Huertero continues, "But Brian ungallantly seeks to cast the blame on Elizabeth. Brian tells me that Elizabeth warned Bobby of my plans for him. If that is true—as perhaps it is—then I can only tell Brian that he was negligent in sharing my plans with Elizabeth here, especially if he knew that she and Bobby were at one time lovers. If that is true, then both Brian and Elizabeth are at fault."

Huertero sets his cup and saucer on the side table and sharply orders Elizabeth, "Stand up."

She gets out of the chair and Johnson sees a tremble pass over her body like a shadow across the desert.

"Turn around."

Elizabeth turns her back to them.

"The robe."

She shrugs her shoulders and the robe slides down her back. Johnson winces: The woman's back and butt are a raw terrain of welts and cuts.

Huertero calmly says, "Brian is a deeply stupid young man who does not understand—*cannot* perhaps understand—the nature of this kind of woman. I know Elizabeth, you see, Mr. Johnson. She was an old friend of my late daughter's. Her best friend, perhaps. No, Elizabeth? I have known Elizabeth for years; she has been a frequent guest in my home.

"Elizabeth is warm, lovely, charming, intelligent and lazy. She has the body of a courtesan—that is her blessing. She also has the soul of a courtesan, and that is her curse.

"What Brian fails to understand is that such a woman does not fear pain. Does not *like* pain, certainly—I am not suggesting that—but does not *fear* it. She would not betray a love from fear of pain.

"Turn around."

Johnson watches the woman turn to face them. Her voice is steady and cool as she asks, "May I put my robe back on?"

"Please."

She doesn't hurry. In a slow, fluid motion she reaches down, picks up the robe and puts her arms through the sleeves. She winces slightly as the silk falls over her back.

"What such a woman fears," Huertero's saying, "is disfigurement."

Huertero rises from his chair and steps over to her.

"Look at that face," he says. "Beautiful. What such a woman fears is being ugly," he says. He takes his index finger and slowly runs it from her forehead to her chin. "A deep scar from here to here, perhaps. With the blade of a dull knife so that no surgeon, however skillful, could . . ."

He forms his large hand into a fist, softly touching her face as he says, "Or perhaps her cheekbones smashed, or her nose, or the orbital bones of her eyes. Painful? Oh, yes, but that is not the fear that would cause her to betray a lover, no. Only the fear of disfigurement could do that. The fear of ugliness. Am I right, Elizabeth?"

"Yes."

"Yes?"

"Yes."

"Please sit down."

They both take their chairs.

"With a man such as you it is simpler," Huertero says. "You want to live, yes?"

"Yup."

Huertero nods, then sits with his thoughts to himself, letting the silence get to them. Johnson doesn't like to admit it, but it works—he's about half spooked when Huertero starts to speak.

"So . . . for your betrayals and failures I sentence *you*," he says, nodding to Elizabeth, "to disfigurement. And you, Mr. Johnson, to death."

Johnson sees Elizabeth turn goddamn white and he ain't feeling so hot himself.

"But I suspend the sentence," Huertero says. "Suspended sentence, shall we say, aware that anytime I want you I need only reach out because the world is not big enough for you to hide in. On parole, shall we say, as an expression of mutual good faith?"

"How do we get off parole?" Johnson asks. Gruffly, rudely, because he's tired of this Mexican-gentleman-hidalgo crap and his arm aches.

Huertero feels the rudeness but apparently doesn't care enough to have Johnson swatted like a fly.

"Simple," Huertero says. "You bring me Bobby Z."

"Simple." Johnson laughs.

"You bring me Bobby Z within, shall we say, thirty days?" Huertero says. "Or the sentences will be executed."

Huertero smiles, gets up and walks out, just like that.

"Didn't know you was buddies with his daughter," Johnson says.

"Uh-huh."

"And she died?"

"You heard the man."

"What happened?"

Elizabeth gathered the robe around her and got up.

"She killed herself," she said, and started to leave.

"What for?" Johnson called after her.

"So she wouldn't be alive anymore, I guess."

Johnson walked over to the bar and helped himself to a new bottle of Brian's tequila. Had a feeling Brian wouldn't be needing it anymore. Went out on the porch, sat down and put his feet up.

They had old Brian lying naked in the sun. Standing around him with those cute-ass machine pistols making sure he didn't get up. Old Brian lying there crying and blubbering, his skin already a rosy red. Every time he'd try to cover himself one of the boys would give him a kick to make him straighten out. They'd give him water, too, a couple of gulps now and then, because they didn't want him dying on them.

That Mexico is a hard country, Johnson decides.

Hour or so later, Don Huertero emerges from the house and sees Johnson.

"I don't know what Brian sees in that old film," Huertero says. "I've been just watching it. It's lousy."

"I like that Gary Cooper, though."

"Yes, Gary Cooper is fine," Huertero admits. "But the story . . ."

"Kinda stupid."

"Very stupid."

"Brian just liked that A-rab shit, I guess."

"Do you think that getting drunk will help you to find Bobby Z, Mr. Johnson?"

"I don't suppose at this point it'll hurt."

Huertero shouts some orders in Spanish and the boys start scurrying around. A few minutes later they back Brian's little Toyota four-wheeler up and chain Brian's ankles to the bumper.

Huertero stands over Brian. Brian's burned pretty raw. His face is swollen bad, Johnson sees, and almost the color of his red Brillo hair.

"I cannot tolerate a man who raises his hand to a woman," Huertero says. "And all those *dólares* you keep in holes in the ground . . ."

Huertero spits in Brian's face and yells another order. The Toyota takes off and Johnson can see it racing out toward the brush to where the beaver tail and silver *cholla* is.

Johnson unfolds himself from his chair and starts to amble home. He wants to brew himself some coffee, pack his things and locate Mr. Bobby Z before his thirty days are up. He takes a good look at the house as he walks away. Figures that life here is over.

A damn Toyota, he muses as he shuffles through the dust. In the old days they used horses.

40.

Elizabeth sits applying her makeup in front of the mirror. She can still feel the trace of Don Huertero's fingernail down her face. Can still feel the soft imprint of his knuckles on her cheek, nose and eyes.

She looks for a long time into the glass, then takes a red lipstick and draws a thick vertical line from her forehead to her chin. Stares at her image for several frozen minutes and thinks about herself, Olivia and Angelica.

What a trio. The three best buds. The Mascarateers, they called themselves. Playgirls.

Then.

Now: Herself a homeless whore, Olivia a rehab junkie, Angelica dead.

Angelica, Huertero's little angel. Gorgeous girl, just fucking beautiful. High-flying Angelica.

But Bobby broke her wings.

She had no experience falling so she fell hard. Never learned how to roll so she got hit hard. You fall with your arms wide open, Elizabeth thought, you land on your heart.

The subsequent overdose was just a formality—the period to the sentence.

Elizabeth washes the lipstick scar from her face, redoes her makeup, then eases into a soft denim blouse, jeans and boots. Brushes her hair out and starts to pack. Although well practiced at packing, she takes almost two hours to clear out the walk-in closet of her things. She has a lot of clothes and anyway it still hurts to move.

She doesn't bother to ring for anyone to carry her bags down. All the servants are gone and the house is deathly quiet except for the drone of the television in her room. Some afternoon talk show—she doesn't even know which it is except that some trailer trash is screaming at some other trailer trash for sleeping with her trailer-trash husband.

It's on her second trip out to the car that she sees Brian's body, or maybe just Brian because it's possible he's still breathing.

He's just lying there in the courtyard, skin red and body grotesquely swollen, and he looks like he's been shot with a thousand miniature arrows.

Next time down she takes a different route to the car.

It's a red Mercedes. She puts the last bag in the trunk, sets the radio for some light jazz and drives away. Keeps her head pointed in front of her so only peripherally sees Don Huertero's men loading the illegals back into the trucks.

For Lord knows where, she thinks. For Lord knows where.

She stops on the main road and pulls the car over to look back.

The black smoke mixes with the rosy-gray sunset, fades into the blackness of the mountains beyond, then disappears into the darkening sky. Fire tops the walls of

Brian's old Arab fort. The orange towers of flame shooting above the parapets remind her of the Arabian doorways. Tear-shaped, almost.

Beau geste, Brian, she thinks.

Some funny joke, old pal.

41.

Ten days later Tim's pouring out the last of the Corn Pops into his and Kit's bowls while they watch a cartoon called *Double Dragon*, which Kit thinks blows but Tim thinks is at least all right.

They're living in the last cabin of eight cedar cabins gathered in a meadow on the western side of the Sunrise Highway on Mount Laguna. Mount Laguna's nowhere near and has nothing to do with the town of Laguna or Laguna Beach, but still it's enough of an echo of Bobby Z to keep Tim focused on his main problem in life.

Which is the fact that for all practical purposes he *is* Bobby Z and Don Huertero is terminally pissed at him.

At least Mount Laguna's not a desert mountain. It has real fucking trees, for one thing: big tall piñons, cedars, hemlocks, and even oaks. *Shade* trees, and the Knotty Pine cabins—at fifty-seven bucks a week off-season the price is right—sit just off the road flanked by a stand of giant pines. It's cheap, quiet and private, and the owner doesn't ask a lot of questions even if he does notice that the customer's shirt is stained with dried blood. Doesn't matter, as long as he pays. Also there are no other guests in the other seven cabins, which Tim really likes, so even though it's kind of a toilet it's about perfect for him to sit for a while and figure out what to do.

And it's like kid heaven for Kit, who's just out of his skull to be around a man for a change and is really into the "just us guys" thing, and gets to eat as much junk as Tim can buy from the general store about a mile up the hill.

So it's been Corn Pops, Pepsi, chocolate milk, hot dogs, peanut-butter-and-jelly sandwiches, Hormel chili, Dinty Moore beef stew and stacks of frozen pizza, and all the television he wants to watch.

The kid's into it.

He's also into the spy thing.

The spy thing is Tim's version of hide-and-go-seek.

"We're playing spies now," he informs Kit after first getting the key from Macy, the old man who owns the motel.

"How do you play spies?" Kit asks.

"First of all, we need different names."

"Why?"

"You can't be a spy and have your own name," Tim tells him. "Everyone will know who you are and then you can't spy."

Kit thinks this over and asks, "What's your name going to be?"

Tim pretends to think and then says, "How about Tim?"

"Good."

"Who're you gonna be?"

"Mike."

"Mike?"

"Mike."

"Mike's good, I like that," Tim says. "Now the game is that the bad spies are after us and we're hiding until . . ."

"Until what?"

"Until we can find where the secret formula's hidden."

"Is that our cabin, Tim?"

"Yes, Mike."

"Can I open the door?"

"How come?"

"Just want to."

"You know how to use a key?"

"I'm *six*."

"Okay with me."

So Kit runs ahead to the cabin, throws open the screen door and struggles with the key until he pushes it open. Tim doesn't get it that six-year-olds are just crazy about doing that kind of thing, but it's okay with him.

The cabin's small. There's a kitchen counter with a small stove and an oven, a sitting area with a ratty old couch and a rocking chair, and a bedroom with bunks in it. The bathroom's big enough to turn around in and has a shower but no bath.

Place has a TV, though, and it has "Bobby," which is about all Kit cares about, so he's happy. And if he has the bloody night in the desert on his mind, he isn't saying anything about it and it sure isn't affecting his appetite any the way he puts down pizza and ice cream.

After about a week Tim's getting tired of hiking back from the general store with groceries and also figures he's going to need transportation to find out the next step to being Bobby Z, so he decides to get a car.

His first thought is to steal one, of course. Hang out by the gas pumps at the general store until some citizen leaves the key in the ignition while they're inside buying their beef jerky, but then he thinks better of it. It's a small town—shit, the general store *is* the town, that and a biker bar across the road—and the victim is bound to see his missing vehicle parked at the Knotty Pine Motel. And the last thing Tim needs is to wind up back in the system where Gruzsa and the Aryan Brotherhood will be happy to greet him.

And then there's the kid. What's going to happen to the kid if I get nailed? Tim wonders. So he goes against his better nature and decides he'd better just buy some old heap.

And there *is* an old heap, a plug-ugly lime-green Dodge, been parked in the gravel parking lot since they've been there, so Tim tells Kit to finish watching the cartoon and he'll be back in a few minutes.

Tim goes to the cabin that serves as an office and says hello to the owner. Macy grunts a hello back and returns to reading *The Star* newspaper.

"That old Dodge?" Tim starts.

"Yeah?"

"Been parked out there awhile," Tim says. "You know who it belongs to?"

"Yeah."

"Who?"

"Me."

Fucking old coot, Tim thinks. Has to make this hard.

"I'm looking for a vehicle myself," Tim says.

Old bastard looks up from his paper and says, "Nine hundred."

"I don't want it *bronzed*," Tim says. "I'll take it as is. Give you five."

"You won't give *me* five," the old guy says. Sits for a minute, then says, "I'd take eight-fifty."

"Yeah, I bet you would."

Tim stands for a minute while the guy finishes his article. When he looks up again he doesn't seem all that thrilled that Tim is still there.

Tim says, "I'll give you six."

Man thinks about it for a while and says, "I won't take a check."

"I was thinking of cash."

Tim doesn't like saying it and doesn't like the look in the guy's eye. Old man running an out-of-the-way dive has to wonder why white trash would have that much cash on him. Wonders where he got it and probably wonders what kind of reward there is on a poor man carrying that kind of cash.

But it can't be helped, Tim thinks. We need a car.

"Go get the cash, I'll go get the keys," the old man says.

Tim reaches into his pants pocket and pulls out six bills.

"I'll go get the keys," the old man says. He goes into the back room and returns a minute later and tosses the keys on the counter. "Pink slip's in it. You're not checking out, are you?"

"Not yet."

Tim's halfway out the door when the old man asks, "You need anything else?"

"Like what?"

"Like a gun."

Tim doesn't tell him that he already has a gun, thanks. Tim left the M-16 smashed up under a rock as he came out of the desert, on the theory that even in Southern California it's hard to hitchhike with an automatic rifle slung over your shoulder. But the pistol, even now, is tucked inside the waistband of his jeans.

"Why would I want a gun?" Tim asks.

The old man shrugs. "Protection."

That's what the old geezer says, Tim thinks, but what he means to do is sell Tim a gun so Tim can go rob something else. Long as it's not him, the old man doesn't give a shit. Long as it pays the rent.

"I always have a piece handy for protection," the old man adds, making sure that Tim knows it's *not* okay to rob *him*.

Nobody robs their hideout, Tim thinks with disdain. Even asshole Wayne LaPerriere wouldn't be asshole enough to rob his own hideout.

"I think the car's enough, thanks," Tim says.

He goes outside, climbs into the driver's seat and is nicely surprised when the heap starts up first turn of the key. He calls Kit outside to help him check the brake lights, taillights and turn signals, then double-checks the registration sticker and emission-controls stickers. Tim does not want to get pulled over for something stupid.

Specially as he doesn't have a driver's license.

Kit's way juiced about the car.

"Is this a *spy* car?" he asks.

"Don't say it so loud."

"Sorry."

But there's a grin all over the kid's face and Tim decides that the boy leads a rich fantasy life.

"Let's take her for a spin," Tim says. "We need groceries."

They go up to the general store to lay in a fresh supply of junk. Tim decides he needs another week or so of quiet to decide just what the hell to do next.

Also figures it'll be time to move on soon, before the old man finds a buyer to sell him to.

Tim's thinking these weighty matters over as he and Kit put the groceries in the car. Problem is, Tim's been out of the joint just long enough to let his paranoia get rusty, so he doesn't notice the biker across the road giving him just that extra-second glance. In all fairness to Tim, it's cold up on the mountain, there's still patches of snow on the ground—and the guy's got an Australian herder's coat on over his colors.

The biker notices him, though, although he has to chew on it halfway back to El Cajon before it hits where he knows this guy from. The kid threw him off at first, but then he remembers he has an image of Tim on the yard in San Quentin.

And because it never hurts to do a good one for the brothers in L.A. he calls one of the clubs up there and a couple of hours later that ugly prick Boom-Boom calls him back.

"Yeah?" Boom-Boom says, like he's pissed off he's been taken away from something more important.

"Guess who I saw earlier today."

"Who?"

Real bored-like.

"Tim Kearney," the biker says.

Then Boom-Boom gets a whole lot more interested.

Chatty, almost.

42.

Tim figures it's about time he called the Monk, because life ain't gonna let him live unless he squares things with Huertero. Piles Kit into the car and they drive up to Julian, about thirty miles away, to make the call.

They do this because Tim figures it would be a stupid, moke thing to call from the phone booth at the motel, and he's doing his best to quit being a stupid moke and fuck you, Agent Gruzsa.

Kit picks up on it, though, when they pull into Julian, which is an old gold-mining town in the mountains that hit the skids and now sells apple pie to tourists. Place still *looks* like an old western town, though, so the phone booth Tim pulls up to looks out of place.

"We came here to make a *phone* call?" the kid asks.

"Yeah."

"Uh, there's a phone booth at the motel."

With that like *duh* voice kids like to put on.

"This is a spy thing," Tim answers. "What if they traced the call?"

"Cool."

"Way cool," Tim answers. "You wait in the car."

"Why?"

Kid is seriously annoyed. Kid doesn't want to be left out of any spy action.

Tim's about to answer *Because I told you to, that's why,* but then remembers his old man and thinks better of it. So he says, "What if you get captured?"

"Captured?" Kit looks a little pale, like he's forgotten this is a game.

"Yeah, captured," Tim says. "You can't tell what you don't know."

Which isn't strictly true, Tim thinks, because he knew lots of guys in jail who were all the time telling the DA's office things they didn't know. Usually worked, too, because the DAs always believed them, because it let them jam up some poor jerk they didn't have enough evidence to convict. Much easier to haul some jailhouse rat in to say, "We were sitting in the jail cell and this guy told me he did it."

Anyway, he doesn't think he should share this miserable fact of life with the kid—who just doesn't have the soul of a rat anyway—so he repeats, "You can't tell what you don't know."

The kid bites, saying, "And anyway, someone needs to guard our spy car."

"Right."

"Look out for bad guys."

"Right."

"What do the bad guys look like?"

Tim wants to answer *If you don't see him in your mirror you better assume it's a bad guy* but instead he says, "They're driving silver cars."

"Silver?"

"Yeah."

"Okay," Kit says seriously, and he gets busy watching out for silver cars.

Tim goes to the phone and dials the number Elizabeth gave him.

Tim's heart is like fucking racing because he doesn't know who's on the other end of the line.

Three rings and a flat voice answers, "Yeah?"

"Yeah, it's me," Tim says.

Long fucking pause during which Tim thinks maybe he better hang up and race out of there. He's a heartbeat from exiting stage left when the voice says, *"Bobby?!"*

Like he just can't believe it, right? Like he's beside himself with fucking joy.

Like someone's come back from the dead, huh?

"Yeah," Tim says. "Bobby."

Then he takes a huge chance.

"Who's this?" Tim asks.

Another pause.

Run away, Tim thinks. But he hangs on.

"It's me, man," the voice says. "The Monk."

The Monk? Tim thinks. The Monk is like the guy, right? Bobby's right-hand man. Man who knows where everything's hidden.

"Good to hear your voice, man."

"Good to hear *yours*," the Monk says. "Where have you been? Your mother and I have been worried sick about you."

"Where *haven't* I been, man?"

"You sound different."

Shit. Run away, Tim thinks. Get in the car and drive as far as it'll take you.

Which is like maybe El Centro, right? Which just ain't

gonna cut it. Gotta get through this, Tim tells himself, so he makes his voice kind of hip-annoyed and growls, "You'd sound different, too, man, you been where I been. You ever seen a Thai jail, Monk?"

"I've avoided that pleasure so far, babe."

Babe. Fuck you, babe.

"Yeah, well, that's a good idea," Tim says.

"You coming in?"

"I'm too hot, man."

You can like *hear* the guy thinking over the phone.

"What do you need?" Monk asks.

"Cash," Tim says. "And a new passport."

"Ask and ye shall receive."

"I'm asking," Tim says. "I need about twenty K for starters."

"You want to meet at the old place?"

Sure, Tim thinks, except that nobody told me where the old place is.

"No," Tim says.

"Okay, where?"

Someplace crowded, Tim thinks.

Someplace I can bring a kid.

"The zoo," Tim says.

"The *zoo*?"

"San Diego Zoo," Tim says. "Tomorrow. Two o'clock."

"Where, exactly?"

Tim's never been there but he figures every zoo's got elephants so he says, "Outside the elephants."

Plus Kit'll like the elephants, right? Kids like elephants.

Tim can hear Monk thinking again.

Then Monk says, "I'll bring the stuff in a plastic Ralph's bag. Can you get one of those?"

"Sure."

"Two o'clock."

Tim decides to take another chance.

"Also," he says, "I need some information."

"Shoot."

"What'd we do to Don Huertero?"

Using the "we" to drag old Monk into it. Give him more than just a rooting interest.

And Monk thinks it over for a long time. Unless he's tracing the number.

"So?" Tim asks.

"Nothing I can think of."

"Do we have something that belongs to him?"

"Nothing *I* know about."

"Work on it, huh?" Tim orders. "Talk to you tomorrow."

Tim hangs up. If Monk was tracing the number it was time to leave. Also, Kit is hopping up and down in the seat because there's a silver car coming down the street.

"Bad guys," Kit whispers as Tim gets in the car.

"We'll have to lose them," Tim whispers back.

"Can we do it?"

"Oh, yeah."

I'm Bobby Z, right?

Tim finds a hardware store, where he buys some PVC pipe, a hacksaw and some steel wool. At the general store back on Mount Laguna he buys the usual crap, some chocolate-chip cookie dough, and the thinnest cookie sheet they have.

He's struggling with all this shit when Kit runs ahead to the cabin so he can unlock it.

It's funny, Tim thinks, what little stuff'll make a kid happy.

They bake cookies that night. Kit does, anyway—Tim doesn't have a fucking clue how to bake cookies. He tried to get a job in the kitchen at Quentin but they put him in the license-plate factory instead.

43.

The Monk hangs up the phone and looks out over the ocean. The living room has floor-to-ceiling windows, so this isn't too tough to do. House sits on the edge of a point with rock cliffs on three sides, so if you want to see ocean you can see ocean without straining your neck. You can see El Morro beach to your right and Laguna Beach to your left. House has a million-dollar view, which it should, because it cost three times that.

Dope money. Bobby Z money.

Problem is, now he's back.

What's shaking Monk up is not so much that Bobby is back—that's a problem in the physical world—it's that One Way's prophecy is being fulfilled.

You take a hike on God, fulfilled prophecies are bound to make you a little hinky.

The zoo? The Monk thinks. Since when does Bobby go to the zoo? Why not meet in the cave at Salt Creek Beach like they used to? Or the steps at Three Arch Bay? Why the zoo?

Because he doesn't trust you, Monk thinks. He wants a public place.

Paranoia, Monk sighs as he slides the glass door open and steps onto the deck. The bane of the drug market.

Twenty K and a passport. Twenty K? Lunch money to Bobby, but he sure seems sweaty to get it. And a passport. Bobby's splitting the country again, so that must mean he's feeling heat from the Heat and not just Don Huertero. You just can't get out of Don Huertero's jurisdiction. Not breathing, anyway.

And who's Bobby kidding with this *what'd I ever do to Don Huertero* bit. The Monk wonders if Bobby didn't have someone listening to the conversation. Like maybe Huertero already has Bobby and he's setting *me* up.

There's no loyalty, Monk sighs, in a godless world.

Because the fact is that Monk ripped Huertero off bigtime. And Bobby, for that matter. Bobby took the old Mexican's money—three million *yanqui* dollars—for some Thai opium and delivered it to Huertero's boys in Bangkok. But Monk ratted them out to the Thai police, then split the opium and the profits with the Thais.

Sorry, Don Huertero, but the Thai police busted your boys. Say *adiós* to your investment. Bad luck.

Well, Monk thinks as he watches some surfers catch the reef break down on El Morro, Huertero must have figured it out.

And he's mad.

And now Bobby's in trouble and he wants to know why. Will want to have a look at the books. Will probably want to give the money back.

I don't think so, Monk thinks.

He drives into town and cogitates on the universe over an Italian cappuccino. He still can't figure out how that acid casualty One Way knew that Z was back.

It spooks him.

Spooks him so much that he drives down to Dana Point to check on the boat.

Looks over his shoulder as he strides down the slip. Doesn't see One Way or anyone else so he starts to figure that even a lunatic gets lucky every once in a while in the old prophecy business.

True? If a hardcore schiz like John the Baptist can hit it, maybe One Way can, too. So relax.

Monk goes below and starts in to work with a screwdriver and woodworking knife. Two hours later he removes a section of plank and reaches into the hull.

Feels the nicely wrapped packages of cash.

Works diligently to replace the plank and while he's working he's thinking.

Maybe it's time to sail away.

But first he has to give Bobby his chump change and his passport.

Then kill him.

44.

Gruzsa's pissed because he's getting ashes all over his new shoes.

He's standing in the ruins of Casa Brian Cervier and the wind's blowing ashes all over his brand-new pair of cordovan Bostonians that he got on sale at Nordstrom.

Gruzsa's also unhappy because Brian got whacked almost two weeks ago and no one thought to tell him about it until now. So now he's standing out in the middle of fucking nowhere ruining the shine on his shoes and looking down at the crispy remains of major-league pervert and skell Brian Cervier, who looks like he's been napalmed, and Gruzsa figures that with a disaster this big that stupid moke Tim Kearney just *has* to be involved.

"Carbon in his lungs?" Gruzsa asks the young DEA agent whose name he's already forgotten and who looks like he's been on the job for maybe a month.

"The ME says no."

"So Brian got lucky," Gruzsa says. "Died before the fire. What, did his clothes all burn up?"

"No, he was naked."

So there's luck and there's luck, Gruzsa thinks.

"And they say Bobby Z was here?" Gruzsa asks for about the fifteenth time.

"We rounded up some of the household staff in Borrego Springs and they all say that a Señor Z was a guest at the house."

"But we haven't found Señor Z's body," Gruzsa repeats.

"No."

Because Señor Z is a trickier motherfucker than I thought, Gruzsa admits to himself.

"What about this dead Kraut?" Gruzsa asks.

"Engine failure," the kid says. "It looks unrelated."

"What are you—stupid?" Gruzsa asks. "You got a crispy-critter drug dealer and slave merchant, his Heinrich business associate dropped out of the sky like a meteor, you got some big rock in the middle of the desert with dead Indians all over it like it's a John Wayne movie, and you think anything's unrelated? You think, what, the house gets hit by lightning and goes up like Nagasaki? Where are you from, Iowa?"

The kid stands there turning red and it isn't from the sun.

"Kansas," he says.

"This is fucking great," Gruzsa says. "I'm going up against fucking Don Huertero and fucking Bobby Z and fucking who knows who else and I've got some goober from Kansas on my side. Say the truth, they have drugs in Kansas?"

"Sure."

"Sure. What do they have?"

Kid starts listing drugs but Gruzsa's not listening. He's thinking that now this all-American loser Kearney starts believing that he *is* the great Bobby Z and starts leaving bodies in his trail like bread crumbs. Fucking asshole thinks he's Hansel or something out here. Well at least he's left a trail.

". . . crystal meth, Ecstasy, cocaine, crack cocaine . . ."

"Shut up."

The agent shuts up.

"Can't you tell I'm fucking with you?" Gruzsa asks. He's well and truly aggravated. If he'd been told about this right away, Kearney's trail would still be hot. He could still pick him up and deliver him to Huertero.

But now . . .

"I want this cleaned up," Gruzsa says. "Like yesterday. You tell the park rangers nothing ever happened here. You bury those fucking Indians, you ship that Kraut back to Frankfurt, you blow up those bunkers, and you send those beaners back to Mexico. Can you do that?"

"Yes, sir."

"Don't call me fucking sir," Gruzsa says. "I look like some kind of officer to you?"

Gruzsa scans the debris again.

A-fucking-mazing, he thinks. Huertero comes across the border like it's eighteen-whatever, kills the gringo, burns the place to ashes and then slips across the border again.

Fucking Don Huertero is a serious man.

So I can't fuck around, Gruzsa thinks. He looks down at Brian's body—if you want to call it that—and can see what happens to someone who disappoints Huertero.

What I need to do—and quickly—Gruzsa thinks as he gets back into his car, is to deliver young Timmy Kearney to Don Huertero.

Dead on delivery, so he can't open his stupid mouth.

Problem is, Kearney's turning out to be a tougher take-down than I thought.

Semper Fi, huh.

Gruzsa looks down to see that the ashes from his shoes

are now on his carpet and he just vacuumed the goddamn thing. He's in one murderous fucking mood when the phone rings.

"Hey, cocksucker," Boom-Boom says.

"What do you want, lard-ass?"

"I found your boy."

Suddenly Gruzsa's feeling a little better.

"No shit," he says.

"No shit."

So then Gruzsa's not feeling so bad about his shoes. Fuck the shoes, he thinks, I can buy lots of shoes.

Pretty soon I'm going to be rich.

45.

Tim gets Kit to sleep after *Baywatch* is over. *Baywatch* is one of the shows they both like. Kit gets off on the rescues and saving people and all that happy shit, and Tim gets off on the women jogging around in wet bathing suits. He figures that these are the kind of women who jog around in wet bathing suits on the beaches that Bobby Z would frequent.

They had a lifeguard at the public pool in Desert Hot Springs, he remembers. They called her Big Blue because she wore a bright blue one-piece bathing suit. No one ever actually saw her swim—the popular theory was that if anyone started drowning Big Blue would just jump in and raise the water level so that the drowning person would just sort of wash up on the edge of the pool. No one ever volunteered to test the theory, though, so Tim's memory of Big Blue was her sitting up in that big chair reading *Mademoiselle* magazine while chewing on beef jerky.

Tim doesn't think that any of the girls on *Baywatch* would even know what beef jerky is.

Anyway, he finally gets Kit to bed so he can get to work. He takes the section of PVC he bought and saws off a straight one-foot piece. He stuffs rough-grade steel

wool into the pipe and then screws the end-cap down
onto it. He fits this onto his pistol barrel until he sees it'll
fit nice and snug, then takes off the pipe.

46.

Tim pays for the bag of Oreos, bottles of water, cheese snacks, loaf of bread and jar of peanut butter, and the bagger asks, "Paper or plastic?"

"Plastic, please."

He and Kit leave the Ralph's and get back in the car.

"What's the surprise?" Kit asks again as Tim pulls out of the parking lot and works his way back to the freeway.

"If I told you, it wouldn't be a surprise."

"Oh, maaaan . . ."

"Oh, maaaan . . ." Tim mocks him. "You'll know in a few minutes."

"So it's someplace in San Diego . . ." Kit says to himself.

Kid's having a great time.

Tim wishes *he* was. Fact is, he's scared shitless. Doesn't know what he's walking into, doesn't know if the Monk is righteous, doesn't know who is going to be waiting by the elephants. Just doesn't know and that scares him shitless.

Except it is kind of fun to take the kid on this surprise. It doesn't seem like anyone's ever done that for the kid before, because Kit is like out of his skull with excitement.

Tim turns off the 163 where the sign says "4th Avenue—Balboa Park—Zoological Park."

Kit's pretty smart and he sees the "zoo" in "zoological."

"We're going to the zoo!!!!!" he screams. "That's the surprise, isn't it?! The zoo? Right?"

"Maybe."

"It is! I know it!" Bouncing up and down. "The zoo!"

"You never been to the zoo before?" Tim asks.

"No!"

"Neither have I," Tim says.

They drive through Balboa Park and follow the signs to the zoo. Drive around the huge parking lot until they find a spot.

"Okay," Tim says, "your job is to remember what row we're in. The ostrich row."

Picture of an ostrich on top of a big pole on their row.

"Ostrich row," Kit repeats.

"Ostrich row."

Because that would be the shits, Tim thinks. Pull this off and then not be able to find the car. That would be a classic Tim Kearney fuck-up.

Tim buys their tickets and can't believe it costs fourteen bucks to get into a fucking zoo, but it does and he pays it. First thing he does inside is look at the map they gave him with the ticket. One of those cutesy fucking maps with pictures of all the animals and he looks for a picture of an elephant.

Next thing he does is get the lay of the land. The zoo sits on the slope of a big hill and the footpaths switchback up and down. There's also one of those gondola cable things running from the bottom to the top. There's only one exit and that's beside the entrance where they're standing.

"Can we ride that?" Kit asks, pointing at the cable car.

Tim consults the map and says, "Sure, why not?"

They have plenty of time because he's made sure they're early.

"Goody," Kit says.

Goody? Tim thinks. Take the kid to the zoo and the kid turns into a kid.

"I think it's a good idea," Tim says, and they go over to the gondolas and get in one of the open-top little cars. Tim's not thrilled that the thing rattles and shakes as it climbs up the hill, but it does give him the unexpected advantage of aerial surveillance.

So up they go. Kit's looking at antelope and buffalo and birds and stuff and Tim's looking over near the elephants for someone carrying a white plastic Ralph's bag. Someone who looks like he's not all that interested in the elephants.

Thinks he sees a tall thin guy who fits the description but isn't sure, so when they get to the top they get out onto an observatory deck and Tim puts quarters into the big binoculars. Has to take turns with Kit so it costs about seventy-five cents for Tim to get a good enough look at the guy to decide it's the Monk.

He isn't fat, he isn't wearing a brown robe and a hood, and he doesn't look like he's out of a Robin Hood movie, but Tim decides this guy's the guy.

Plum Polo shirt, khaki Dockers, black baseball cap, John Lennon shades. Moccasins with no socks. White plastic Ralph's bag.

Very hip. Standing there looking a little nervous and a little bored. Of course he's there early, too. Half an hour early and the guy's there already, which makes Tim even more edgy.

Tim would like to know if the guy's alone, but there's a crowd down there and how can you tell who's just there and who's, like, *there*. He's scoping out single men—no families, no girlfriends—when the image goes dark.

"I'm out of quarters," Tim says.

"What do you want to do?" Kit asks.

"Did you ever," Tim asks, "play 'Spy at the Zoo'?"

Kit smiles like the day just got more perfect than he thought was possible.

"How do you play that?" he asks.

"First we have to find a guy carrying a white plastic bag," Tim says.

"Is he a bad guy?"

"Dunno," Tim says.

But he thinks he's probably going to find out.

47.

Boom-Boom watches the old fucker drive off in his car. Old coot steams off like he's got a woman waiting, so Boom-Boom figures he got himself some time.

Ain't gonna need a lot of time to do this, though, he thinks. Cheap old door—you could spring the lock with a snowball. Boom-Boom lets himself in and closes the door behind him. He's relieved that there's still food and clothes and shit there, so he ain't too late.

Kearney's a dead fucker.

Boom-Boom works fast. He has nimble hands for a fat man. He shapes the plastique into a thin line and molds it across the top of the door frame. He gently closes the door and tests its play. Then he runs a thin wire across the inside of the door, strips the end, runs it through the blasting cap and sticks it into the plastique.

When Kearney opens the door, what he'll be doing is like pushing a plunger.

Ka-fucking-boom.

His body's gonna be standing there wondering where its head went.

And Stinkdog'll finally get to lift a brew down in hell.

Be nice and ready to welcome Kearney when he gets there.

Boom-Boom takes the screen off the bathroom window and squeezes out. He can sit and have a beer down the road and watch for Kearney's shitty car to come back.

Follow Kearney back up and watch the fun.

Watch the boom-boom.

48.

Macy drives down to the biker bar and sees the man sitting in a booth in the corner. This has to be the man because he doesn't look like a biker. He looks like a man who's waiting to meet somebody.

That someone is me, Macy thinks. I'm ready to make some money. He looks at the man and the man points with his eyes to the seat across the booth. Macy sits down.

"Are you the guy who's looking for someone?"

"You got something for me?" Johnson asks.

"That depends."

Johnson isn't in the mood for games. His shoulder hurts and he's tired. He's been combing the countryside for twelve long days and nights now, asking in every shitty bar and tavern, putting it out on the circuit that he's looking for someone. Then he gets the word that some old man is trying to sell somebody except he don't know who and what for.

Anyway, it seems to be a match—a seller looking for a buyer.

Only I ain't in the mood for bargaining, Johnson thinks.

"Depends on what?" he growls.

"On the price," the man says. Then adds, "My name is Macy."

Sticks his hand out. Johnson just looks at it.

"How much do you want?" Johnson asks.

"Five thousand," Macy whispers. His eyes light up with greed.

Johnson laughs.

"I don't have five thousand on me," he says.

The old bastard's face looks disappointed.

"But I have it in my truck," Johnson says.

That gets Macy smiling again.

"Half now," Johnson says. "Half when I get my man."

"Getting your man is *your* problem," Macy says. "I'm not going to lose out just because you can't do your part. Half now, half when you identify him as the man you want."

Macy describes him. When he's done Johnson asks, "Man I'm looking for is alone. Your man alone?"

Johnson sees a cloud come across Macy's face.

Macy says sadly, "This man has a kid with him."

Johnson smiles and asks, "Little girl?"

"Boy," Macy says.

Johnson smiles and says, "Mister, thank your stars you got an honest streak in you. That's the man I'm hunting."

Macy grins like a butcher's dog.

"That man's at my motel," Macy says.

Johnson says, "Come on out to my truck and I'll give you your money."

They go out to the gravel lot and Macy hops in the passenger seat.

"Lock your door," Johnson says, and Macy pushes the button down.

Johnson reaches across into the glove compartment

and takes out a white envelope. He hands it to Macy, who tears it open. Macy counts the money and asks, "What's this?"

"It's five hundred bucks. It's what you're getting."

"Now listen, mister . . ."

Johnson takes his good right hand, grabs Macy by the throat and shoves the man's head back into the window. Once, twice, three times—real hard—until a stain of blood shows up on the glass.

"No, *you* listen, mister," Johnson says. "Five hundred's what you're getting and you'll be happy with it. You're also going to keep your mouth shut or I swear I'll come back and beat you into a pulp. You understand? Now where is he?"

"The Knotty Pine, just up the road. Cabin 8," Macy croaks. Johnson's hand is still tight around his throat.

"He there now?" Johnson asks.

Macy shakes his head.

"You telling me the truth?"

Macy nods.

"Where'd he go?" Johnson asks, alarmed because maybe Bobby's luck is holding and he's already taken off. Johnson almost can't stand the thought.

"Don't know," Macy croaks.

"Shit," Johnson says, releasing him.

Regrets it the second he does because the old bastard starts to reach behind him and Johnson realizes he must have a pistol stuck in his waistband.

Johnson doesn't have time to pull his own gun so he throws his weight across the seat and slams Macy into the door, pinning the old man's hand behind his back. Johnson keeps pushing so the old man can't bring that gun around and the old man keeps trying to get his arm out so he can shoot Johnson.

The windows start to fog up as the two men struggle and suck air and Johnson watches Macy's eyes get real wide as the old man realizes he's fighting for his life. Johnson digs his feet into the floor and pushes harder.

Goddamn shoulder hurting like hell where he's pushing, but he needs his good hand to get the pistol from its hip holster and he does and Macy's eyes get real wide like a horse that's seeing a saddle for the first time and just figured out it's going on *him*.

Macy's eyes are that wide when Johnson takes the .44 barrel and shoves it through the old man's teeth. Macy makes choking noises and shakes his head wildly back and forth and Johnson has a tough time holding the barrel in there as he pulls the trigger once and then again.

Johnson holsters the gun, starts up the truck and drives out of there. There's blood, hair and brains all over the passenger window, but he figures he can clean that up when he gets to the motel.

He wants to be sitting in that room when Bobby gets home.

He pulls his truck into the Knotty Pine Motel, looks around, then carries Macy's body into the motel office. Sits him down in the back room and puts the pistol in his hand. Looks for and finds the keys to Cabin 8. Drives the truck down the road a piece and leaves it at a scenic turnout. Hikes back up to the cabin and puts the key in the lock.

49.

Tim parks Kit by the gorillas. There's a bench there on the little knoll and it's an easy place to find.

"Don't move from here," he tells the boy. "I'll only be a couple of minutes."

"Why—"

"Do not move from this spot," Tim says.

"Okay, okay."

Kit's pissed off but Tim doesn't care. If everything's cool at the meet he'll be right back; if things are uncool there's no reason to walk the kid into it.

The kid sits on the bench and won't look at Tim.

"I'll be right back," Tim says.

Kit just stares toward the gorillas.

Tim stops in a men's room on his way down to the elephants. He goes into a stall and fits the homemade silencer over the pistol barrel, jams it into the front of his pants under his denim jacket. Then he takes the cookie sheet from the bag and sticks it into the back of his pants and pulls the jacket down over it.

On the way out he steps in front of the mirror to see if he looks like he's walking anywhere close to normal. Decides he is—maybe a little stiff—but also decides it's gonna play hell on any hopes of a future sex life if that pistol goes off accidentally.

The elephant exhibit turns out to be a good choice. It's on the end of a broad, straight walkway that allows Tim a good view on his approach. The Monk's still standing there, the white bag dangling from his wrist.

Tim tries to look around to see if there's anyone else at the meeting who shouldn't be, but he doesn't see anyone too obvious just hanging out. Mostly it looks like foreign tourists and school groups and old people. He doesn't know what he's looking for, really, but there's no guys with shades, radios and machine guns standing around so he decides to go ahead in.

Anyway, Monk spots him, takes off his shades and gives him as hard a look as you can give to a man you're pretending not to see.

Monk checks him out and then turns to the elephants and leans against the railing. Tim steps up beside him.

"Good to see you, man," Monk says. "It's been—how long?"

"Long time," Tim says.

"You look—"

"Changed, Monk," Tim says. "So do you."

"Time . . ."

"Yeah," Tim says. "Monk?"

"Yeah?"

"Don't look down, but I'm holding a silenced 9mm pointed at your gut."

"You don't trust me, Bobby?"

"I don't trust anybody, Monk," Tim says. "Let's swap the bags now."

Tim can't see through Monk's shades but there's that slight motion of the head that Tim's seen a few hundred times on the yard. That look over the shoulder of a con who's about to get it from behind.

He sees it a fraction of a second before the blade of a heavy knife hits the cookie sheet over the small of his back. The point slides off where it was aimed but slices the side of Tim's stomach. Tim looks down and sees the bloody blade straight under his right arm. He traps the attacker's elbow under his own right arm, then grabs the guy's wrist with his left hand. He presses down with his left and up with his right until he hears the guy's elbow snap and then he lets go.

And Monk is like *gone*.

Tim's walking away before the would-be killer hits the ground.

He hears some old lady yelling, "Somebody's fainted!" and he guesses that the elephants are shook up, too, because they're making those noises from the old Tarzan movies, and then Tim realizes he still has the knife in his hand and he tosses it on top of a pizza box in a wire trash basket.

Another classic Tim Kearney fuck-up in progress, he thinks as he notices the warm sticky feeling of blood coming from his right side and realizes that he would be like fucking *dead* if he hadn't taken the precaution of that old trick from the prison kitchen. Remembers that goof from Fresno and the surprised look on his stupid face when he went to stab Johnny Mack and the cheap shiv just bounced off the cookie tray and Mack turned around and like put his lights *out* and stomped him until the guards got there, and Johnny Mack was one big fucking black man, too.

And why the hell am I thinking about that, Tim wonders,

'cause this is no time to daydream, because they're coming after me.

Tim's trying to think—shit, trying to stay conscious—and walk and look behind him and even in the crowd he can make them out now. Three guys dressed like dorky tourists, one with an I ♥ San Diego T-shirt, another one with a Sea World T-shirt and a third with a Padres cap, and Tim doesn't know how he missed them except that he's a world-class fuck-up.

Now Tim knows he's truly out of his league, because there's just too much going on for him to handle. Maybe Bobby the great Z can deal with this shit, Tim thinks, but I can't. Like, there's getting away with my ass, and finding Kit, and now we're going to be out of money and out of chances and I'm going to get whacked at the fucking *zoo*, for chrissakes. And is that a pisser, or what? I mean, you live through three stretches in the joint, the Gulf War, the whole fucking scene in the desert, and you're going to buy it at the zoo.

But then he thinks *Would these guys really take you out in broad daylight in a public place?* And then he thinks *Well, I guess so, because they just tried it, didn't they?*

Life blows big-time.

What Tim would like is to sit down and keep moving at the same time, which even he knows is a contradiction, but then he remembers the cable cars.

Doesn't think it through, though, and only figures out when he gets *on* one that he's now fucking well trapped, because only two of the guys get on the car behind him and the third one goes racing up to meet them at the top.

Anyway, there's nothing to do about it so first Tim pulls out his shirt to check his side and there's a nice five-inch cut bleeding like a son of a bitch and starting to burn. But it isn't too deep, he sees, and figures he won't bleed to death if he can get it bandaged pretty soon, so he tucks his shirt back in and starts looking around for Kit.

Who isn't at his bench by the gorillas.

Tim feels this fucking terror shoot up around his heart because the kid isn't where he's supposed to be.

Tim's looking wildly around and can't spot Kit's blond head anywhere, and now he feels like he can't breathe, and while he's cranking his head around he sees the two guys in the gondola behind him just grinning. Tim looks up the hill and sees Mr. Sea World leaning against a tree screwing a sniper rifle together, and Tim knows the guy doesn't have to be Lee Harvey Oswald to put two nice shots into Tim as he steps off the gondola onto that nice flat platform.

You dumb moke, Tim tells himself. You monumental fuck-up. You blow the money, you lose the kid, and you get yourself killed. Just another day's work for Tim Kearney, three-time loser.

So Tim's riding up to his death like he's on a conveyor belt at a slaughterhouse. Like, he's a hundred feet in the air with nowhere to go except the target range and like what's he gonna do, *jump*?

Which is what he does.

Later his pursuers will tell Monk that Bobby Z flew— fucking *flew*—through the air. Just climbed up onto the edge of the rocking gondola, kept his balance and fucking *flew* across to the car coming down the cable on the other side.

They'll tell Monk that all of a sudden it was the Ringling Brothers Barnum & Bailey Circus up there, because the few people who happened to be watching at the time *screamed* like they do at the circus when they think the trapeze guy has terminally fucked up and there's no net. Which there like *isn't* at the San Diego Zoo, just hard ground and spiky fences and man-eating animals and shit. In fact, one of the hitters will tell Monk he saw the lions look up in anticipation when Z leapt from the gondola, but Monk would put that down to literary license. Anyway, the fact is that anyone who drops out of one of those gondolas at the San Diego Zoo isn't likely to pop up and go like *Ta-da*, and jumping from a car going up to a car coming down is something only an idiot or a lunatic would attempt.

Or a legend.

"I can see now why the guy is a legend," one of the hitters will tell Monk, who will not think this is literary license but will nevertheless be annoyed by the remark.

"He flew," the hitter will add in awed tones. "Like Superman."

Anyway, people are screaming—including Tim—as he jumps out of the car and he's in air for what seems—especially to Tim—like a long time, then he's grabbing the edge of the descending gondola and holding on by the fingertips and the two guys chasing him are too shocked to shoot him which would have been easy except that a couple of dozen people are now paying intense attention.

People screaming, lions roaring, elephants trumpeting, security guys on the run, and Tim finally gets a leg up and over and pulls himself into the gondola.

Landing with like a thump.

But alive.

At least for the time being, because Tim knows that when he reaches the bottom landing there'll be security cops there, which could mean the slammer, which will mean death. And anyway, Mr. Sea World is probably right now madly unscrewing the sniper rifle and trying to get back down the hill to greet Tim at the successful conclusion of his ride.

So there's nothing to do but jump again before he gets to the landing, although Tim waits until it's about a ten-foot drop before he does the Geronimo bit and just hopes that whatever's down there is either like a Bambi or something or has already had its lunch.

It is some sort of weird deer, as it turns out, that looks real startled when a human drops from the sky. It looks at Tim for a split second, then runs like hell away, which Tim also thinks is a fine idea, and he starts to climb the fence.

Tim can hear the pitter-patter of little security feet—a familiar sound from his youth—running around looking for him so when he gets over the fence he gets into some thick bamboo and starts to make his way to a path on the other side, where maybe he can get away.

Going through the bamboo is such a good idea that the sniper thought of it, too, and they're each a little surprised when they come practically face-to-face. Tim hits him with three short, chopping blows to the face and the guy drops. Tim keeps moving, thinking fuck it—if I get out of here, I'm going to find the kid and move to Oregon because you have to fight too many people when you're Bobby Z.

So he decides just to start another life altogether. How to finance it is a different story, and he thinks maybe he'll stop in Palm Springs on the way out.

But first he has to find Kit, because although the smart thing to do would be to just get the fuck out of there and leave the kid, this is no time in his life to start doing the smart thing.

Anyway, he just can't do it for some reason, maybe the old impulse-control thing, so even as he hears the security cops in the bamboo yelling *We found him! He's hurt!* Tim heads not out but up toward the gorillas to see if Kit has maybe gone back there.

He hasn't and Tim goes on your basic whirlwind tour of the animals of the world as he strides past gorillas, orangutans, chimpanzees, the rest of the primates, across the Asian steppes, through the jungles of India, down by hippo beach, into the snake house, and he can't find Kit.

Tim's like *panicking*. He's not even thinking that the hitters might still be cruising around looking for him, he's just got tunnel vision for his kid and he can't find him. He sees a sign for "Petting Zoo" and makes a dash for that, figuring that no kid can resist petting goats and sheep and other smelly shit, but Kit's not there either, and now Tim thinks that somehow Monk knew about the kid and has grabbed him as a hostage.

And Tim's thinking about shooting Monk in the kneecaps as he goes out into the parking lot to drive off and phone Monk and make a deal, and then he can't remember where he left the car.

Parking lot the size of like Rhode Island and he can't remember where he left the car.

Some kind of bird.

Tim can't remember the actual bird. What he can remember after some effort is Kit saying "The ostrich row," he has a real clear memory of Kit's face as the kid repeats it to himself, so Tim looks around until he spots the ostrich on the pole and he heads for the car, only remembering that Kit has the keys when he sees the boy sitting in the passenger seat.

With a white plastic bag on his lap.

"You're hurt," Kit says when Tim slides into the driver's seat.

"I thought I told you to wait at the gorillas."

"Good thing I didn't," Kit says, pointing to the bag.

"How did you get that?"

"I followed you to the elephants."

"You did?!"

"And then I followed the guy with the white plastic bag," Kit says, "and I grabbed it and ran."

"You shouldn't have done that."

Kit shook his head. "No guy is going to chase a kid through a zoo. They'll figure he's a pervert and beat him up."

Tim looked at the kid for a long moment and said, "We're moving to Oregon."

Kit hands him the keys.

50.

Johnson's been sitting in the cabin for hours and he's starting to get worried that maybe Bobby's smelled out the trap and taken off. The thought aggravates Johnson, because he's tried to be real careful. He even decided against going through the front door, because Bobby might well have been cautious enough to leave a hair or something across the door and would check it. So Johnson went through all the hassle of climbing through the back window and now he's sitting there with his cocked rifle across his lap and maybe his man ain't coming after all.

The same thought occurs to Boom-Boom, who's spent the entire afternoon draining beers and eating pork rinds and waiting for that faggot lime-green car to come rumbling up the road. So by nightfall Boom-Boom's drunk and ugly, much drunker than really behooves a man about to commit a murder, even by remote control. He just sits there by the window, staring out, and it's almost too dark to make out the lime-green car when he does see it head up the road.

Johnson sees the headlights as they turn into the parking lot. The lights flash across the window and change shape as the car turns in. Johnson sits up in his chair and damn near stops breathing, he's so afraid Bobby Z can hear him.

Johnson gets up and moves against the wall. He hears the car pull in and the motor stop, so he raises the rifle to his cheek and waits for the son of a bitch to come through the door.

Listens real hard for the sound of footsteps.

Hears car doors open, and one car door close, and hears the boy yell, "I'll unlock the door!"

51.

Tim lets Kit run ahead. It's taking Tim a little time to turn his sore body sideways and ease out of the car, especially with the bandages and tape that Kit plastered all over his side after they stopped in that drugstore in El Cajon. Also, Tim needs to get the bag full of money out of the trunk, but then he realizes that Kit has the key.

And Kit's running for the door.

"Hey, I need the keys!" Tim yells.

But Kit keeps running and yells back, "I have to go to the bathroom!"

Tim figures the bag can wait for a second. He starts to follow Kit when he remembers something. Remembers he left the light on over the sink and the cabin is totally dark.

"Stop!" he yells to Kit, and Tim starts running to catch him, because the boy is just giggling and running to unlock the door before Tim can catch him.

"Last one in is a rotten egg!" Kit sings out.

Then the night turns bright white.

52.

What happens is that Johnson risks a peek out the window and sees Bobby Z chasing up the path after the boy, and he hears Bobby yell "Stop!" and he just knows Bobby ain't coming through that door.

But Johnson figures he can shoot over the boy's head and hit Bobby smack in the chest, so Johnson cradles the gun in one arm and pushes the door open with the other. He's standing in the doorway lifting the rifle to his cheek when there's this moment of stillness like the world is frozen, and then the blast takes his head from his shoulders.

Tim keeps pushing through the light that's turned from white to red as the cabin catches fire. Half blinded by the explosion, he screams, "Kit! Kit!" and a couple of thousand nights go by until he hears the boy cry, "Bobby!"

Tim has an image of the boy maimed: legs blown off, or arms missing or face burned to jelly and it's at least another thousand hours before he has Kit in his arms and the boy is crying and his hair is a little singed but he seems all right.

And for some reason Tim keeps repeating, "I'm sorry, I'm sorry, I'm sorry," and Kit just keeps sobbing but between gulps says, "It's okay."

"Are you okay?" Tim asks.

"I think so."

"Thank God," Tim says. "Thank God."

He holds the boy tighter and is sitting in the wet grass cradling the boy to his chest when he hears the motorcycle pull into the parking lot. Recognizes Boom-Boom straightaway and realizes he has problems he didn't know he had.

Boom-Boom comes waddling up the path, a beer bottle clutched in one fat fist. It's the beer bottle that kills him, because when he recognizes Tim huddling on the ground the smile comes off his face but he forgets he's holding the bottle as he goes for the gun in his belt.

In that second Tim shoots him three times, the silenced pistol sounding mute and hollow against the crackling fire. Boom-Boom finally drops the beer bottle, then sits down heavily on the lawn and tries to figure out why he feels so sick and tired so quickly, and he just watches as Tim Kearney runs by him with what looks like a large package in his arms.

Boom-Boom hears a car trunk open and close, then hears his own bike start up and roar off and figures that he should do something about that. But it seems like so much work to get to his feet, and the fire is so pretty. So he just sits staring at the cowboy boots on the porch and admiring his own handiwork, and that's the way the volunteer firemen find him when they get there a few minutes later.

Kit's holding on to Tim for all he's worth and it's like that first night they escaped from Brian's except this is no dirt bike but an all-American Harley hog and Tim is *pushing* it down that mountain road.

Because Tim Kearney knows that the Angels'll never

quit now, and Huertero won't quit, and Gruzsa won't quit and there isn't going to be any new quiet life in Oregon.

Not for Tim Kearney or Bobby Z.

Or for the kid.

So Tim pushes the hog down the mountain road and then heads west. West and north and west again.

If there's no escape from being Bobby Z, he'll just have to *be* Bobby Z.

Be Bobby Z and beat 'em all.

Become a legend.

And that means going to Laguna.

53.

Under normal circumstances Tad Gruzsa would have considered attending Raymond "Boom-Boom" Boge's wake a pleasure trip. Few things would have improved a soft California evening better than seeing that slimy bag of guts laid out in a cheap casket while his mourning brethren drank, smoked and fucked around him.

Gruzsa would have enjoyed tilting a couple of beers, insulting the assembled scumbags and tripping back out into the night.

But the evening is spoiled for him now by the knowledge that Tim Kearney is once again on the loose and that everyone who gets too near him ends up taking a dirt nap.

Tim's leaving bodies scattered behind him like Little Johnny Stiffseed. A regular one-man crime wave, and Gruzsa's not too thrilled by the prospect of explaining why he turned this career felon loose on the public.

And someone's bound to figure it out, because Timmy-boy is leaving quite a trail. First you have the great Anza-Borrego Desert Massacre—Parts One and Two—then an otherwise inexplicable fiasco at the San Diego Zoo, then you have a quiet mountain cabin motel turned into a funeral home slash crematorium.

The owner commits a very dicey suicide, shoving a pistol through his own teeth and getting two shots off. Then you got a headless cowboy whose good-old-dead-boy truck ID's him as one Bill Johnson, former ranch manager for known livestock merchant, the also late and unlamented Brian Cervier. Top that off with the body of Boom-Boom, found sitting at the fire scene like he's roasting marshmallows, except that he's got three bullets in him in a tight pattern.

Like, Gruzsa thinks with some pride, a Marine might fire.

"Shame about Boom-Boom," Gruzsa remarks to a silver-haired Angel sitting on a stool by the casket, which is resting on two sawhorses. The Angel is old enough to look like he plays for the Grateful Dead, but Gruzsa knows that Duke, as the head of all the Southern California chapters, has serious juice. Which is why Gruzsa's here in the first place.

"Fuck you, Gruzsa," Duke says. "Did I mention I fucked your mother and your sister?"

"My mother's dead and my sister's a dyke," Gruzsa answers. "So it sounds like you."

He reaches into the cold water of the garbage can, pulls out an icy bottle of Red Dog, snaps the lid open on one of the casket handles and says, "Boom-Boom makes a lovely corpse, though, don't you think, sweetheart?"

"What brings you here, Gruzsa?"

"Other than the joy of seeing Boom-Boom laid out?" Gruzsa asks. "I'll tell you, this has been a banner year for wakes. First Stinkdog and now Boom-Boom. I'm telling you, Kearney's taking out the whole family, huh?"

Duke glares at him. "Kearney did this?"

"I thought you knew that," Gruzsa says. "I thought you knew everything, Duke."

Gruzsa lets him sit with this and takes a look around. It's not a wake any Polish boy would recognize. Music blasting, booze and reefer reeking. Over in the corner two mamas are dispensing blow jobs while in the other corner there's a polite line for gang bang, although Gruzsa can't see the bangee.

"Did you set Boom-Boom up?" Duke asks.

"No, I set *Kearney* up," Gruzsa answers. "*For* Boom-Boom. But the dumb prick fucked it up. I have to tell you, Duke—and not to speak bad of the dead—but I think the Boge family stands about ankle deep in the old gene pool, you know?"

He drains the beer and reaches for another.

"Help yourself," Duke says.

"Thanks." Gruzsa wipes his wet sleeve off on the edge of the casket. "I were you doofs, I'd look around Laguna."

"They only got fags in Laguna."

"Yeah, well, to date this fag has greased the entire Boge family, half a fucking tribe of Indians and some cowboy from East County who was supposed to be a pretty tough hombre," Gruzsa says. "So when you're cruising around Laguna, watch your ass."

"You know where he is, why don't you just pick him up?"

"I don't want him picked up," Gruzsa says. "I want him dead."

Duke smiles. He has chipped front teeth and long canines, makes him look like an old wolf.

"We can make him dead."

"That's what Boom-Boom said."

"Boom-Boom went out alone."

"So?"

"We're going with an army."

Gruzsa tosses the empty bottle into the casket and walks out.

The Death and Life of Bobby Z   279

In San Juan Capistrano. He'd spent most of the...

Church Street and Park...

54.

Tim finds the trailer on the beach.

It's like a mobile home, he thinks, not much different from the one he grew up in—or failed to—in Desert Hot Springs. A fucking mobile just like any trailer-park trash would live in, except this one sits on the beach in El Morro Canyon. Sits among about twenty others in an isolated curve where the beach rounds into a huge rock cliff. And on top of the huge rock cliff is an enormous white house with two-story glass windows that look out over the ocean on three sides.

So it's a little different from the mobile home where Tim grew up—or failed to—which had a view of five other mobile homes and a junked-car lot.

Anyway, it's real pretty there. The ocean's pretty, the beach is pretty, the big rock cliff is pretty, and Tim Kearney is finally living on the beach.

Which is a bitch, Tim thinks. I gotta have half the world trying to kill me before I finally get to live on the beach.

It's taken him some time to get up here. After racing off Mount Laguna, he'd dumped the motorcycle in Carlsbad and caught the late Amtrak train, which he rode to San Juan Capistrano, Kit asleep most of the way and real quiet anyway.

Tim got off the train in San Juan Cap, walked a couple of blocks in the barrio and in forty-five minutes flat had the pink slip to a rebuilt '89 Z-28 muscle car, which maybe even had had other owners who at one point in time had reported it missing.

Then Tim drove down to the Pacific Coast Highway through Dana Point, Monarch Bay, Salt Creek, Aliso Niguel, South Laguna and into the town of Laguna Beach.

Gets weird fucking vibes in Laguna, like it's, you know, Bobby's town and Bobby's ghost is hanging out, and Tim's a little spooked by everyone he sees, especially in the all-night 7-Eleven where he buys a couple of hot dogs for himself and a bean-and-cheese burrito for Kit.

They get back in the car and drive north out of town until they spot the sign for El Morro Canyon and Point Reef Beach, and there's a dirt road that jogs back north at a sharp angle and takes them to the back of the mobile homes that line the cove by the rock cliff.

They find number 26, and it's basic but well kept. A kitchen with a sitting room, two small bedrooms and a bath. Nice covered porch on the beach side.

A nice getaway, and Tim can't get it out of his head that this is where Bobby and Elizabeth used to come to screw and it must have meant something to Bobby because he holds on to it.

Tim figures that because he *is* Bobby now, the place belongs to him, and it'd be nice to live in a place like this. This place would do him just fine, man. Simple, basic and on the beach, and there's a school right across the road that he could like *walk* Kit to. Maybe he could even learn to surf and teach Kit, who should be like a natural, right, and it's then that Tim figures out what the place smells like.

Wax.

Surfboard wax, and Tim pictures Bobby just coming here to chill before he split. Place to get away from being the great Z and just sit here and wax your board and go out and ride the waves and come back, sit on the porch and have a cup of coffee, watch the sun go down. Maybe then go back into the bedroom with Elizabeth—and I could get into that life. Make dinner for the kid, sit down and eat, talk about school and surfing and comic books and shit. And Kit would grow up to be one of those *cool* California kids, man. Kid who grows up on the beach in maximum-cool Laguna.

I have to cut this fantasy shit out, he thinks. There isn't going to be any staying here, living here, walking Kit to school, surfing and boffing a beautiful woman with a long back, flat stomach and shiny hair. There's just going to be getting stiffed out unless I can find what I need to get to Huertero, and then there's still Gruzsa, and the Angels and maybe now this fucking Monk.

So what I need to do is be thinking about how to find out what I need to find out and then get the *fuck* out.

And get the kid back to his mom, which is like where the kid should be, I guess.

So how to learn what I need to learn, Tim is thinking as he puts Kit to bed and sits beside him. Same old Tim Kearney, man, behind the learning curve again, and I guess what I have to do is I have to call old Monk and find a way of getting him to tell me what he knows.

And Kit, poor little bastard, has hardly said a word

since almost getting blown up and like, big surprise, right?

"You okay?" he asks the boy.

"Yeah," Kit says—kind of defensive, like he wouldn't admit it if he wasn't.

"What'd you see back there?" Tim asks, hoping the kid saw a bright white light and nothing else, because Tim can still see Johnson's headless body and those cowboy boots and while he saw a lot of that kind of shit in the Gulf, it's nothing a kid needs to have in his head.

"Nothing," Kit says.

"This'll be over soon, man," Tim promises. "I'll get you back to your mom."

"I don't want to go back to her."

"Yeah, well, we'll talk about it, okay?" Tim says. "You better get some sleep. I'll be right here."

He gives the boy a hug and a kiss and feels the kid's lips on his cheek, which feels like real weird but all right. He's about out the door when he hears Kit ask, "Why do people want to kill you?"

Tim's not real sure himself but he has the general answer to hand: "Because I've done some bad things in my life."

"You fucked up?"

"Don't use that kind of language," Tim says. "But, yeah—*big*-time."

Seems to satisfy the kid, seems to be enough.

"*I've* done that," Kit offers.

It's generous of the boy to say that, thinks Tim, who hasn't been real familiar with generosity in his life.

"It'll be okay," Kit adds. Then he rolls over and pulls the blankets over him.

Which is real nice of the boy to say, Tim thinks, but he'll be damned if he knows how it'll be okay.

He knows he has to get out there, meet Monk again and find out what he knows. Get his hands on enough money to get lost and stay lost *and* deliver the kid back. All of which is impossible enough but really impossible with a kid in tow.

And I'm just not going to bring him into the line of fire again, Tim decides. I know that.

So he's going to have to find a baby-sitter, and he's sitting looking out the window watching the moonlight on the waves and thinking about how the hell he's going to find someone he can trust, when there's a soft knock on the door and it's Elizabeth.

55.

Tim puts his forefinger to his lips and says, "The kid's asleep."

She shuts the door softly behind her and takes off her vinyl windbreaker. Tosses it on the old couch under the window.

"How'd you know I was here?"

"I didn't," she says. "I've been driving by checking for lights every night."

She looks great. Got on some silky kind of emerald green blouse tucked into stonewashed jeans. Boat shoes, no socks. Skinny little gold necklace that dips down from her throat to the rise of her breasts.

"How's Kit?" she asks.

"Pretty shook up," he answers.

"You mind if I sit down?"

"I don't mind."

She sits down on the couch and her jeans crease into a sharp V between her legs. She stretches one arm out along the back of the couch and says, "Don Huertero's looking for you."

"No shit."

There's that sparkle of laughter in her eyes that for some reason makes him add, "So's Brian, for that matter."

She shakes her head.

"Brian's dead."

"No shit?"

"No shit," she answers. "Huertero gave Brian what he wanted to give you. He left him naked out in the sun for a few hours, then tied him to the bumper of a four-wheeler and took him for a spin through the cactus. Be glad you weren't there."

"I am."

"Huertero sent Johnson to hunt for you."

"Johnson found me."

He watches her eyebrow curve into an elegant arch of curiosity.

"But a booby trap took his head off before we had much of a chance to talk."

She looks really alarmed.

"Christ," she said. "Kit didn't see that, did he?"

"I don't think so."

"Christ."

He sits beside her on the couch.

"Casa del Brian is all burned down," she says.

A flicker of something . . . suspicion, maybe . . . flicks across his stomach, and he asks, "How did you get out?"

"Well, Brian beat the shit out of me and that seemed to satisfy Don Huertero."

"He just let you go?"

"No," she says, looking him in the eyes. Giving him that cynical, intelligent, kind of angry look. "He didn't just let me go."

"What does that mean?"

"You know what that means."

They're staring at each other and then he's like watching his hand reach out and undo the top button of her blouse and he's wondering like where'd *that* nerve come from? But she doesn't do anything to stop him, so he undoes one button at a time and reveals her breasts in the skinny black bra and feels that wonderful heat come over him.

He lifts one beautiful breast from the bra, and then he's leaning over and softly kissing a nipple, and he feels her long fingers on the back of his head as he feels the nipple get stiff and fat on his tongue. He leaves it and pulls her blouse from her jeans, then slides down to the floor and takes her shoes off, and he's still wondering who the fuck is this person doing this, because it ain't me.

But he gets the shoes off, and she's still leaning back into the couch, and he slides her jeans off her wonderfully long legs, and then the black panties, which are so soft even against the soft skin of her legs. He follows them down with his eyes—off her feet and onto the cheap rug on the floor—and then he looks up to see the precise triangle of auburn hair between her legs. He slides his hands up her legs to gently part them and then dips his head down. Her hands grip his shoulders as he touches her with his tongue and licks up and down as slowly as he can. Even though he's trembling and hard under his own jeans, he licks her slow and soft because she's been hurt and he figures she deserves slow and soft and besides, he can *taste* the reward of his patience on his tongue.

And she's making soft noises because the kid is asleep in the other room, but the soft sound of her voice could make him come as he parts her lips with one hand and flicks at her with his tongue. Taking his time still, because this is a fine place to be, he looks up at her face and can't believe that it's him doing a woman this beautiful and she's liking it, and he watches her face as she has one hand on his shoulder and the other pinching her nipples. He's still watching her face a few minutes later as she twists away from but also *into* his tongue and he puts a finger into her and gently presses inside the top of her and he like can't believe it but he comes at the same time she does.

But she takes his prick—semi-hard and sticky—from his jeans, and he twists out of his clothes and quickly he's hard again and inside her and she pulls her knees up and back so he can be deep. At first he cups her small ass with his hands, but later they have their arms wrapped tightly around each other as they rock back and forth, and this time she cries when she comes but keeps rocking and squeezing as he comes, and he can feel the wetness on her cheeks as he lays his face on hers.

They're lying there soft and quiet for a while, he feeling the warm dampness of her skin and listening to her breathing, and life feels calm to him for a change.

He's feeling all calm and safe when she murmurs, "So tell the truth."

"About what?"

He's feeling sleepy.

"About who are you, really?" she asks.

Which kind of wakes him up.

56.

"I'm Bobby Zacharias," Tim says.

"No, you're not."

It's her fucking confidence that undoes him. He's sitting on the toilet watching her clean herself with a warm washcloth.

"How do you know?" he asks, but it's not as much a challenge as it is a request for information.

"Baby, a woman knows," she says.

Tim doesn't want to pursue that angle, so instead he asks, "How long have you known?"

"Moment one."

"Moment one?"

She smiles at him and nods.

Which moment one? Tim wonders. Like the moment he came out to the pool at Brian's or the moment she took his dick out of his pants? But again he decides that's not something he really wants to know, so he asks, "How come you told me about Huertero? Why didn't you just keep your mouth shut and let them kill me?"

She towels herself off and starts to slide her jeans back on.

"It didn't seem fair," she says, "to let you get killed for something Bobby did."

"What did Bobby do?"

She slips into her blouse and buttons it up as she says, "You first."

"Me first what?"

"Like who the hell are you?" she asks. "And what are you doing running around pretending to be Bobby? And where's Bobby?"

She's looking serious for a change, Tim thinks. The mocking smile is gone and there are little wrinkles around her eyes. She looks older than he's seen her. Older and prettier.

"Did you love him?" he asks.

"Once."

"Still?"

She shrugs.

Tim takes a deep breath, then says, "My name is Tim Kearney and I'm a three-time loser. The DEA made a deal with me: Pretend to be Bobby so they could trade me for an agent that Huertero's holding."

She just stares at him, waiting for the other shoe to fall, because she asked him three questions and he answered two. And he doesn't want to answer the third. He'd rather lie and tell her he doesn't know, but the woman did him decent back at the old ranch and she was a stand-up guy when Brian took a belt to her, so Tim figures he owes her the tough answer.

"And Bobby is dead," Tim says.

He gets up, ready to catch her if she like *faints* like they do in the movies, but she keeps her feet and gets right to the bottom line.

"How'd he die?"

He can tell from the tone of her voice that she thinks Bobby got whacked, and he's about to say "natural causes," when he remembers that in the drug business getting whacked *is* a natural cause.

So he says, "Heart attack."

"You're kidding."

"In the shower," Tim says. "The DEA had him and they were going to swap him and he died of a heart attack in the shower."

"Just like that."

"Just like that," he says. Then asks, "You okay?"

She says, "Yeah, I'm okay. I just never pictured the world without Bobby. I mean, I haven't seen him for years, but he was always there, you know?"

"Sure."

She's talking now. Tim's seen it before in the joint: Guy doesn't say a word for months and then he just goes on a jag, starts just speaking what's in his head without thinking about it.

"Even when I was in trouble, you know," she's saying. "You know, out of money, or some guy's hassling me, or the CHP finds a roach in the car, all I had to do was like call the Monk and it was taken care of. I was taken care of, and that's Bobby, reaching out from wherever the hell he is."

"Yeah."

"And I was there for him, too," Elizabeth says. "I mean, I didn't, you know, *see* him, but sometimes he'd need someone he trusted and he'd get word to me and I'd do the errand, whatever it was."

"Two-sided deal."

"And now he's gone."

"Right."

"*Really* gone."

"Uh-huh." Tim's just making sounds, letting her work it out.

"It's like the world can't ever be the same again."

And that's no shit, Tim thinks, for her and me both.

"So why don't you just tell them?" she asks.

"Tell who what?"

"Tell Huertero you're not Bobby," she says. "That Bobby's dead."

He shakes his head. "Won't work, there's been too much blood, and besides, it still leaves me with the DEA on my ass."

Not to mention, which he doesn't, the Hell's Angels.

"No, I gotta work it out," Tim says. "Make it right with Huertero and then get my ass out of the country somewhere."

"How are you going to do that?"

"Dunno," he says. "Anyway, you better take the kid back to his mother."

She snorts. "Olivia doesn't even know he's gone. Olivia couldn't care less."

"Anyway . . ."

"He wants to be with you."

"So?"

"He thinks you're his daddy."

"He knows?" Tim asks. "About Bobby?"

"He's a kid," she says. "Not a moron. Of course he knows. Poor little bastard grows up knowing his dad is some sort of legend, then the legend shows up and takes his side for once? Scoops him up and blasts him out of that lunatic asylum like some comic book hero he sees on TV? Who do you think he wants to be with?"

"Christ, who turned you on?"

"Well, you just can't play with a child that way," she says. "Shuffle him back and forth."

"Like you been doing?"

"That's right . . . So what are you going to do?" Elizabeth asks a few seconds later, after they've been staring at each other.

"I'm gonna go see the Monk," he says. "If I'm gonna get out of the country and support a kid and keep the kid safe, I'm gonna need money. Lots of money. Money to pay off Huertero, money to run with, money to hide with, money to live on. And Monk's got the money, right?"

"Bobby's money."

"Fuck that," Tim says. "*My* money. I get Bobby's enemies, his problems, his blues, his child—I get his money."

"How about his woman?" she asks.

He looks her dead in those green eyes.

"That's up to his woman," he says.

Then walks out of the room while he's still feeling tough and strong. Figures that was about the best exit line he's going to get off.

Elizabeth takes the warm cloth to her face. Feels the soothing water and looks in the mirror. Runs her long fingernail down her face from forehead to chin and stares at the faint red mark it leaves.

You've done some dumb things in your so-called life, she thinks, but letting this sweet boy out of Brian's was the dumbest. Letting him get away again would be, well . . .

"Dumb, dumb, dumb, Elizabeth," she says into the mirror. What's the matter with you these days, you can't ball a guy without getting stupid and falling a little in love?

"Shit," she says. "Love?"

As the lady says, *What's love got to do with it?*

From the bedroom she can hear the sound of the child's breathing.

57.

Monk jumps a little when the hotline rings. It's not so much a ring as it is a purring vibration, but it still jars. He sets his latte down and picks up the receiver.

"You're dead."

"Bobby?" Monk asks. "Thank God it's you! Are you all right?"

Tim can't believe how smooth the guy is. He's standing at a phone booth on the public beach in Laguna listening to this shit, and he just can't believe what he's hearing.

Anyway he says, "Monk, one of your guys tries to stick a knife in my back and you're asking about my health?"

Monk just ignores the accusation.

"Bobby, who were those guys? Huertero's people?"

"I notice you didn't stick around to find out."

"I was hoping to draw one or two of them off," Monk says. "You know, split them up."

"Yeah, and how many followed *you*?"

"We have to be more careful," Monk says. "One of them got the money, Bobby, and the passport. I'm sorry, but what could I do, he had a gun. It's only money, right? Where are you, Bobby?"

"So you can send someone?"

"You bet," Monk says. "Get you in a safehouse until we can figure all this out."

"I figured it fucking out," Tim says. "You ripped off Huertero, kept it to yourself. And the money."

Monk's voice sounded hurt. "Would I do something like that?"

"I don't know."

"Bobby . . ."

Monk's looking out the window while he talks. The marine layer is still in, but he looks down through the mist at the beach below the cliff and sees a woman playing Frisbee with a kid. The child should be in school, Monk thinks.

"I want you to look me in the eye and tell me, Monk," Tim says. "Look me in the fucking eye and tell me you wouldn't do something like that."

"I would welcome that opportunity."

"Cool," Tim says. "Salt Creek cave tonight. Eleven o'clock. Be motherfucking alone this time."

"Salt Creek cave?" Monk laughs. "What is this, Bobby, *Treasure Island*? What are we, kids again?"

"You know what I think, Monk?"

"What do you think, Bobby?"

And there's like an edge to it, Tim thinks. Like the guy's willing to fuck with Bobby a little bit. Like the guy figures he has the juice, he *can* fuck with him.

"I think you're like a bank," Tim says. "Like you've been taking care of my money so long you get to thinking it's *your* money."

"It's all here for you, Bobby," Monk says. "Metaphorically speaking. I mean, most of it is liquid, so you can have it when you want it. Other monies are in long-term investments—mutual funds, real estate holdings—"

"I'm interested right now in the liquid," Tim says, "which like better *flow* in my direction. Some of it maybe oughta drift back to Huertero."

"Well, render unto Caesar . . ."

"Yeah, whatever," Tim says, not giving a shit about whatever the hell some guinea has to do with it anyway. "You be there tonight, you bring me some cash, you come alone. Or you're a dead fucker. *Capisce?*"

"I understand."

Monk hangs up the phone and walks out onto the deck. The sun is starting to burn through the fog and it's going to be a typically sunny Southern California day.

Just another day in paradise, Monk thinks.

58.

Tim's sitting on the deck of the trailer watching Kit and Elizabeth goof around on the beach.

He's sitting there in these cool shades he picked up in downtown Laguna and he's got his face toward the sun, which is like *baking* him, and he's digging on the blue water and surf that's so regular it looks like someone's drawing a line of white chalk across the blue rectangle of ocean. This is *cool* California.

Tim thinks that life, if he can hold on to it, is a pretty good thing.

Kit's running around grinning. Kid can't throw a Frisbee to save his life, but he sort of flings it at Elizabeth, who isn't much better or is pretending not to be much better. She throws it back and the kid goes running, chasing the rolling Frisbee, and he's laughing like an idiot and screaming in delight when he has to chase the Frisbee into the cold ankle-deep water.

And even a three-time loser, officially antisocial career criminal like Tim Kearney knows this kid is sky-high because he's got himself a real mommy-daddy-kid combination plate for at least a little bit and is making the most of it.

Tim takes off his shirt and lathers his body with Bain de Soleil. He's just grooving on sitting in the sun, listening to the surf, smelling the salt air and feeling the cool breeze wash across his chest, and he feels like fucking relaxed for maybe the first time in his life.

Knows, too, that it's dangerous to feel relaxed but doesn't care at the moment. Like tonight he has to go back to being a skell and doing skell things, but right now he's got himself a place on the beach and a beautiful woman and a terrific kid, and sitting in the joint looking at his life sentence he didn't even *dream* that life was ever going to look like this.

Then Kit notices he's relaxing and figures that's against the rules and calls to him to come play. So Tim puts up the expected token resistance and then trots down onto the sand and starts tossing the Frisbee with them. Elizabeth's looking at him with sweet sexy eyes, and the kid is just sky-high as they do this family beach thing.

Tim thinks like, Thank you, Bobby Z, wherever the hell you are.

Problem is, of course, that you can be getting royally fucked without even knowing it and that's what's happening to Tim as he tosses the Frisbee on the beach.

Sometimes you get remote-control screwed just for nothing at all, just because that's the way the world spins, and sometimes it's because you fucked up in the smallest way. It's the latter that's happening now, a long way anyway from Tim's little seaside domestic scene.

What Tim did to fuck up was that he shouldn't have bought a car in the barrio.

Because what's happening right now is the kid who sold it to him gets the word that some serious people in

East L.A. are looking for a guy who looks like the guy who bought the car. Paid cash and was in a big fucking hurry. No test drive, no haggling, no questions: just money, the keys and the pink slip, *ese*.

So the kid in the barrio in San Juan Cap thinks that maybe he can do himself some good and makes a call to a guy, and that guy makes a call and *that* guy makes a call and pretty soon the kid's on the horn with Luis Escobar, who the kid knows is serious people in East L.A.

So Tim's indiscretion gives Luis Escobar a description of the vehicle and a fucking license-plate number and a he-went-that-a-way, and while Tim's having himself a good time on the beach, Luis Escobar is dispatching the troops in search of that vehicle.

Luis does something else.

Luis Escobar is a careful man. Luis believes in *planning*. Planning and the right tool for the right job, and he decodes that the right tool for this job is a *cholo* from Boyle Heights who isn't some gang-banging child but a "precision matters" pro, name of Reynaldo Cruz.

The point about Reynaldo Cruz is that Cruz can *shoot*.

Cruz was the star of the sniper school at Pendleton. His Marine instructor said that Cruz could shoot the balls off a flea. Cruz goes to the Gulf with his unit and makes his bones picking off Iraqi officers from long range. Like one second the Rack is walking around doing the *Allahu Aqbar* thing and the next second he's like *with* Allah. Compliments of R. Cruz, Boy Sniper.

"DFN Cruz," man, was what the rest of the platoon called him. "Death from Nowhere." That night of Khafji, man, all hell breaking loose in the black sky and Cruz just lies there in the prone position like he's on his couch in the barrio, dealing death from nowhere. Plinking Racks like in a video arcade, except Cruz never runs out of quarters. *Plink, plink, plink*—one bullet one corpse—and like DFN Cruz is the all-time Mortal Gulf Kombat cham*peen*.

And cool. Maximum cool. DFN Cruz doesn't even sweat. In the fucking desert. Just puts that scope up to one stone-cold black eye and *plink*. Death from Nowhere. DFN Cruz is as crazy in his way as Corporal Tim Kearney, who is also a crazy fucker. Night of Khafji, DFN is lying in the sand plinking Racks and Kearney's running around in the open like bullets can't touch him. Running around blasting away, throwing grenades, dragging the wounded out from under the Rack tanks. Like Kearney's out there yelling, "Medic!" at the same time he's blasting Racks with his free hand, and it was some videogame out there that night, you got crazy Tim and DFN Cruz on the same screen.

Two Navy Crosses for the unit that night, man—Kearney and DFN Cruz. Some crazy motherfuckers, Semper Fi.

And those two like *ripped up* Kuwait City. Cruz is in fucking sniper heaven, man, playing pop-up in those blasted buildings. Fucking Rack shows his head and his head is like bye-bye, and then DFN and Kearney start working as a team. Kearney is so loopy he plays like *bait*, getting the Racks into a running firefight until one of them pops up to make the kill, and it's welcome to paradise, Ahmed.

And Kearney thinks it's like funny, man. He comes back to the firing line all laughing and juiced, and everyone figures Kearney's heading for another Cross, and then he smacks that Saudi officer and that's that.

The Saudi colonel is beating the hell out of this Palestinian kid he finds hiding in the rubble, and Kearney just gets up from where he's eating his meal and puts the Saudi *down*. Like one punch—*whack*—and the Saudi colonel drops, but Kearney's not finished, because he like stomps on the colonel's balls, and the Saudis, they want to decapitate Kearney right there and then.

It's like some old movie—the Saudi MPs actually pull out those monster curved swords and they're looking to sever Kearney's head from his body. Would have, too, except that DFN Cruz is sitting back against a wall with his weapon across his lap and smiling and shaking his head, and the Saudis get the message that DFN Cruz doesn't care *who* he kills.

So Kearney gets to keep his head, but he sure as hell doesn't get another Cross, and the brass don't want like an international incident or a public relations disaster by court-martialing an honest-to-God hero, so they settle for a DD and Kearney becomes a civilian.

So does DFN Cruz. Becomes just Cruz again and goes back to the old neighborhood. Where Cruz has like nothing to do because there are no frigging jobs and he can't get into the police academy. And Cruz, he's thinking about becoming a mercenary and he's showing a classified ad from *Soldier of Fortune* to Luis Escobar one night, and Escobar, he says, basically, *What do you want to go and work for strangers for?* so Cruz goes to work for Luis Escobar.

As a precision tool.

Escobar's been thinking this thing through. What Escobar thinks is that killing Bobby Z is a long shot. Literally—because no one is going to get close enough to Z to do the bang-bang thing in the back of the head, because this Z is just too good. So it's going to have to be a long shot, a bullet that comes from nowhere.

So when Escobar gets his lead on Bobby Z, he goes to talk to Cruz, who's hanging out waiting for his next assignment.

Stand by, Escobar tells him. We're going to do this job right. Find this piece of garbage, throw a net around him and then you can come in and do your thing. Death from Nowhere.

This makes Cruz happy, because he's very good at his job and takes a professional's pride and gets bored and unhappy when there is no work. Also he has enormous respect for Luis Escobar, who is not only his *patrón* but is also a man.

Also, Cruz can use the money. He's saving up for one of those giant big-screen TVs like they have at the sports bar, and he wants to hook up a monster Super Nintendo system to it so it's better than real life.

Cruz misses the war.

Tim doesn't. Tim would be perfectly happy to live the rest of his life quietly on that beach with Kit and Elizabeth, even though he knows that isn't going to happen.

What he doesn't know is that he screwed up this one detail. What's flirting around the edge of his consciousness is something else that just doesn't square, and that isn't about the car, it's way back on that first night on the border when Jorge Escobar bought the farm. Tim can't dump this image of Escobar's brains bursting through the front of his skull. The *front*, man, like he was shot from behind. From the U.S. side.

But this is just too fucking confusing for Tim to deal with at the moment, what with the sunshine, the woman, the kid and everything. He just dismisses it all, so even as he and the woman and the kid go inside to make some sandwiches, he doesn't get that the world is fucking him in fresh and imaginative ways.

59.

What's bothering the Monk is One Way's John the Baptist routine. Monk strides through the streets of Laguna searching out this wack job who predicted the return of Bobby Z.

Monk just can't get it out of his head, because it smacks of powers cosmic and supernatural, which of course is the very stuff that the Monk decisively dismissed that warm morning in Tucson.

So Monk is desperate to hear a rational, scientific explanation exhale from the otherwise foul breath of Laguna's resident bard and public nuisance. But just at the unprecedented moment that someone in the community actually *wants* to see One Way, the perverse madman has seemingly disappeared.

Just dropped off the screen.

The cops and the merchants are delighted, of course, One Way's sudden disappearance being an event devoutly and daily wished for by the entire law enforcement and business communities. Even the other street people are relieved by One Way's absence, because the loony fucker like *just cannot shut up*, so they welcome the unusual quiet.

They all have different explanations for the disappearance.

The cops—and one of them even got on the horn and radioed comrades in Dana Point and Newport Beach—are betting that One Way's decomposed body will wash up on the beach or become entangled in the nets of the commercial fishermen off Dana Point. The merchants are speculating that One Way has migrated south to the larger vagrants' community in San Diego's Balboa Park. The street people, generally a more imaginative lot, are at the point of deciding that One Way has been abducted by aliens, the only point of debate being whether or not One Way put up any struggle.

But none of the above are obsessed with the mystery. The street people have the daily challenges of food and shelter to obtain, the merchants are busy doing mercantile things with the throngs of tourists descending on the town, and the cops, well, the cops are having a busy day keeping an eye on the unusual influx of bikers into the community. The cops are always wary of any confrontation between motorcycle gangs and the town's large gay community, which would present them with the double dilemma of (a) how to tell them apart and (b) who to root for.

The cops are also freaking a little bit on an unusual increase in cars with Mexicans in them cruising around. The Laguna cops call their brethren in Newport Beach—jaded types who ask what the fuck they're being bothered for—and their more jejune colleagues in tiny Dana Point, who have nervously noted the same phenomenon.

So the street people are busy, the merchants are busy, the cops are very busy, and the only person obsessing on

One Way's apparent disappearance is the Monk, who has his own explanation.

Which is basically like *paranoid*.

What the Monk is thinking as he's pacing around the community not finding One Way is that Bobby's behind the whole thing. Bobby contacted One Way and told the freak to spread the word of his return just to spook the Monk, and now One Way is in hiding somewhere at the behest of Z in a conspiracy so diabolical that Monk does not stand a prayer of unraveling it before he's undone.

So the Monk is in a sweat to find One Way and rattle the truth out of him before it's too late. But Monk can't find him and Monk starts freaking. It's like Bobby's everywhere and sees everything. Monk starts thinking about how that knife just bounced off Bobby at the zoo and how Bobby flew through the air and then disappeared.

And Monk starts losing it, like he can never go against Bobby Z, and as Monk's walking around he starts losing it worse and worse and finally he goes into a phone booth and drops a dime.

Starts babbling into the phone some semi-coherent shit about how One Way has gone into hiding with Bobby Z.

The truth is that One Way *is* hiding.

One Way is squatting in a cave on the beach with his hands over his ears, because the surf won't stop talking to him. The surf won't stop talking and the sunlight reflecting off the uneven surface of the cave wall sparkles in shifting diamond shapes before his eyes.

What the surf is telling him is truly horrific. The surf is screeching that Bobby Z is in danger. Mortal danger and One Way must warn him.

And One Way is squatting in this cave, hiding from Z's enemies lest he be captured before he can deliver his jeremiad, and he's crying. Crying in frustration and the fear of an unfathomable failure.

One Way is weeping because he must find Bobby Z to rescue him, but he doesn't know where he is.

60.

Kit's pissed because Tim is leaving.

"It's just for a while," Tim says to the boy, who's fighting hard not to cry. "Elizabeth'll be with you."

"You're leaving," Kit insists.

"I'm coming right back," Tim says. "I just have to talk to a guy."

Kit shakes his head and closes his eyes.

"C'mon," Tim says. "You and Elizabeth'll have fun."

Tears spill over this time as Kit asks, "Why can't I come with you?"

Because it's too dangerous, Tim thinks, but he doesn't want to scare the boy. It's dark out now. They've had supper, and done the usual thing of settling in for some TV, some wrestling on the floor and a comic book or two. Then they'd put Kit to bed and Tim had hoped to sneak out and back before the kid woke up, but with that eerie kid ESP the boy had woken up, is some fucking upset. Tim doesn't want to scare him on top of it.

So Tim says, "It's grownup stuff."

"I can help you!"

"You probably could."

"I helped you at the zoo!" Kit cries. "Who got the money?"

"You did," Tim says. "You're my man."

"So why can't I come *with* you?!" Kit cries, and he throws his arms around Tim's neck and holds on hard.

Tim rubs the boy's back for a few seconds and whispers in his ear *I'll be back soon* and pries Kit's arms from his neck and hands him to Elizabeth. Kit buries his face into her neck and sobs.

"I'll be back in a little while," Tim says quietly.

Elizabeth nods and holds the boy tightly. Tim looks at her green eyes and sees something sad.

She's hurting for Kit, he thinks. So am I, but I need to go do this thing.

In the kitchen he checks the load on his pistol and sticks the gun in the back of his waistband. Then he gets in the car and follows Elizabeth's directions to this cave they all hung out in when they were kids. He parks on a quiet side street off the PCH and follows some old concrete steps that curve down to the beach. Seems to be about a million of them, but he's edgy and wired so it probably just seems like a lot. The steps end suddenly at a big broken hunk of concrete, and he has to make a little jump onto the sand.

The beach is a narrow strand at the base of a steep sandstone bluff. There's just enough moonlight for him to see where he's going, and the moonlight is flickering off the water and the big rocks that set just outside the break line.

The beach seems deserted. Of course, it's almost eleven and the beach is officially closed, but Tim had expected at least a few horny couples or drunks. But the beach is quiet.

Tim doesn't like it. Feels too exposed out here, when he realizes he'd be an easy shot for someone sitting on the bluff with a nightscope, so he finds a worn footpath on the edge of the slope to take away that firing angle if the Monk is setting him up for a pop.

Bad fucking idea, he thinks now, to meet in this cave. Can't blame Elizabeth because she hasn't led the life, you know, but still, the approaches to the meet are too dangerous, too exposed, and it's a bad fucking idea.

But too late now.

He edges his way along the path until it ends back at a tiny sliver of beach on a point. The cave's in front of him.

It's bigger than he thought—about ten men wide and at least ten feet high at its highest and shaped like a big bowl. He can see the faint glimmer of a flashlight in there and a person's shadow. Tim pulls his gun, holds it low on his side and goes in. His shoes crunch on the small rocks that make up the cave floor.

"Bobby?"

It's Monk's voice.

Tim doesn't answer. Doesn't want his *yes* to be answered with a bullet in the chest.

"Bobby?" Monk asks again. "Is that you?"

Tim waits for his eyes to adjust to the cave's dim lights. He waits until he can clearly make out Monk, and from what he can see Monk is alone. Standing alone in the cave with a flashlight in his hand and a gym bag at his feet.

"Hi, Monk."

"You are a sight for sore eyes, Bobby," Monk says and he comes forward with his arms open for one of those guy hugs.

Tim raises the gun.

"Uh-uh," he says, shaking his head.

"Oh, Bobby," Monk says, hurt and disappointed like. "You're being paranoid, old friend."

"What's the beef with Don Huertero?" Tim asks.

"I don't know anything about it," Monk says. "I asked, I did research, I talked to all our distributors. *Nada.*"

"Say good night, Monk," Tim says. He points the barrel between Monk's eyes.

The man's knees start to knock. Really actually fucking knock, and Tim thinks it's a good thing Monk never had to go to the joint, because he'd've been like a universal bitch, man. Everybody's girlfriend, and Tim realizes that if Monk knows the truth he's going to spill it.

"You fucked me, Monk," he says. "You fucked me with Huertero."

"Didn't happen, Bobby."

But his voice is getting thin and reedy.

"Did you jam me with the Thais, too?" Tim asks. "Get me popped in Bangkok?"

"Bobby . . ."

"You ever see the inside of a Thai jail, old friend?" Tim presses. "Not a day at the beach."

"Bobby, I—"

"You better get right with God," Tim says, starting to squeeze the trigger, "because you're going, Monk."

Monk like *freaks*. Drops to his knees and starts praying, "Oh, my God, I am heartily sorry for having offended thee. And I do repent all my sins, not for the fear of the fires of hell, but because they have—"

This is not the confession Tim has in mind, so he sticks the gun into Monk's forehead and says, "Talk to me, Monk."

Monk looks up with big eyes and says, "I took the money, Bobby. I took Huertero's money and arranged with the Thai police to arrest Huertero's men after they picked up the dope. I split the take with the Thais, but I didn't give you up, Bobby, I swear."

"Why, man. *Why?*" Tim asks. Like suddenly he's feeling like he *is* Bobby, and he's actually hurt. Like why did Monk have to go and fuck up a good thing. "Didn't you have enough, man?"

"Greed, Bobby," Monk says sadly. "The worst of the seven deadly sins."

"Least you could have split it with me," Tim mutters.

"I wanted you to have deniability."

Whatever the fuck *that* means, Tim thinks. Well, at least now he knows what the beef is and maybe he can make it right.

"How much we owe Huertero?" he asks.

"Three million."

"We got it?"

Monk's still sniffling, but he casually shrugs and says, "Of course."

"Can we lay our hands on three mil cash?" Tim asks. Now his voice is shaking because this is a little different from boosting TV sets and liquor.

"Yes," Monk says.

"Where?"

"On the boat."

"On the *boat?*" Tim asks. But he doesn't want to ask like *what boat*, because it sounds like he's supposed to know. So he asks, "Where is the boat now?"

"Dana Point Harbor," Monk says. He starts praying again, but Tim's not listening. He's thinking if he can get his hands on the cash and get in touch with Huertero he can give the money back and maybe take a stroll on all this. With enough cash left to have a fucking life somewhere.

Like maybe he can pull this whole thing off without fucking up.

So he's trying to think about how to do that when Monk finishes praying and asks, "What are you going to do, Bobby?"

"The fuck you think?" Tim asks, annoyed. "I'm going to try to make this right with Don Huertero."

"I mean about me."

Good question, Tim thinks. He knows he should get the name of the boat and then cap Monk. Like if this was the joint he'd lose respect—terminally—if he didn't cap a guy who did what Monk did.

"Monk, say the truth," Tim says. "Was it you set me up at the zoo?"

Monk's voice quakes, "Yes."

"For you or someone else?" Tim asks. "The truth."

"For myself," Monk says softly. Tim feels the man's body tense in anticipation.

"Fuck, man," Tim says.

"I know," Monk whispers. "I have the soul of a Judas. There *is* a God, isn't there, Bobby?"

"I guess."

"I'm ready, Bobby," Monk says. "Thank you for the time to get my spiritual matters in order."

"Sure."

Tim lowers the gun.

"Pick up the bag and walk," he tells Monk. "C'mon, get up."

"Really, Bobby?"

"Take me to the boat," Tim says. "C'mon, Monk, move."

"You want me to go first?" Monk asks.

"No offense, but I'm not real comfortable with you behind my back," Tim says. He gestures Monk forward and the tall skinny man picks up the gym bag and starts to walk.

Funny thing is, the guy's knees start knocking again.

Tim thinks this is weird but tots it up to sheer relief on the guy's part until a gunburst hits Monk square on and the guy folds to the sand.

Tim doesn't even think about going for the gym bag, he just hits the deck and crawls like a motherfucker back into the cave.

Knows instantly why Monk's knees were knocking. Monk had set him up to leave the cave first. Carrying a gym bag.

Soul of a Judas.

Tim wastes a few seconds wondering which of his enemies is out there then decides it doesn't matter anyway, because in a few seconds they'll be down to collect the prize and will realize they got the wrong guy and they'll be coming into the cave.

Meeting at this cave, Tim thinks again, was a really shitty idea.

So how the fuck to get out? Tim thinks. Always the question. Part of him starts wanting just to go out the front of the cave blasting away, man. He's pissed off and he's like just fucking had it, and if he's going out he wants to go out like Butch and Sundance, man. Out the front shooting into a blaze of gunfire.

That's what he's feeling building up inside him, but then he told Kit he'd be back, so he stuffs his anger in and starts feeling his way back toward the other end of the cave to see if there's another way out.

Feels like a chickenshit as he sneaks toward the back of the cave, which seems pretty solid, and it's looking like it's going to be the old Butch and Sundance bit after all when he spots a sliver of moonlight.

It's a crack in the cave wall, but it isn't wide enough to walk through. He edges in sideways and feels the cold salt water come up over his shoes, and then he's stuck.

Great, he thinks. This might be the most humiliating fuck-up of a life of fuck-ups, and he tests the side of the wall with one shoe and finds a foothold. Sticks his gun back in his pants, digs in with his other foot, then stretches his arms out akimbo and finds that the cave wall bows outward and he can work his way out by pressing hard against the wall with his hands while working his feet forward.

It's taking time, though, and he doesn't know if he has time, because he hears an angry voice back on the beach yell, "Shit!" and Tim figures that Gruzsa just realized he shot the wrong man and is probably keenly disappointed.

All of which gives Tim some motivation to press forward, like literally in this case, but then the space narrows and he can't get through and he hears footsteps running up the rocks on the beach, so he starts seeing if he can climb *up*.

Climbing up works but it's like *slow*, and he can hear Gruzsa's cautious footsteps coming into the cave.

So Tim climbs, trying not to make like a fucking sound. Climbs with his feet dug into the rock and his hands pressing against the sides to hold him up and it like hurts, man, because his arms are just straining.

Thinks again about just dropping down and shooting it out with Gruzsa, like do a Clint Eastwood thing and be finished with it. Gunfight in the OK Corral, man, and it'll just go down the way it goes down but he doesn't do it. He gets as high as he can and stops. Hangs there like some bat, man, still as he can, his arms quivering now with the strain, and the beam of Gruzsa's flashlight passing around the cave like the spotlight on the prison yard.

And through the crack in front of him the moonlight's shining soft and silvery on the open water.

Looking like freedom.

Tim presses his hands harder against the wall. Gruzsa spots him up there, he'll take like a hundred years not to miss the shot, and Tim wonders now if that's what happened that night on the border, that Gruzsa was trying to shoot him and fucked up, killed his buddy instead.

Easy mistake to make at that range at night.

But why the fuck would Gruzsa want to grease me or Bobby? Right when he was about to make the swap for Art Moreno?

Doesn't make any fucking sense, Tim thinks. One thing for sure, Gruzsa won't miss if he sees *this* shot. The bullet-head motherfucker will just laugh and call me a moke and *bang*.

Dead fucker.

61.

One Way is shivering through a serious psychotic episode.

He has witnessed bursts of flame blaze in the darkness that destroy Bobby's high priest. Even now the surf begins to lick at the priest's lifeless body and the crabs left behind by the tide start to click their way toward a fortuitous meal.

One Way presses himself even tighter against the soft soil of the bluff as the man comes running past, the man holding a gun, the man One Way recalls talking to many times on the streets of Laguna. The man who always seemed legitimately interested in the story of Bobby Z. One Way recognizes the man as the one who would go into a restaurant, emerge with a grilled-cheese sandwich encased in a Styrofoam box and give it to him as encouragement to tell more tales.

No wonder, One Way thinks now in horror. No wonder the man was so interested.

One Way is in serious pain. The pain shoots through his brain as if nails were being driven into his skull.

He has—albeit unwittingly—betrayed Bobby.

Told this man—this Caiaphas, this Pilate—all about

Bobby, and now the man has killed Bobby's priest and is racing into the cave to kill Bobby.

And it's my fault, One Way thinks.

I have sold Bobby for a grilled cheese—with cottage fries—and a box of nonbiodegradable Styrofoam that lives forever.

The pain increases.

One Way knows from whence it comes. It is the pain of guilt, the pain of shame, the pain of failure. It is the pain of paralysis, because One Way cannot bring himself to move. Cannot throw himself from these shadows into moonlight to go and fight for Z. Knows he should race after the man and throw himself on his back. Grab his arm and stay the fatal shot. Take, if necessary, the bullets meant for Z.

But he's afraid.

The pain of fear.

One Way huddles in the shadow of the bluff, holds himself and rocks in rhythm with the waves. Listens for the shot that surely must echo in the cave, the explosion foreshadowed by the relentless pounding in his brain, and knows that he'll live with that forever.

Styrofoam.

I am so weak, One Way thinks.

And my weakness betrays Bobby Z.

Then he feels the voice build inside him, build like a sudden cyclone in his stomach, twirl and twist out of his mouth. He isn't responsible for it, doesn't think it, doesn't will it. It's happening on its own—not by him but *through* him. The voice forces itself up through his throat just as his mouth opens and his body unwinds and moves upward like a cyclone coming up from the water.

And he's standing—inexplicably on his feet—legs planted in the sand as his voice—bass and treble both to the max—hollers, "I SEE YOU!!!"

62.

Tim almost falls, the high-pitched, wailing scream startles him that much.

Who sees who? he wonders. He doesn't think that anyone can see him, because if they could he'd have a couple of rounds in him by now, so whoever is screaming out there is either having a serious case of the DTs or is maybe yelling at Gruzsa.

Apparently Gruzsa thinks so, too, because Tim hears him mutter "Fuck" and start to ginger-foot his way out of the cave the way he came in. So Tim figures if he can hold on in this position for another minute or so, he just might live to fuck up another day.

Gruzsa, he's so pissed off and confused he can barely contain himself. For one thing, he's greased the only guy who could positively nail down where Tim Kearney is. Second, Kearney has apparently disappeared into thin air—a Bobby Z sort of thing to do—because he sure as hell didn't come out of the cave and he sure as hell isn't in it, either. And three, some voice comes out of fucking nowhere and starts proclaiming himself as a witness and Gruzsa all of a sudden is thinking he might have to whack not one but two people tonight, and neither of them is Tim Kearney.

Gruzsa checks his load and starts for the sound of the voice that's wailing like a siren.

63.

Tim works his way toward the moonlight.

It's like some obstacle course only the most sadistic Marine DI could have dreamed up, and Tim's muscles are maximum-strained and his hands are bleeding by the time he makes it to the edge of the cave and hears a shot from the beach behind him.

He jumps out onto the beach, which is like water by now, because the frigging tide's come in. The beach at this little cape is all rock anyway, and Tim slips and falls on the slippery rocks about three hundred times before he comes onto a footpath that leads back up toward the top of the bluff.

He staggers up, tired and scared because he knows Gruzsa's on top of him now and he isn't going to have time to work this thing out. As he works his way through the back streets and along the PCH back toward the trailer, he's trying to think of the next move.

The next move is clearly like "out," man, but the problem is how. As usual in the so-called life of Tim Kearney, the problem is getting out, the exit stage left, and he's thinking, just bundle Kit up in a blanket or something, see if they can use Elizabeth's ride and like just drive, man. North or east, because Huertero's to the south and he's run out of west. So by the time he gets back to the trailer, he's made his mind up to do just that. Get Kit and Elizabeth—if she wants to come—and drive toward the Great Plains somewhere. Find some little town in Kansas or something and grow wheat.

Except that when he lets himself into the trailer, nobody's home.

Kit and Elizabeth are gone.

64.

Tim's lost.

He's like suddenly free of everything and he doesn't know what to do. Like Gruzsa's on fucking top of him again and he has to split and the last fucking thing he needs in the whole wide world is a woman and a kid, but that's what he wants.

And they're gone.

Gone in a heartbeat, man, because they hardly took shit with them. A few of Kit's clothes and his toothbrush, that's all, and the kid's comic books are still in a pile beside his bed.

Elizabeth's makeup sits by the bathroom sink.

Tim wants to just sit down and fucking cry, man.

Go out and drop onto the beach and howl his pain to the moon. Howl until Gruzsa comes up behind him and puts a round in the back of his head.

Maybe Gruzsa's already got 'em, he thinks. Gruzsa comes back up the beach and figures if he can't get Tim he'll get Tim's family. Call Tim up and cut a new deal. Gruzsa'd do that. The DEA would do fucking anything.

He knows he should split, too.

Take off and don't look back like *now*, because maybe Elizabeth split for some reason other than he's a hopeless dickhead. Maybe she got scared and ran, maybe they've tripped onto the place and he's a sitting duck if he doesn't get out.

But he's in that give-a-fuck state of mind, so he doesn't take off. What lifelong loser Tim Kearney does is he opens the fridge and pulls out three cervezas. Holds the necks between the fingers of one hand and goes and sits on the beach. Watches the silver flicker on the water, drains the beers and goes back in for the survivors of the six-pack and a bottle of tequila.

Takes the phone out with him in case they call.

But knows they're not going to call, so he's out there trying to actually drink himself to death—your basic lack of impulse control—and doing a pretty good job of it.

He's lying there on the beach, looking up at the stars and he's laughing at himself for thinking that he could have his little family of Elizabeth and Kit and him in some *Lassie Come Home* town in the Midwest. Just laughing his ass off that loser Tim Kearney, All-World Fuck-Up, All-Universe Loser, could pull that off, he's just laughing till he cries and cries until he passes out. Comes to when an acrid foul smell jolts him awake. When he opens his eyes there's this goat bending over him grinning at him.

He smells the goat before he sees him, just smells this smelly old goat, so he opens his eyes and, sure enough, this goat's staring down at him and Tim's wondering what's a goat doing in Laguna Beach like unescorted when the goat starts to talk.

"Bobby?" the goat asks. "Bobby Z?"

Tim sees it's not really a goat but a person who looks and smells like a goat.

"I'm not fucking Bobby fucking Z," Tim says.

"Yes, you are."

"Not."

"Are."

"Leave me the fuck alone."

But the guy starts picking him up, getting underneath his arms and saying, "We have to get you out of here."

"My kid and my woman split," Tim says. "I'm going to die here."

"Right, you're in danger," the guy says, and he manages to get under Tim and lift him. Starts dragging him across the beach. He drags Tim to the base of the bluffs where they're out of sight and plops him down.

"You've gained weight, Bobby," he complains.

"Who are you?" Tim asks.

"I don't remember exactly," One Way says. "But they call me One Way."

"You're the acid casualty," Tim says.

"That's what they say," One Way admits. "They think I'm crazy."

"You *look* like a lunatic."

"I *am* a lunatic," One Way says. He pauses with a poet's dramatic timing. "But I know things."

"What do you know?"

One Way's eyes flick up and down the beach. Then his eyes sparkle in the moonlight and he smiles a sly, snaggle-toothed grin.

"I know," he says, "where your unfaithful priest hid your treasure."

65.

On a boat, One Way tells him.

"Which boat?" Tim asks.

There are only about twelve thousand in the marina.

One Way blinks his eyes rapidly.

"*The* boat," he says mysteriously.

"And the boat is called . . ."

"The *Nowhere*," One Way whispers. "A square-rigged sloop moored in Dana Point Harbor. I watched him bring the money there."

"He's dead," Tim says.

"I know," One Way answers. "I heard everything. Well, almost everything. The rest the moon told me."

"Sure it did," Tim says. "This is the money Monk ripped off from Don Huertero?"

"If you say so."

"My kid is gone," Tim cries. "My kid and my woman."

"We'll get them back," One Way says soothingly.

"How?"

"I don't know."

"Great."

"But we will."

"How do you know?"

"Because you're Bobby Z," One Way says.

One Way takes the blanket from his shoulders and wraps it around Tim. He lifts Tim's head and puts it in his lap and cradles him as he says, "Because you're Bobby Z and the child is your son. Or your daughter. Whatever. You have a woman and a child and that's life's sacred rhythm. Endless, repetitive, like the beat of the ocean, which is like you, Z. They can't stop the beat of the ocean. The surf will rise and crash, life will be born from water. You glide on the ocean, man. From it you spring and to it you shall return."

He strokes Tim's head and intones, "To it you shall return. With your wife. With your son. Or daughter. Whatever."

Then the phone rings.

66.

Tim picks up the receiver and just listens, praying it's her. Just wants to find out *Where is my kid, is like my kid all right?* He thinks he hears her breathing over the phone and knows she's doing the same thing, wondering who's on the other end of the line.

She jumps in first.

"Hello?"

"Is Kit okay?"

"Yes."

"Are you okay?"

"Yes."

But it sounds tentative. He reads in her voice like *I'm okay now,* but like he can feel Gruzsa in the background, sitting behind her, smirking . . . So he waits for her to go on.

"They have us," she says.

"Who does?"

"Don Huertero."

"How's the boy?" he repeats. Because he thinks he knows what's coming.

"Scared but all right," she says. "He's a tough kid, you know."

"Yeah, I know." Tough little monkey. The kid like *shows* you something.

"If you don't come," Elizabeth says, "they say they're going to kill him."

"I'll come."

"They'll—"

"I know," he says. "Tell them I'll come. Tell them I have their fucking money. I'm giving it back."

He hears her start to talk to someone and then the someone gets on the line.

"Bobby Z?"

"Yeah," Tim says. "Is this Don Huertero?"

"Never mind who this is," the guy says. Mexican accent, but sounds rougher to Tim than Don Huertero should. "You come or we kill the kid."

"Where are you?"

"Fuck you," the guy says. "You think we're stupid?"

"I can't meet you if I don't know where you are."

"You got the money?"

"I got it stashed."

"Somewhere near the money," guy says. "Somewhere quiet."

"Hold on."

Tim holds the phone close to his shirt and asks One Way for a quiet spot with a good view of the boat.

"The Arches," One Way tells him. "Park at the end of Blue Lantern Street. Take a left on the Bluffside Walk. Down a slope, across a wooden bridge over the canyon. Three concrete arches, all that's left of a luxury hotel got half built before the crash of 1929. You can see the boat from there. You can see everything."

Tim tells the guy and says he'll be there in an hour.

"In the morning," the guy says. "We're meeting you

nowhere at night. People get dead they approach you in the darkness, Bobby Z."

Tim wants to talk to Kit but the Mexican hangs up.

"They have Kit," Tim tells One Way. "They say they'll kill him."

"We'll save him," One Way says. "We'll give them the money and then . . ."

One Way's eyes shine with a fanatical joy.

"Then what?" Tim asks.

"Then sail away," One Way says.

"I don't know how to sail."

One Way smiles like a lunatic cherub.

"I do," he says.

"Could you sail *this* boat?"

"Anywhere."

"And you'd do that?" Tim asks.

"Joyfully."

Then One Way frowns. His smile collapses into a shame-faced grimace. "There's a problem."

Of course there is, Tim thinks.

"What's the problem."

"The cop."

"Fat cop?" Tim asks. "Shaved head, like a bullet?"

"Yeah."

"Ugly mouth?"

"A mean cop."

"I know him," Tim says. "What about him?"

"He said if I found you I should tell him where you are," One Way whispers. "Or he'll kill me."

Tim thinks about this. Then he says, "So tell him where I am."

"No!"

"Yeah," Tim says. "Tell him exactly what I'm doing.

Tell him I'm turning myself in to Don Huertero for Art Moreno and my kid."

"Don Huertero . . . Moreno . . . kid."

"Just don't tell him about the boat."

"What boat?"

Tim sighs. "The boat that . . ."

One Way stops him with a hand on his arm.

"I know," One Way says.

He gives Tim a stage wink and runs off down the beach.

67.

As Tim packs his shit he knows what he should do.

What he should do is he *should* get on the boat like *tonight* and sail away with a cool three mil. You can hide forever and hide goddamn well with three mil in cash. Even with a nutball as your captain. You can hole up on some Caribbean island, sip drinks with umbrellas in them and fuck tanned, long-legged women until you die. Eighty-three years old, tan, rich and relaxed, and die of a heart attack in the saddle, man. Give some Caribbean honey a story to tell her grandkids. Leave fucking Don Huertero sitting on his ass, leave fucking Gruzsa eating his own liver, leave Bobby Z's problems to . . . Well, let the dead bury the dead. *Adiós,* motherfuckers. For once in his whole fucked-up life Tim Kearney has the exit, man. He has the loot and he has the exit and he should for once take it. That's what he should do.

But even as he's stuffing his sweatshirt into his duffel, dumb fucking Tim Kearney knows he isn't going to do what he should.

Big news, right? Like that's a first, Tim Kearney taking a pass on the smart thing. But that's how you get to be a three-time loser, right? Knowing the smart move and doing the opposite.

It ain't for the woman, either. He knows that's what they'll all think. That every con will stick his dick in the wringer for some pussy. Especially *that* pussy. But that ain't it. Although he sure as shit loves her, he could walk away from her.

It's the kid.

Goddamn it, goddamn it, goddamn it, and it isn't even his fucking kid.

Three million dollars and the lifetime *out* and he's probably going to get killed for the kid.

Because Huertero's probably gonna whack me anyway, Tim thinks, soon as he has the cash in hand.

So what I should do is split.

Tim finishes packing, shoves his pistol into his belt and gets in the car.

Says so long to the trailer and the beach where he could have lived happily.

Just wasn't meant to be, he thinks.

68.

The doorman won't let One Way in and threatens to call the cops.

"They know me," One Way says.

The doorman threatens to just beat the crap out of him, but One Way tells him just to ring Gruzsa's room or he'll just sneak out and take a dump in the parking lot.

"But if you do ring his room," One Way says, "I'll never forage in your Dumpsters again."

This is a big sacrifice, because the Ritz-Carlton Dumpsters are among the finest on the south coast. It's been One Way's experience that rich people tend to send a lot of food back just to show that they can, so the Dumpster is a mecca for a gourmand of recycled haute cuisine.

The doorman tells One Way to go hide in the shadows somewhere downwind and keep his fucking mouth shut, and it's only about ten minutes later that Gruzsa comes huffing out and spots him.

Gruzsa hauls him into the parking lot and pushes him up against a Mercedes 510 SL.

"What?" Gruzsa asks.

"It's about Bobby Z," One Way says.

"You saw him?"

"In the flesh."

"Fucking where?!"

"Fucking Laguna Beach," One Way lies. "He's going—"

Gruzsa smacks him across the face.

"He still there?" he asks.

"How should I know if he's there?" One Way answers. "I'm *here*."

"Was he still there when you left?"

"Oh, yes."

Gruzsa ponders this for a second then asks, "What's he going to do?"

"I heard him over the phone say he's going to turn himself in to Don Huertero in the morning."

Gruzsa looks around the parking lot, doesn't see anyone, then pulls his automatic and shoves it under One Way's chin.

"You fucking with me, nutball?" he asks. "This some kind of a trick?"

"It's the gospel truth."

"Why the fuck would he wanna do that?"

"They have his son."

"His son?" Gruzsa says. "I didn't know he had a fucking son."

"Don Huertero will phone you when the deal's complete," One Way says. "They'll release Moreno at the border."

"No shit."

"Completely shitless," One Way says.

Gruzsa puts his gun away. "You ever say anything about this to anyone, I'll find you and *really* scramble your brains. You got that?"

"Aye-aye, sir."

Gruzsa mumbles *Fucking nutball* and shoves him away. Watches as One Way runs off.

A few minutes later Gruzsa goes back to his suite and says to the guy lying on the bed watching TV, "Congratulations, you're a dead fucker."

"Really?"

"First thing in the morning."

Gruzsa pours himself a tumbler of single-malt Scotch from the honor bar and says, "Did you know you had a kid?"

"No."

"Well, I guess you got a kid."

"So?"

"So nothing. You got a kid, is all."

Guy shrugs and goes back to watching TV.

69.

When Tim pulls up to Blue Lantern Street there's a limo already parked there. Darkened windows so Tim can't see in, but he's pretty sure Kit's in the car.

Big fucking hump of a Mexican with a lump in his jacket points down Bluffside Walk.

Tim checks the view out as he walks down. It's misty in the early morning, but you can still make out the harbor below even though you can't see individual boats yet. He can only hope like hell that One Way is on that damn boat with the money.

Tim goes down some steps where he can see three concrete arches that look funny just sitting there. Like someone took a piece of Greece or something and plopped it down in Dana Point. What's left from someone's wet dream after the crash. Tim knows how the poor loser felt, especially because some guy's standing at the near end of the bridge. Guy takes him by the arm and leads him *off* the walkway, under the bridge. Where no one can see, Tim thinks, so he knows he's in for an ass kicking.

There's a little flat spot under the bridge, a square of dirt worn down by people coming to drink, screw, smoke dope, or all of the above. There's a residual smell of stale piss and beer. Spot is perched at the edge of a steep ravine. At the bottom, big date palms rise up through boulders.

It's gonna be an ugly fall, Tim thinks.

A little knot of people standing under the bridge.

Guy in a gray suit, three bodyguards in dark suits and Elizabeth.

The guys in the dark suits all have shades on and they're talking into little bodyguard microphones just like in the movies. Tim knows they're cutting the walk off.

Ain't no civilians going to take a stroll on this part of the bluff walk until the business is over.

Elizabeth looks like shit. She's dressed to fucking kill, Tim sees, but her green eyes look dull. Tim's seen the look before, on the yard, just before some guy gets it. She steps up and throws her arms around him and Tim knows without anyone saying anything that she's set him up.

"Thank God you came," she whispers in his ear.

She kisses his cheek and holds him tight and Tim braces for the shot he knows he's going to take. It comes right behind the ear, and smooth as shit the second Mex slips his gun from him before his knees hit the ground.

Tim sees Elizabeth's spinning face mouth, "I'm sorry."

You're sorry, Tim thinks.

70.

Escobar's troops are out early.

They're out there like hounds with a scent, because the car's been spotted heading south from Laguna on the PCH. Which is good news for Escobar's troops, because Dana Point has a barrio just off the PCH, up the hill from the harbor. So there's a frigging platoon of young Chicanos walking the town looking for the car. Some of them are on bikes, *ese,* because they're too young to drive, and they're all juiced because the rumor is that DFN is on his way from East L.A.

And the word is out: Don't anybody lose his cool and blow it, *ese.* Don't nobody decide to be a hero and go in blasting, because even if Bobby Z don't take you out, Luis Escobar will, you blow the shot for DFN Cruz.

It's two older boys with a ride who are cruising slow along Santa Clara and one of them jerks his head over to Blue Lantern and laughs. "Check it out."

And they can't like fucking believe it because the car is just sitting out there in the open like this guy has some *cojones, ese.* Next to a big black limo, so the guys, they punch in Cruz's number and then get out of the car to check it out.

The limo driver, he reaches into his jacket as the two

men come up, and they put their hands up by their shoulders and just ask, "What's happening?"

Driver has some stones himself, because what he says is, "What's happening is you're going to get your asses away from here, is what's happening."

One of the cruisers, he says, "We just want to take a walk, *ese.*"

And the limo driver answers, "Take a walk in the other direction."

So they do. They smile and move backward slowly to show they're not afraid. They get back in the car and DFN Cruz's driver checks in and they tell him *Get over here,* ese. *Something's going down.*

So Cruz starts putting his piece together and checking the sight, and the driver hustles the car toward Santa Clara and Blue Lantern.

And the two cruisers, they pull out and cruise down Santa Clara to Golden Lantern, where they can get into the park from the other side because they just know that the legendary Bobby Z must be doing some business on the Bluffside Walk.

And they wanna be there when DFN Cruz does Bobby's business, *ese.*

71.

"The great Bobby Z," Huertero says. "The legend."

Don Huertero, he shakes his head, then kicks Tim in the face.

One Gucci fucking loafer right between the eyes, square on the nose where it joins the skull. One inch either way with that pointed toe and Tim loses an eye, but this way it only breaks his nose, so he can still see through blurry eyes as Huertero yanks his head up by the hair, glares at him, coughs up a big ball of phlegm and spits in Tim's eyes.

Tim can feel the warm spit merge with the blood oozing warmly down his face and with the tears, because his eyes are overflowing and while he isn't exactly crying, he isn't exactly *not* crying either.

Huertero jerks his hand away.

One of his boys is quick with a handkerchief. Huertero wipes his hands and tosses the handkerchief on the floor.

Tim manages to find Elizabeth with his eyes and asks, "Where's Kit?"

"In the limo," she says. "He's all right."

Then she adds, like she's begging him, "I'm sorry, Bobby. I had to."

Of course she did, he thinks. She knew I was going to get nailed one way or the other, so she has to do what's best for the kid. Save herself so she can be a mother to the boy.

"It's cool," he says.

"Your son?" Huertero asks.

"Yes."

Huertero nods silently and seems to lapse into thought. Tim figures he's thinking about how to whack him.

But he ain't going down quite yet.

"I have your three million," Tim says to Huertero.

Huertero raises an eyebrow and smiles.

Encouraged, Tim adds what he knows. "It's on a boat in Dana Point Harbor. Right down there. Give me my son and we can walk right down and get it."

"Is that so."

"I want to pay you back," Tim says. "One of my men—"

Huertero bends down and slaps Tim so hard it knocks him over. When Tim opens his eyes, Huertero's standing over him, his face red and angry.

"You talk to me about *money*?!" Huertero yells. "You dare talk to me about money?! You stole my *treasure*!"

Tim's confused as hell, and he hears Elizabeth murmur, "Oh, shit."

Then Huertero says, "You stole my child."

What the fuck?

Huertero adds, "You stole my daughter."

"I don't know—"

"And you killed her."

Tim's like fucking reeling.

"And, yes," Don Huertero says. "You *will* pay me back."

And Huertero launches into the story of Angelica Huertero de Montezón.

72.

Her father's treasure, his only child.

No male children to carry on the line, the one sadness of Huertero's life, but then there was Angelica, his angel, born to marry some young hidalgo and carry on the blood if not the name.

A beautiful child, this his angel, with hair as soft and black as a Sonoran night and eyes of purest starshine. A smile that brought the sun to him, a laugh that made the air sing.

A beautiful child.

Growing to womanhood, his Angelica, and as she grew she developed the strong will of her father rather than the docile compliance of her mother. It infuriated him but made him proud, her strong stubborn will, and he had to admit that he could refuse her nothing. Not toys or dolls, or jewelry or friends, or dangerous horses or dangerous men.

He tried to keep her away from his business, he did. But how to give her the riches he made without exposing her to the seamy shadows? Had she been more compliant, less spirited perhaps, he might have managed to keep her in, to lock her up inside the hacienda and let her be trained to the domestic arts. But she had the spirit, this

Angelica. The proud spirit of a hidalgo, of countless generations of conquistadors, and she was born to ride and roam and he acknowledged that.

As with a spirited horse, one tries to guide. To let it run but choose the fields, as he tried to choose her friends, and he liked Elizabeth and Olivia, even though they came from the drug demimonde. They were courtesans, after all, were they not? Sophisticated college girls, smart enough to keep up with Angelica, loyal enough to protect her.

Had he not even, as it were, sampled Elizabeth? Taken her to bed and sensed her spirit. Rewarded her with a generous stipend and a secret job. The days of black-draped chaperones were long gone, he knew, but perhaps Elizabeth could keep an eye on Angelica? Be, as much as one could in these modern times, a chaperone to this modern girl?

They roamed the world, these three. Three spirited young ladies with wealth and breeding, but these are different times, freer times, one would have to be a fool not to acknowledge that reality.

And he had told her—his angel, his wild child—that she may have her wild years. Her parties, her dances, her shopping sprees. She may go on the cruises, shop in Paris, dance in Rio, flit from club to club in Cap Ferrat, in Cannes, in Manhattan, in Los Angeles.

She may play the Anglo princess, but deep inside she must remain a Latina. She must—no matter what her loose Anglo friends did—remain a virgin until she married.

And that man would be a Mexican.

A Mexican and not a hated *yanqui.*

And then she met Bobby Z.

He would never forgive Elizabeth for that. Could

never fully take her in again, for Elizabeth should have stopped it. Or at least come to him so that he could have stopped it.

He would have forgiven her, too. Taken in his fallen angel, even as she was ruined, and brought her home to him. His hopes for a good marriage dashed by the fall of his high-flying child, he still would have cherished her and they could have spent their years together as the last of their family.

Had he only known that they were Bobby Z's harem, the three girls. Elizabeth and the poor drug-addicted fool Olivia, and, yes, Angelica.

But of the three, only Angelica fell in love. Only Angelica had the tragic purity of heart to fall hopelessly in love. She alone could not give herself to a man without *giving* herself to a man.

"But you destroyed her," he said to Tim.

Tim shook his head.

"You used her the way a man might use a whore and you left her," Huertero said. "Her heart was broken, her spirit was broken, her soul was broken. I tried to touch her, to reach her, but she knew that she was not the girl that I had raised. She could not face me in her humiliation at your hands. She could not look me in the eye.

"And then she disappeared. From me, she disappeared. I had her tracked to Los Angeles, to New York, to Europe. For *months*. Then she simply disappeared.

"Why? I asked myself. Why? I summoned Elizabeth here and finally heard the truth of what you had done. Heard that you had *had* her. Used her, played with her, led her to believe that you loved her, and then left her. Tossed her away like garbage, and that is how she felt. No wonder she could not stand to look me in the face. And you talk to me of *money*?!"

Tim braced himself for the kick that didn't come. Realized that Huertero was too deep inside himself to lash out. That would come later.

"When they found her it was in Crete," Huertero said softly. "She had died of a heroin overdose. Can you imagine a better way to punish her father than to die of an overdose of Mexican Brown? I can see her lying on that cold stone floor. In her own vomit and her own shit. I see this every time I close my eyes for six endless years. For six long years I ask Why? Then I find out that it was you."

He pulls a pistol from his silk jacket.

Tim flinches when the cold metal touches the front of his skull.

"Look at me," Huertero says.

Tim looks up. He's trying not to shake but it isn't working.

He jumps at the sound of the hammer clicking back.

"We will meet in hell, Bobby Z," Huertero says.

Tim sees the man's finger tighten on the trigger.

Just do it, he thinks.

Nike time.

Over.

Just do it.

He hears Elizabeth's soft sobbing.

Waits for the last big bang.

Closes his eyes and sees Kit's smile.

73.

Life hasn't been good to asshole Wayne LaPerriere.

Like he's been long overdrawn in the bank of karma but he never thought it would come to this.

Room service fucking waiter at the fucking Ritz-Carlton.

Which was the idea, you know, so he could spot those rich dickheads too stupid to put their valuables in the safe-deposit box at the front desk. Humiliating, bringing omelettes de fines herbes and smoked salmon fettuccine to rich assholes who sometimes don't even bother to stop fucking in the bedroom while he sets the tray in the sitting room, but remunerative when he can turn Al Matteau on to a score and get a piece. And sometimes he got a look at some tit or some pussy, and once he even thought he was gonna get laid but her limpdick husband came wheezing in.

So it wasn't all that bad, but on this particular morning asshole Wayne LaPerriere almost swallowed his teeth when he went to deliver goddamn fucking early-morning coffee and croissants and Tim Kearney's standing there.

Now the last time Wayne had seen Kearney was when he picked him up from the joint and did a Gas n' Grub on the way to a bar where they got drunk and arrested. And what Wayne did was Wayne got right on the train the detective offered and put the gun in Tim's hand and walked away with nine months on the farm.

Last person in the goddamn world Wayne wants to see is Tim Kearney, who Wayne heard was in the deepest of possible shit having slicked a very large Hell's Angel named Stinkdog in the yard, but there's fucking Tim at the fucking Ritz-Carlton, real as life.

Longer hair and gained a little weight maybe, but it's Kearney, and Wayne slips his hand under the linen napkin and reaches for the knife.

But Tim doesn't recognize him.

Asshole Wayne LaPerriere can't fucking believe it, but the arrogant bastard doesn't recognize his old best friend. Just juts his chin and says *Set it down over there* and goes back to shaving.

And some guy in the bathroom is yelling to eat his fucking croissant in a fucking hurry because they got to get to the fucking harbor, and Tim tells the guy to go fuck himself.

And goes on shaving like Wayne's invisible.

Uppity son of a bitch. If Kearney, who is as big a loser as was ever born, is ordering up room service at the fucking Ritz-Carlton, he has to be on to a very large score, and the least he could do is share it with his old buddy, Wayne thinks. Who the fuck gave him a ride home from the joint? Kearney's own parents wouldn't pick him up, but there was old Wayne, and how does Kearney treat him now?

Like some loser, that's how.

Fucking Kearney's too good for him now.

So asshole Wayne LaPerriere is like steaming as he goes back to the kitchen. He's pissed and he throws his faggoty little waiter jacket to the floor and says he quits this asshole job.

And what Wayne does is he goes right out to a phone booth and calls an Angel buddy who sells him some meth from time to time and says, "Don't you guys have a beef with Tim Kearney?"

"Yeah, what about it?" his buddy asks.

"He's at the Ritz-Carlton."

And the Angel like snorts and says, "Tim fucking Kearney is not at the fucking Ritz-Carlton."

And laughs, which makes Wayne all the madder.

"Yeah, well, then I saw a fucking ghost," Wayne says. "Anyway, in case you're interested, he's going to the harbor."

And his buddy says, "You didn't see a ghost, you saw a fucking dead man."

Few minutes later there's an army of bikers headed for Dana Point Harbor, and asshole Wayne LaPerriere, he's happy and relieved that Tim Kearney is about to be a dead fucker, because it really takes a load off his mind.

74.

Huertero's hand quivers.

Then the finger lets up on the trigger.

Huertero's shaking his head.

"It's not enough," Huertero says sadly. And Tim figures like Huertero's gonna shoot him in the belly and leave him or set him on fire or something. He's getting ready for it when he hears Huertero order, "Get the boy."

Hears Elizabeth shriek, "No!"

One of Huertero's boys grabs her and clamps a hand over her mouth.

Huertero lifts his chin, looks in Tim's eyes and says, "A child for a child. You will watch and then perhaps I will give you the mercy of death."

Tim lunges for him but Huertero's boys are too quick, too good.

When they let Tim up he sees Kit standing there.

Looking so scared.

"Don't do this," Tim says to Huertero.

"It's horrible, isn't it?" Huertero asks. "Horrible even to contemplate."

"I've met some low motherfuckers in my life . . ." Tim says.

Huertero gestures for them to take the boy to the edge of the ravine.

Tim imagines the bullet in the back of the head and Kit's body flying off the edge.

"He isn't my kid," Tim says.

"Yes, I am!" Kit shouts.

Huertero kneels next to the boy.

"Son," he whispers, his words a fatherly caress, "you will tell me the truth and I will spare this man's life: Who is your father?"

"Kit—" Tim warns, but Huertero's man clamps a hand over his mouth.

Kit looks Huertero in the eye and says proudly, "Bobby Z is my father."

"This man?"

And Kit looks at Tim with a look that Tim recognizes as like pure love, man.

And says, "Yes."

Huertero looks at Tim and asks, "Would you deny such a brave son?"

Huertero puts his arm around the boy and ushers him toward the bridge.

Kit balks. Tears himself from Huertero's arms and attacks the man holding Tim. Goes for the back of his neck and tries to haul him off his father. Bites, scratches, kicks and punches. Screams, "Let my daddy go!" and wails away and Tim's just trying to reach around to hold the kid's arms, just hold him so they'll at least have to do them both and maybe he can hold his hand over Kit's eyes as they fall, be X-Men or something so it won't be real until the kid wakes up in heaven.

But he can't hold on and feels the kid slipping away from him. Kit's played out, and when Tim can get his head turned to see, one of Huertero's men has the boy in a bear hug. Both of Kit's feet are off the ground and kicking.

Like a hanged man's feet.

"You look for me in hell," Tim tells Huertero. "I'll be coming for you."

"You haven't *seen* hell yet," Huertero says.

"Daddy, help me!" Kit's screaming, and Huertero smiles at Tim as if to say *that's* hell, and Tim reaches for him but can't get there. As they carry the boy to the edge, they lever Tim's head up so that he has to watch.

Elizabeth says to Huertero, "You won't hurt the boy."

"You underestimate my grief."

"He's your grandson."

Everything stops.

75.

Escobar's put the whole move into a freeze.

He's got a net thrown around the Bluffside Walk, and no one, not even the legendary ghostman Bobby Z, is getting out of there.

So Escobar's standing on a knoll with DFN Cruz and Cruz is checking out every possible firing angle and Cruz, he's in heaven. Escobar, he's looking down at that harbor. He can see the whole thing and as usual he's thinking ahead.

What he's thinking is that Bobby Z is a dope smuggler who's been bringing his product in from the sea. And what's good for bringing in is good for getting out, so Escobar decides it's a good bet that Bobby is going to finish his business and get on one of those boats.

He points this possibility out to DFN Cruz and they talk it over like two professional men. How Cruz can get a shot on whatever dock Bobby has to walk down to get on his boat. If he misses, Escobar says, talking over DFN Cruz's objection, the boat has a long way to go to get away.

Boat has to pull out of the slip, then cruise slowly on the inside of the long stone jetty that forms an oval ring around the harbor. A long way inside that quiet strip of water, then under a bridge until it gets to open water.

"Can you hit that far?" he asks Cruz.

"Won't have to," Cruz says.

"That's not what I asked you."

"I can hit that far."

Escobar's getting anxious.

"Would it be better from the bridge?" he asks.

Cruz shakes his head.

"It would be a good shot," he admits. "But I want to get away."

Everyone and his fucking mother would see you shoot from that bridge. You'd have to be a crazy motherfucker to shoot from that bridge. He doesn't say that to Escobar, though. Escobar is an intelligent man but a little uptight right now.

Besides, there's a whole line of bikers sitting on that bridge, and the last thing Cruz wants now is a hassle with a bunch of bikers.

"I'll take the shot from here," Cruz says.

Death from Nowhere.

76.

"She was pregnant," Elizabeth says. "That's why she ran from you. She was afraid. I tried to get her to have an abortion but she wouldn't. So we concocted a plan. She would go away and have the baby as Olivia. Everyone would believe it: Olivia was the most promiscuous of us. Olivia would raise the baby as the awkward result of one of many affairs. I would help.

"It worked as far as it went. We fooled everybody. But poor Angelica . . . You were right, she couldn't fool herself. She yearned for Bobby, she yearned for her son. She would have taken the boy back but she was so afraid of your anger. Afraid of what you would do . . ."

Elizabeth juts her chin toward the bridge. "She was half afraid that you would kill the child."

"Kill my grandson?" Huertero blinks. *"Mi carnal?"*

Elizabeth looks at the thug holding Kit and snaps, "Put that boy down."

Kit runs to Tim and throws his arms around him. Digs his face into the man's chest to hide.

"Olivia couldn't raise a kid," Elizabeth snorts. "Olivia couldn't raise a houseplant. I should have known that. Her eighth rehab or whatever and I was planning to take him myself. Then *he* shows up and I thought, you know, *fuck* it, he should know he has a kid."

"A grandson," Huertero mumbles. His eyes fill, then overflow with tears. He's weeping as he says, "A grandson. A treasure."

Tim can't believe like what the fuck he's hearing and why Elizabeth like didn't mention this tidbit maybe a little earlier, and next thing he knows, Huertero's sitting on the ground beside him trying to get Kit's attention, saying, "You'll have everything. Toys, boats, games, *horses*. You will have a stable of horses to ride, you will be like a prince from a fairy tale. We will ride together early in the mornings and I will tell you stories of your ancestors and how they conquered Mexico and how they fought the Comanches and the Apaches and the *yanquis*. And you will have a sweet woman to teach you Spanish and Elizabeth will be your nanny. Would you like that?"

He's reaching around and trying to hold the boy or just to touch him, but Kit clings to Tim and buries his head further into his chest. Blood drips from Tim's nose onto the boy's hair.

Huertero gets up and tries to brush the dirt from his slacks.

"Take the boy," he orders.

"The boy stays with me," Tim says. "Take your money and go."

Huertero just smiles and says, "Take the boy."

"Slip ZZ," Tim says. "The *Nowhere*. You can be on it and out of here, but leave me the boy."

Elizabeth starts to say something but Tim snaps, "Shut the fuck up!"

Because he like knows it's over. Knows Huertero's going to get the kid and the money and whack him. And the kid's going to have a rich, shitty life but at least he can go through it knowing his father wanted him.

Ain't that much for a kid to ask.

"I'll go with you," Kit says to Huertero. "I want to go with you."

"Kit—" Tim says.

He hears Kit saying, "If you don't kill him."

Kit's a smart, tough little fucker, and he's saying, "You can't take me if I don't want to go. I'll start screaming and yelling and you can't stop me. And I'll tell them you kidnapped me and you'll go to jail."

Tim figures Huertero'll like freak, but the old fucker like *beams* and says, "The boy has spirit."

"The boy is serious," Kit says.

And the boy has sat up a lot of late nights watching movies on television, because the boy says, "I want a letter from him every year, and him and I have a code so I'll know if it's faked. As long as he's alive I'll stay with you."

"You have your mother's blood," Huertero says.

"And my dad's," Kit says.

Huertero solemnly sticks out his hand and Kit shakes it.

"We have an understanding," Huertero says. "My word of honor."

"Word of honor," Kit says.

And Tim doesn't say anything, because he wants the kid to think what he wants to think. Like he saved his daddy's life, but Tim knows Huertero's honor is worth absolute shit.

But there's Kit standing in front of him trying to be brave, and Tim puts his arms out and the kid hugs him and Tim whispers *I love you* and Kit whispers *I love you, too* and it's like *fuck brave*, because they're both crying.

Next thing Tim knows, Elizabeth's taking Kit by the hand and taking him away, and Tim touches Kit's fingers and then they're gone.

And Tim's kneeling in the dirt, crying.

On the way to the car Huertero mutters to his head honcho, "After we get on the boat, kill him."

The man nods. "I'll wait here."

Huertero shakes his head.

"You won't have to," he says. "He'll be coming."

"*¿Sí?*"

Sí, Huertero thinks.

Huertero knows men. He knows that man will be coming. A son such as that, the man will be coming for him.

And while he's saying this, lifetime loser Tim Kearney is letting himself slide over the edge of the ravine. Toward the top of the palm trees, toward the sharp rocks, Tim Kearney doesn't care.

Tim Kearney's sick of losing.

Semper Fi, man.

77.

One Way's getting the boat ready.

Feels good to him, too. Feels like old times, and it's coming back to him, the lines and the rigging. He's spent the night working on the engine, getting it humming and throbbing, and One Way has to wonder what he's been doing all these years in between.

It's been like one long weird trip, you know, and now he's ready to leave it behind. Sail away, man. From the Hotel California.

So he's standing on the deck looping the spare lines into neat coils, feeling the sun on the back of his neck, and he's waiting for Bobby to come and hand the money over so they can leave it all behind. Him and Bobby and Bobby's woman and kid, and One Way's blissed out on the thought of teaching the young Z how to sail.

Then he sees them coming and alarms go off in his head because Bobby isn't with them. A long black limo like a hearse pulls up and the boss Mexican gets out with a bodyguard and a woman and a kid. And One Way only has to get a glance at the kid to know it's the little Z, and here they come walking down the dock toward the boat, but Bobby isn't with them.

The old Mex looks at him and pushes the kid onto the

boat and orders, "Take him below!" so One Way does. But the bossman Mexican stays on the dock. Like he's waiting for something.

One Way's getting pins and needles through his stomach. Something's real wrong here, so he runs below and starts the engine in case they have to get out of here quick, and when he comes back up he sees Bobby come onto the deck with Gruzsa coming up behind him.

And Escobar and DFN Cruz up on the bluff and the Angels on the bridge, they all see the same thing. DFN Cruz has the crosshairs straight on Bobby's back, and the Angels have their AR-15s laying on the rail of the bridge, and Huertero's man, he has his pistol drawn, and Bobby, he seems to feel it because he stops and turns around.

Just as Tim Kearney staggers out from the ravine. He's standing at the base underneath a big palm and he looks straight across at the dock and his eyes meet Bobby Z's for just a second.

They give each other the funniest damn look, and then Tim hears Gruzsa screaming, "NOOOOO!" and Tim suddenly gets the whole damn setup. Like Gruzsa set him up to take the rap for Bobby Z and then Gruzsa and Z go sailing away with the three million, so it's like this sudden moment of enlightenment and then *wham*, the world opens up.

Like one second Z is standing there and the next second he like just dissolves, man, so many rounds hit him from so many angles.

It's like he's just *gone*.

And Gruzsa, Gruzsa, man, he sees Don Huertero standing there between him and his money and he goes for his gun as Huertero's man goes for his reload, and Huertero's man is a beat faster.

Gruzsa goes down on that dock but is like too fucking mean to die before he puts two shots into Huertero's man, who staggers off the dock into the water.

One Way hears all this and all he knows is he has Bobby's son to protect, and he guns the engine. Comes up on deck and starts to pull the *Nowhere* out of that slip and head toward the open water, because Bobby is dead. One Way can see what's left of his body on the dock and One Way knows he has to get that kid to safety somewhere, and safety for any son of Bobby Z's is on the water.

So the boat starts pulling out, and the old Mexican in the suit starts to get on board, but Bobby's woman has a blade that flashes like a sunbeam down his face from his forehead to his chin.

Huertero's standing there looking at his own blood flowing into his hands when Elizabeth plunges the knife into his chest.

And she just stands there waiting for the cops, and she's not going to have long to wait, because the sirens are already blaring.

It's like fucking chaos in Dana Point Harbor.

Escobar's crew is speeding out of town in the knowledge that they've avenged their *carnal*, and DFN Cruz is happy but a little weirded out because the target looked so much like that crazy fucker from the Gulf whose name he can't remember.

And the Angels are roaring off that bridge. Just dumped their weapons in the harbor and now they're riding like to San Berdoo or someplace to celebrate the death of Tim Kearney and the fact that their brothers can now party in hell.

And One Way, he's tired of the chaos. He just wants to

get out of fucking California, man, out of the trip, and he has a job to do. A lifelong job, which is to take care of Z's kid.

And Z's woman, so he jumps off the boat, grabs the woman and hauls her on board, and then steers the *Nowhere* out toward the open ocean while Bobby's woman holds Bobby's crying kid.

As the sirens wail and the cop cars skid into the harbor, One Way just calmly steers the *Nowhere* under the bridge and out to the open sea.

To like disappear with the legend of Bobby Z.

The Death and Life of Bobby Z

78.

Tim watches the boat go.

Stands there and watches the boat slip away and head for the open ocean.

Knows he's lost again, because there's like no way that boat can come back into the harbor to pick him up and they all get away. Cops like fucking everywhere because there are bodies all over the place, and dead bodies draw flies and cops.

So Tim is like *stuck.*

Of course, he thinks. Of fucking course.

But he's seen Elizabeth and Kit get on the boat. And there's lots of money on the boat and they'll live happily ever after with One Way and the smart thing to do is to forget about them, and he's thinking like *go boat go.* Get the hell out of here.

And besides, he thinks, I'm dead.

Whichever the fuck person I am, I'm dead.

Tim Kearney's dead and Bobby Z is dead, and so it looks like I get a fresh start.

Head up to Oregon, get a new name and a new life.

Because the money and the woman and the kid would have been nice, would have been a *dream,* man, but losers don't get dreams.

Losers have to settle for real life, and now at least I got one of those.

So he watches the boat sail away. Figures he'll watch it until it disappears over the horizon. Then creep back into that jungle of a ravine and disappear.

That'd be the smart thing to do.

Then he figures like *fuck that*.

And starts to run.

Starts to jog toward the harbor and the stone jetty. No one's gonna notice another jogger on the beach in California, man. The cops are too happy with the bodies and the ambulances and shit, and the crowd forming over there, and Tim just jogs right past it toward the jetty.

Gets on those rocks and starts hustling toward the ocean, toward the boat, and now he's slipping and falling on those rocks and the waves are crashing and threatening to take him off, but he keeps going.

And no one looks up, not the cops or the ambulance attendants, or the joggers or even the surfers braving the big waves on the other side of the jetty.

79.

It's Kit who sees him, of course.

Kit's standing on the deck, sobbing into Elizabeth's stomach, and he looks out and sees him running on the jetty. And Kit yells to One Way.

Who looks over, and this ain't no trip, man, but Bobby Z's risen from the dead.

Risen from the dead and running toward the open ocean, and One Way pulls on a couple of lines and tells Elizabeth to pull on a line, and she and the kid are tugging away and the sails come up and One Way has that boat turned around and he's steering it to run parallel with the jetty.

Tim, he's working his way down the rocks now, trying to find a place where he can jump into the water, and it's a scary fucking jump from anywhere on these big sharp rocks into that surf, and Tim stands there trying to get the courage.

Because he can't swim.

Lifelong loser, world-class fuck-up Tim Kearney has come this far, from the middle of the desert to the edge of the earth, and he can't make the last hundred or so yards because it's water. And the boat can't come closer because it'll crash onto the rocks.

Tim sees Kit on the deck of the boat, jumping up and down and waving his arms, and he thinks he can hear the boy yelling *Come on!* and he jumps.

Like just fucking flies over the rocks into the surf.

And starts to go down.

And he doesn't know what the fuck is going to happen to him.

What happens is that lifelong loser, world-class fuck-up Tim Kearney gets lucky for once in his fucked-up life.

What happens is that there's a goofy-footed surfer out there trying to catch the point break and he's a cocky little bastard. Thinks he's going to be the next Bobby Z, man, he thinks he's that good. So sure of himself he doesn't even have his leash on because this kid doesn't think he can fall. So he's sliding across the roof of this right-breaking wave, he's on top of the world, he's going to be the next Z. But then he wipes out big-time and his *board* . . . his board just goes *flying*. Shoots up into the blue sky like it's a missile, man, and lands flat in the water in front of Tim Kearney.

Who's just smart enough to climb on board.

How Tim gets to the boat is he climbs on that board and starts to paddle like hell.

Paddles like hell and holds on for life over the top of the swells. Just riding those waves, man, not in but out. And only lets go when Kit and Elizabeth grab him and haul him onto the deck of the *Nowhere*.

Three lifelong losers and a kid on that boat.

A life sentence, Tim thinks as he rolls around the deck with the kid in his arms and that treacherous, lovely woman looks on crying, and that wonderful goddamn lunatic smiles and steers the boat.

I'm doing life.

Later that day, miles away on the open ocean, the setting sun turned the boat and everything around it into the purest gold.